P9-DHO-445

GHOSTS OF EDEN

GHOSTS OF EDEN

T. M. Gray

Five Star • Waterville, Maine

First Edition
First Printing: January 2005

Published in 2005 in conjunction with Tekno Books and Ed Gorman.

Set in 11 pt. Plantin by Minnie B. Raven.

Printed in the United States on permanent paper.

Library of Congress Cataloging-in-Publication Data

Gray, T. M.
Ghosts of Eden / by T.M. Gray.—1st ed.
p. cm.
ISBN 1-59414-304-8 (hc : alk. paper)
1. Psychiatric hospital patients—Fiction.
2. Mount Desert Island (Me.)—Fiction.
3. Bar Harbor (Me.)—Fiction. 4. Haunted houses—Fiction. 5. Summer resorts—Fiction. I. Title.
PS3607.R397G48 2005
813′.6—dc22 2004057535

For Mary Jayne, my best girlfriend,
who acted as midwife at the birth of this novel.
I love you, always will.

ACKNOWLEDGMENTS

With deep heartfelt thanks to Larry and Joy, Alice and David Beaney, and Diane Cowperthwaite; and in respectful devotion to the people of Bar Harbor, Maine, my birth town, especially to those brave men, women, and children who fought the fire, as well as those who survived and remember.

Grateful acknowledgment is made for permission to use the Smokey Bear logo catch-phrase; with sincerest thanks to the Fire and Aviation Management division of the Forest Service, and Max Farrow, Smokey Bear Licensing Project Manager, LISBOA, Inc.

And to my wonderful first readers: Mark, Alice, Dave, and MJ. I also want to thank Deb Brod, my editor at Five Star, along with John Helfers and Ed Gorman; you folks made this book possible. And to Rick Hautala and Brian Knight, true guardian angels for their sound advice, and last but not least, Bob, my loving soulmate, whose companionship is always a pleasure, especially on those many trips to Mount Desert Island during the research for this novel.

Because this is a work of fiction based on the events of a Maine community in 1947, none of the main characters resemble any real persons, living or deceased.

CHAPTER ONE

1

The rain stopped on June 28, the day Saxon Faraday left the hospital. It had poured nearly every day that soggy spring of 1947, but now the sun was shining, bright and golden in the sky, causing wavy mirages on the highway, its heat making the long-soaked pavement steam. Saxon rolled down the car's window and let the wind ripple through her hair. It felt so good to be free at last! And the sun was shining, too—how could you beat that?

Life, she thought as she drove, *is a process of give and take, of checks and balances, and of all things coming around full circle. Maybe this glorious day is nature's way of making up for such a short, practically snowless winter and such a long, rainy spring?*

Or perhaps nature had freely given what it was about to steal away in the long, dry months to follow? The drought that summer would be among the worst on record, and the wildfires it spawned that autumn would never be forgotten.

But none of this had yet happened; nor was such a disaster conceivable, however, it was not by chance that the weather changed the very day Saxon returned home. *Things happen for a reason;* she believed this to be one of the great truths as well. Some might consider it a mere coincidence that her release from the Eastern Maine Insane Hospital occurred on the same day that the sun finally decided to show its face. Others might see it as destiny: the merging of two distinctly different worlds, one physical, the other metaphysical, that would briefly collide and merge at summer's end, changing both in ways that could not yet be imagined.

But all was not so bright and sunny as it seemed on this day.

Saxon Faraday was aware that she could never feel truly safe and at home until she came to grips with her past. Maybe, just maybe, she could come out on the other side as a whole person, strong of mind and spirit, free from the demons that tormented her. The decision to return home had not been hers; it had been forced upon her with a clean bill of mental health. She was elated at her release, but home was the only place left to go . . . and what awaited her return? Her parents were gone. Father was cold in his grave on Summit Hill, and Mother was probably somewhere in her native Florida, trying to forget she ever had a daughter. There were no other relatives in Bar Harbor and very few friends. Saxon wondered how many people still blamed her for what happened to her family, and she dreaded their accusations. Most would dare not voice them out loud, due in part to a stern Yankee politeness that visitors often mistook for aloofness, but she knew she'd be able to read it in their eyes . . . the blame, the unanswered questions. *Why'd you do it, Miss Faraday? Why'd you shoot your father? Do you still play with razor blades, Saxon?*

Scenarios played in her head as she drove down from Bangor, along Route 1A. She passed through the sister city, Brewer, over the rolling hills of Lucerne, Ellsworth with its bustling Main Street, and onto Route 3, driving through the farming towns of Lamoine and Trenton, then crossing the bridge onto Mount Desert Island.

There was more traffic than she remembered. She slowed down, wanting to drink in all the sights and familiar landmarks. Mount Desert was Maine's biggest island, her birthplace, and coming back to it felt both right and wrong.

But she couldn't go home just yet.

A lump caught in her throat as she passed the intersection at Hulls Cove connecting Route 3 with the Crooked Road, aptly named for there wasn't fifty feet of it that bore any resemblance to straight. She needed to go to the ocean first and Bay Drive was where she'd find it. She felt it essential that she stop there, to rest for a while and take it all in, to reacquaint herself with the Atlantic, after all, she'd been five long years without it. Oh, there had been group walks along the Penobscot River, "nature hikes" as they were called, provided once a month to exemplary patients at the hospital, but as big and mighty as the river was, it was no ocean. She parked her car in a puddle of a turnout atop The Bluffs, a precipice of granite cliff overlooking Frenchman Bay. Rain had poured steadily, nearly every day, from the beginning of April until today, swelling riverbanks and washing out roads; but now the morning sun finally burnt through the clouds, casting sparkling glints on the waves below. It was so clear and crisp, refreshing.

From her vantage point, she could see the old familiar landmarks below: Stave Island, long and narrow, across the bay the bushy, tree-covered sprinkle of Porcupine Isles with the steep cliffs of Ironbound to the east. Bar Harbor breakwater yawned from Bald Porcupine Island toward Cromwell Cove, creating a channel of white-capped blue. Thrumcap Island, bleak and desolate, lay to the south and Egg Rock, equally barren but for its boxy, red and white lighthouse, marked the mouth of the bay. Far off, in the hazy distance between the islands, Schoodic Mountain and the Black Hills loomed blue in the northeast, and in their foothills, the coastal towns of Sorrento, Gouldsboro, and Winter Harbor. Where the sea met granite ledges, slopes, and cliffs, majestic crashing waves sent cold, foamy spray high into the air.

A short distance away, Cadillac Mountain loomed over the town with its bald, pink granite crest and the Summit House Hotel near the very top. Fishermen, even those many miles away, used Summit House as a location marker. A cog railroad wound up the western side of Cadillac, bringing guests to the hotel, who'd come across Eagle Lake by steamship ferry.

Many would consider the mountain and the sea-swept scene breathtaking, and so it was for Saxon, but for reasons entirely her own. The deep blue was a tranquil and welcoming sight in contrast to the dark green of nearby pines, so majestic, but which seemed to whisper to her: *stay away, stay away*. She tried to ignore their warning, blinking at the wetness that threatened to flood her eyes. The ocean wanted her here, but the land, fixed and consistently stable, did not. To her, the bay was like a basin of tears, holding refuge and comfort. She'd experienced so much hurt here, so much pain, humiliation, and terror. She could claim a good portion of it as her own—but not the catalyst that started it all. No, a good share of that, she knew, belonged to Jacqueline Roquefort, whose eyes would never again see the fierce, rugged beauty Saxon was looking at now. *If I had any guts at all,* she thought, *I'd put my car into gear and drive right off the edge of this cliff. Maybe it would be better for everyone if I did?* But they'd taught her differently at the hospital, making her understand that suicide was a selfish, cowardly act . . . and if there was one thing Saxon Faraday wasn't, it was a coward.

She tried to brush away her memories of the hospital: the barrage of psychiatrists, therapists with their inkblot flash cards, needles that stung and then numbed, glassy-eyed patients who shuffled up and down the bleak corridors, antiseptic smells, and the demented screams from nearby rooms that kept her awake during the nights' long hours. The five years following her father's death were days spent seeking the will to live and the strength to try to conquer the part of her past that had damaged her very soul.

Now she returned to face the monster. The Serpent.

Since her parents were no longer here, this afforded some relief. She wouldn't have to face them, for Father was well buried, and Mother had run off to Florida. Maybe the warm sanctuary of the tropical climate was the only way Mother could put it all behind her. Saxon hadn't heard from her since the Christmas of 1945; the card she'd received lacked a return address. Evidently, Mother didn't expect—or want—a reply.

For Saxon, sleeping pills had once been the only means of keeping the recurring nightmares at bay, and eventually her dependence upon them started her on the path of self-destruction. The overdose at the hospital had been her second attempt at taking her own life, and like the first attempt, she'd failed miserably. She no longer needed those pills now; the hazy, dopey days were long gone, but so memorable that she was hesitant to even swallow the occasional aspirin. Recovery exacted a heavy price; last year, the nightmares had returned with a vengeance, but this time, she didn't tell a soul about them. She couldn't. There was only one sure-fire way to put an end to the night terrors once and for all—and it didn't involve pills or razor blades or doctors.

She shielded the sun from her eyes with a gloved hand as she spotted the Tow Path hugging the shore, dotted by wharfs and sea captains' homes with their high gables and widows' walks. In the distance, she could see the roofs of fine houses, which the rich called "summer cottages" and the locals referred to as "mansions."

A. Atwater Kent, radio magnate, and the Rockefellers, Goodrichs, Astors, Pulitzers, Kennedys, Stotesburys, Sears, Morgans, and Vanderbilts, along with Maine's former governor James G. Blaine and his son-in-law, New York symphony conductor and composer, Walter Damrasch, all vacationed here. Their estates had interesting names, too: The Turrets, Balance Rock, Geranium Cottage, Shore Acres, Eden Hall, Edgemore, Reef Point, Breakwater, Wingwood House, Strawberry Hill House, Bide-A-While, Redwood, Kenarden, The Briars, The Doll House, and author Mary Roberts Reinhardt's The Cabbage Key.

Bar Harbor was long established as a summer resort for the wealthy, influenced largely by landscape artist Thomas Cole in 1844, and again in 1850 with his contemporary, Frederick Edwin Church. Mount Desert captured the inspiration and imaginations of both famous painters, sparking outside interest in the island where the mountain met the sea, and by 1890, M.D.I. had become a prime resort location known throughout the world.

This was God's Country, one of the most beautiful spots in New England, but Saxon knew Evil lurked here, for the Serpent never left Eden, which, ironically, had been Bar Harbor's original name until 1918.

God's country, right. With a sigh, she smoothed down her tailored skirt. It was her favorite, a deep, navy blue to complement her silver blouse. Nylon stockings had been hard to come by during the war (some women went so far as to paint their legs, including the neat black seam up the middle of the backs) but she'd saved this pair special for her return home. Her sensible black pumps and black riding gloves completed the ensemble, and although she knew she appeared sharp and confident (that was part of her armor), inside she was quaking with trepidation. It showed in her grimace as she steered back onto Route 3, gently tapping the brake pedal as her car made the downward slope toward town.

No, she couldn't go straight home; first she had to build up courage. Perhaps a drive through town would do it?

My, how Bar Harbor had changed over the past five years! New shops had sprouted up in the very heart of town, many of them catering to the tourists and summer residents. Sidewalks had been laid to accommodate the clientele, and the streets had been widened to afford better access for the newer, larger vehicles.

Some of the stores she'd remembered were still here: there was Sachsman's on Cottage Street, where Father had bought his suits, and Adler's, where she'd worked one summer. They always sold such pretty dresses there. *It would be so nice to stroll along the sidewalk and window shop,* she thought, passing Daney's on Cottage Street. Like Butterfield's, both stores were prohibitively expensive for common folk—and the rich enjoyed the luxury of having their groceries delivered—but Daney's had such wonderful displays. She recalled, marveling at the exotic items she'd seen in their windows in the past, one of them being cans of black tiger meat. *Tiger* meat, imagine that! Turned out, it was canned prawns imported from Siam, but still, it sounded pretty unusual.

The old familiar grocery stores where townspeople shopped were still here: Hatch's IGA and Jordan & Ronald on Cottage Street. The School Street Market. Mom-and-pop convenience stores such as Ora Strout's were down on lower Main, near the hospital.

Hymie Gordon's still sold men's clothing on School

Street, Wards still sold women's clothing, and footwear could be purchased at Franklin Shoes on Main Street, just up from the First National Bank. If you didn't like the shoes at Franklin's, you could try Brown's down on Cottage Street. Up-islanders (people who lived out of town) usually purchased their clothes through mail order from catalogues: Sears, Roebuck, & Co., Montgomery Ward, or for the real fancy duds, Spiegel's.

F. E. Sherman's was still here; photography was done at Brown's Studio on Cottage Street. For the kids, the superheroes—Superman, Batman, and the Lone Ranger—all had homes on the swivel-type wire racks there.

She saw that you could still get your car fixed at Fulton Buzzell's Gulf on Cottage Street. There was also the Ford Motor Company garage on lower Main and a Mobil station across the street from Buzzell's.

Gonya's Drug Store sat on the corner of Cottage and Main. Just up Main Street, one of her favorite stores, The West End Rexall, stood, offering a soda fountain inside where Georgie Marshall used to treat her to Sunday malts (asking for two straws; they'd always share).

She recalled those breathtaking bike rides of his, her seated across the handlebars, the wind whipping through her hair, laughing. Georgie was a careful driver and never dumped her once, although there was that one time when he'd come very close to spilling them both. Mrs. Ferguson on Holland Avenue was learning to drive her new car and apparently had forgotten which pedal was the brake. She'd come barreling out of the garage, swinging a sharp turn onto the street, nearly tilting her car on two tires, and overcompensated by turning the wheel too hard to the left, missing Georgie's front tire by mere inches. Seconds later, panicking, she'd suddenly remembered which pad was the brake pedal. She bounced to a herky-jerky stop right there in the middle of the street, got out, and came running over to see if Saxon and Georgie were all right, and of course they were, although a bit shaken. She gave them each a quarter, which they spent at the movie theater. That had been Saxon's final date with Georgie Marshall, though not by choice. They'd seen *The Mummy* that afternoon and shared a box of popcorn, which they nearly spilled when they first saw the monster.

Monsters . . . she pushed that thought from her mind. Poor Georgie, she couldn't bear thinking about what happened to him, either. Not now. As she passed by The Criterion and The Star Theater, she was nearly overcome with a flood of memories. Not that she had ever been inside The Criterion; The Star was for common folk—whereas The Criterion was for the upper class. She figured she'd like The Star better, anyway, because they often featured thrillers.

She sighed, remembering the movies she and Rob Carmichael had enjoyed at The Star: *Black Friday* starring Boris Karloff and Bela Lugosi (she loved how Rob held her close during the scary parts and how he never laughed when she covered her eyes), *Son of Frankenstein*, *Devil's Island*, and Alfred Hitchcock's *The Lady Vanishes*. Rob loved scary movies, too, but Saxon sometimes wondered if the main reason he enjoyed them so much was because it gave him another opportunity (as if he needed an excuse) to put his arm around her.

The townsfolk also had The Casino, an auditorium-type building with a playbill featuring everything from school plays and speeches to the annual Hayseed Ball. Rob had proposed to her here, on bended knee, knowing he was shipping out a week later—and she'd accepted. He'd joined the Navy and was looking forward to a career in accounting.

First boot camp, then Naval school, followed by a two-year stint at sea, and after that, he'd merit a nice desk job, bringing in enough income to support a wife and family—so his recruiting officer had promised. He didn't have enough money to buy her a ring, but it didn't matter. They were young and in love; they had a dream.

It turned out to be a broken dream, but that hadn't been the recruiter's fault. No one could have foreseen what was going to happen; however, if it were at all possible, Saxon would have never let Rob go. *Time marches on,* she chided herself, blinking back the despair welling up in her eyes. Now was not the time to be crying; she had to be strong. Blinking, she dabbed at her tears with the gloved tip of one finger and drove onward.

The town was growing with the times, spanning outward from the shorefront toward the mountain, and Saxon was glad to see the changes. Visitors sometimes referred to the small, coastal villages of Maine as being "quaint" and oh, how she hated that word! To her, it meant simple and backwards, describing a population unable to progress, doomed by their own ignorance. *Quaint, we ain't,* she thought as she turned her car around. *We may be far removed from the metropolitan areas, but that's what makes us special. That's why people from all over the world come here. . . .*

It was time to go home. She had no trouble finding her way back to Crooked Road and the two marble lion pillars guarding the entrance to Roquefort Manor. She'd never liked those lions much; they looked far too fierce and out of place here, but they'd come with the estate and her father fancied them. Turned out, he'd fancied a lot of things she didn't like.

The driveway was long, narrow, and steep, paved in crushed, pink granite that crunched pleasantly under the tires of her car.

Tapping the brake pedal with the ball of her foot, she slowed to a near crawl as she approached the house atop Paradise Hill. Gorry, but the place looked so forlorn and run-down: the paint was peeling like blistered skin on the clapboards, the windows and doors were boarded up with random slats, and the porch sagged in the middle like a tired old, sway-back nag. She parked her car and gazed up at the house for a very long time, keenly aware of the cold fear coiling in her stomach, threatening to liquefy her bowels. Her grip on the steering wheel tightened.

Even in its heyday, Roquefort Manor hadn't been much of a mansion compared to the summer cottages of the rich and famous, but it was originally an upper-middle class home. Home—no, that was the wrong word for it. It wasn't a *home;* it was a dwelling place for the Serpent and ghosts. Perhaps the entities were gone now that they no longer had anyone to torment?

No, Saxon knew for certain that the Serpent was still here; things hadn't changed *that* much while she'd been away. It was here, all right, biding its time, waiting for her return.

Still, parts of the house looked pretty much the same as she remembered, despite its apparent lack of upkeep. The slate shingles on the gabled roofs still glimmered in the sunshine as if sprinkled with diamonds, but several were missing. The house kept its original color: black, as bizarre and expensive a color choice for the 1840s, when it was built, as it was for now, a hundred years later—and despite the peeling exterior, it maintained a darkness no paint could ever match. And how it rambled! The main part stood three stories high, with double turrets and ells shooting out from three sides. With its expanse of lawn and formal gardens, it clung to an Old World air of elegance and mystique, even if raging weeds and underbrush had taken over. The old family sign, "Faraday," still hung by the front door, although crooked, dangling from a single, rusted chain.

The white porch proved a stark contrast to the darkness of the main house. Its sag had caused some of the support beams to lean at suspicious angles. Was it safe? Or would it topple the moment she walked up to the door?

Saxon pulled her eyes away and gazed down at her gloved hands, prying them from the three-spoke Banjo steering wheel to turn off the engine. It sputtered for a moment and died just as she remembered it doing back when it belonged to her father: the family car, a 1940 Buick. It had cost almost $1,000 brand spanking new, and although they could barely afford it, Geoffrey Faraday was convinced he couldn't live without those sleek, black, graceful lines that boasted good taste, the signature car of a successful man. He'd use his trusty old workhorse, a boxy 1916 Overland hearse, for business, but the Buick was for strictly for pleasure. *His* pleasure. Saxon glanced over at the shed. Was the hearse still parked there? Or had the town taken it in lieu of payment for property taxes? She had no way of knowing—this was something she didn't want to deal with right now.

She didn't want to think about the house, either, and the sorry shape it was in, but the longer she sat here, the harder it would be. *I really don't want to go in there,* she contemplated with some disdain, *but I have to, don't I? It's mine now and this is something I must do.*

She opened the door with a sigh, stepped out of the car, and gingerly made her way toward the porch. As she climbed the granite steps, a sudden, cool breeze kissed her back and she glanced over her shoulder. *I'm being watched,* she thought. *The Serpent knows I'm here, that I've come back, and it's not at all pleased.*

The floor creaked, groaning under her weight, but remained firm, and she almost laughed, in spite of her apprehension, when she read the sign on the door. Typed on card paper, it had been secured by thumbtacks on all four corners. They'd rusted, leaving reddish stains like little rivers: *Red Rivers by I. Bleed Freely.* She giggled at her little joke, but as she scanned down through the words typed on the sign, her jaw became tight, her chin determined.

"Condemned! Too little, too late, I'm afraid—the place should have been condemned *before* it was built," she said aloud, placing her hands on her hips. *Well, if that just doesn't take the cake. I hold the deed to Roquefort Manor, and if memories can't stop me from moving back in, neither can town hall!*

Quickly, she tore down the sign and crumpled it in her fists. She let it drop and kicked it aside with her shoe. *So much for that—just let them try to stop me!*

The boards nailed over the door didn't yield quite so easily, though, and she had to go back to her car to retrieve a crowbar from the trunk. After twenty minutes of straining, pulling, and cursing, she was finally able to pry open the front door.

Noisily, it scraped open, and inside a tomb-like darkness greeted her. *Welcome home to Death House.* Heavy shades had been drawn, and over them, the curtains were closed. The shades were dark green, the same ones used during the war to conceal any light that might otherwise be seen from outside, in case of air raids. Blackout shades, every house had them then. Saxon walked over to the nearest window and pulled the curtains open. At that moment, a flurry of moths fluttered about and she swatted them away. She gave a tug on the bottom of the shade and up it flew with a sudden snap, making her jump. When she opened the next curtain, she stood back a bit and looked around. There, now the room had some light; beams of it shone through the spaces between the nailed boards on the outside.

It only made the room look worse. The boards on the windows reminded her of iron bars, like the kind that had been on the windows at the Insane Hospital. They'd been placed there to prevent patients from escaping—or worse, jumping to their deaths.

She could see that the front parlor was thick with dust; the Oriental rug at her feet was pitifully moth-eaten and frayed. Dingy sheets covered the furniture and there were cobwebs everywhere. The stuffing from the loveseat had spilled out onto the floor in gray piles poking out from under the bottom of another sheet. Soot had blown in from the fireplace, trailing across the floor like black powder, and there were little rodent footprints in it.

The wallpaper, once a luxuriant, velvety material, had curled and peeled away in places, revealing stained and crumbly plaster underneath. Instinctively, her eyes saw a design—or part of a pattern—in an upper corner of plaster, but she turned away, not wanting to look.

This house had a nasty habit of playing tricks on a person, and knowing this, she didn't dare gaze upon anything too long or look too deeply. It reeked with a mustiness that couldn't be denied, permeating everything, reminding Saxon of the dead bats she'd once found in the hayloft of the old barn on the hospital grounds. The entire loft stank of fusty death. She'd been one of the privileged patients, allowed to go on hikes and work on the farm. The work was *therapy,* so she'd been told, but she surmised that it was more a way of helping the hospital help her. But why had all those bats died there? Was the Serpent still trying to reach her, still powerful from almost one hundred miles away?

No, of course not. The bats had likely caught some sort

of disease. Didn't they sometimes carry rabies? *I wonder if there's any bats here?* she thought with a shiver. *Hope not.* She tried not to think about it, and kept her hands busy instead. Coughing and waving at the dust clouds, she pulled the sheets away from the furniture. Water from the leaking roof had damaged much of it. Father's chair crouched against the east wall, its frame warped and bent with joints spread apart, and a pissy stain on its seat looked like a hungry, drooling mouth. *Come sit in me, little girl,* it seemed to say. *Sit in me and let me tell you a bedtime story. How about "The Princess and The Pit Viper"?*

She turned away, rolling her eyes. No, she wasn't in any mood for a story today. Now she noticed the ceiling. What a mess! There was a large, yellow stain in the corner of the ceiling over the baby grand and another over the settee. Parts of it drooped and sagged, gone spongy with mildew.

Her gaze lowered to the plant pots on the floor containing dirt and moldy stems; these had once been her mother's prized Boston ferns, begonias, and coleuses, but the pots had become coffins for their occupants, leaning auspiciously this way and that.

The floor had warped, too, like the rolling hills of the Crooked Road.

Saxon jammed her fists into her hips and sighed. So much work to be done; it would have been easier if there'd been just a little bit of cash to go along with the estate, for she could surely use a hired hand to help her with the heavier jobs.

Still, she couldn't let it get the better of her. *I can do it. I'm young and strong. No spring chicken, perhaps, but I'm sure I can get the job done with lots of elbow grease and time,* she decided on her way to the kitchen. Time was something she had plenty of; as for the elbow grease, well, she didn't have to get everything done at once. She'd chip away at it, little by little and—

—she stopped short. "Well, hell's bells," she said, shaking her head, almost laughing in pity. This room was even sorrier than the front parlor; food had been left in the cupboards and from the looks of it, squirrels, mice, and raccoons had ransacked the loot. There were mummified rodent turds everywhere, dry and pebble-hard, and the only things that had been covered, slightly protected by sheets, were the icebox and the stove. She pulled a sheet away and stared at the stove, stunned by the sudden, searing pain in her palms.

She knew it was psychosomatic, it had to be—but my God, they still hurt. *Damn that stove! After all these years, it still aches to look at the thing.* She felt it whenever she removed her gloves, the old pain whose fire never completely went out. Seeing the stove before her now, knowing it was the source of her discomfort, made her heart skip a beat or two.

It was a grinning monstrosity of black iron, made to burn wood in one half and coal in the other, sporting tiered warming shelves lined with gleaming chrome trim. On the top shelf, the scrolled words: "Home Is Where the Heart Is" mocked her fleeting panic. *Whose* heart? For all she knew, there was a heart here—but it was a Serpent's heart—black and cold, filled with hate and murder. She fought the urge to turn and bolt out the door, never to look back.

But that would have been a cowardly thing to do, and Saxon Faraday was no coward, even though she could hear her father's voice booming in her mind:

"Nasty girl! Idle hands are a tool of the Devil—by God, this'll teach you a lesson!"

What had she done to merit such punishment? She honestly couldn't remember, but it must have been terrible to incite such parental anger, such violence. It had happened such a long time ago, in her early teens, and now all she could recall were the white-hot agony in her palms, her father's angry words, and her quaking fear of him.

She spun away from the stove as if unable to bear looking upon it for another second. That's when she noticed the broken window beside the icebox, revealing the route for the intruding varmints. Mother would have pitched a fit if she'd seen this in her kitchen, of all places. She was always so meticulous about this room—but windows had been her obsession, her constant source of worry. Simply put, they had to be spotlessly clean; it had always taken long hours to polish them with newspaper and white vinegar, a job that might have been easier had they been half- or even quarter-paned—but no, these were the Swiss-style windows of imported, lead glass. Each window contained sixteen diamond-shaped panes, and there were twenty-four such windows throughout Roquefort Manor. Cleaning them was a tedious sentence of torture.

Saxon recalled getting scolded whenever she missed a corner of the glass or—heaven forbid!—when Mother discovered a streak on a window. *If we'd only had more money,* she surmised, *we could have hired a housekeeper to do the job.* But money was always scarce. Father worked as an undertaker and his office was downstairs in the basement. He'd earned a decent living, but it was far from extravagant. Luxuries were few and far between; his grand Buick was a good example of that. Buying it had literally cleaned out their bank account, and if Father had only known the car was now in *her* possession, he'd be twisting in his shroud. *Perhaps,* she thought with chagrin, *he is anyway.*

With a sigh of resignation, she pulled the drop cloth off

the refrigerator and wadded it into a tight ball. This, she stuffed into the hole in the window, a makeshift barrier that would have to do for now. Mother wouldn't have appreciated that, not one bit, but then again Mother insisted on calling the refrigerator an "icebox," even though iceboxes were quite outdated. The tall, white Kelvinator didn't require a block of ice to keep food cold, but it did have a drip pan directly under the upper freezing compartment. Its door had been left ajar, and Saxon could see that at least it had been emptied and cleaned. Of that, she was thankful; there were few smells worse than that of rotten food.

She took off her sunglasses, folded them, and put them on the counter. They were of a Hollywood-style: clear, Lucite frames with silver glints encasing green glass lenses, just like the ones the movie stars wore. This was as close to Tinseltown as she'd ever gotten; her aspirations of becoming an actress were long dead. *I'm too old to be a starlet, and besides, I have a past.*

She blinked, letting her eyes adjust to the light, all the while wondering what other surprises awaited her.

The bathroom was off the kitchen to the left, a tiny room, not much bigger than a closet and furnished with a fat, pregnant-looking toilet, a sink, and a claw-footed tub. She drew a sharp intake of air at first sight of the bathtub, remembering . . .

. . . remembering how at first, she'd thought Mother had died, lying back in that tub, so still and quiet, her head resting just above the water, eyes closed. There was no steam in the air—and there should have been, for it was wintertime and the bathroom was unheated and cold. Mother's lips had a slight bluish tint to them and her skin looked so pale. Frozen.

All at once, Mother had opened her eyes and looked at

her. They were dark blue, sad, beautifully haunted eyes, offset by long, dark lashes. Mother's eyes seldom held joy but now they were full of something else: irritation or distress, Saxon couldn't determine which.

She'd reached a hand out of the water and grabbed Saxon's wrist—and she was instantly stunned by how icy cold her mother's fingers felt. "Mother? Why—"

"Go upstairs," Mother had said with a shiver. "Leave me alone."

But Saxon couldn't leave her alone; she could smell the tang of gin on her mother's breath, and when Mother had explained what she was doing (and why), Saxon had felt chilled to the very marrow of her bones. She'd been merely fourteen then, and already knew what a sadist her father was. No wonder Mother had tried to get away from him a long while back. She'd been told Mother was sick and had to go away, but after she'd come back, things were strange between her parents. The ice baths, for example.

She shivered, trying not to think about her parents now; the task at hand demanded her full attention. All three bathroom fixtures were stained with rust but at least they seemed serviceable. An old box of Cashay tampons and a roll of yellowed, mouse-chewed toilet tissue sat on the shelf behind the commode. The tank itself, above the shelf, was anchored to the wall, a rectangular porcelain water-holder decorated with seashell designs. A brass chain and knob hung from its bottom which, when pulled, would let the water rush down into the bowl to flush. Saxon gave it a tug. Nothing happened.

That was actually good; someone had thought to drain the pipes before closing up the place. Mother? No, more likely one of her friends. Joe Tuttle from next door, maybe.

Saxon shuddered to find that a fat, black spider had

taken up residence in the tub, and she quickly turned away. How she hated spiders! *The Serpent put that spider there,* she reasoned, *hoping to frighten me away. It's so good at mean, little tricks.* A mirror hung over the sink and she paused, catching sight of her reflection.

Her expression was one of frightening resolve. She was a pretty woman, not glamorous by any means, but comely. Her skin was clear and youthful; rosy cheekbones illuminated eyes so dark that her irises appeared black. They were really the shade of bitter chocolate, a perfect match for the color of her hair, and although she liked its color and thickness, she often found her tresses unmanageable—a wild cascade of dark curls, not keeping at all with the tailored, current fashions. When left down, Saxon thought her hair made her look like a pirate's wench, a wild child, a moppet urchin.

Her teeth were slightly crooked, too, giving her a little overbite, which was why she'd trained herself to always smile with her lips closed. She tried it now, thinking, *I'm going to beat you this time, you bastard. You'll not get the best of Saxon Faraday!*

Her smile turned to dismay, though, when she turned the cold water knob on the faucet. First the pipes gurgled, burping air, and then out came a gush of thick, bloody-looking water. She jumped back so it wouldn't splatter her clothes, and after that initial outburst came nothing but air. The pump was off; she knew she'd have to go down cellar to the fuse box to turn on the electricity.

She turned off the faucet and made her way back into the front parlor. Maybe she could call someone and ask them to help her; she really didn't want to go into the cellar. *The basement,* as Father called it. His telephone was still in its place on the corner table by his chair. It was a heavy, black, Western Electric with a brown cloth cord still as tangled as ever. Saxon went over to it and picked up the receiver. There was no dial tone, no friendly operator's voice asking, "Number please."

Only a dead silence . . . and in the background faint white noise, rhythmic, like breath.

The party line, that had to be it. She remembered sharing a line with two other families. She set the receiver back down, waited a moment, then picked it up again and held it to her ear.

"Saxon? Honey, are you there?" the voice was Mrs. Carmichael's, she recognized the low, husky tone at once, but heard a sorrowful, unmistakable urgency there—one that brought another memory flush to the surface, then buried it again in murky depths.

"Mrs. Carmichael? I'm here. I—"

"I'm so very sorry to have to tell you this; you've been like a daughter to me. But I'm afraid it's Rob. Bad news: the Japanese, those planes. Surely, you heard all about it on the radio. He's gone, Honey. His ship went down at Pearl Harbor and they haven't found any survivors. . . ."

No survivors? Saxon dropped the receiver and it fell to the floor with enough force to jar the little bell inside. Backing away, she shook her head, unable to comprehend the impossibility of it. Yes, Mrs. Carmichael had called . . . *five* years ago! Using those same exact words, the same tone of voice.

Maybe the shrinks didn't cure me as good as they thought? she wondered, putting her knuckles to her mouth to keep from crying. *I'm losing my mind again—going over the deep edge—it's all slipping away!*

"No," she said out loud, breathing hard against her fist in an effort to calm herself. "It's just an old, painful memory, that's all. This house is full of them—and if I let them get to me, I really will go crazy." She lowered her hand, staring at the phone, and bent down to pick it up.

She didn't hold it to her ear this time, just replaced it in its cradle.

How long the service had been disconnected? How much money was owed to Ma Bell? The phone itself was rented at the steep rate of four dollars a month. Quickly doing the math in her head, she came up with an outrageous sum of around $240 to cover the past five years. Ma Bell had her by the *calls* for certain. No, she wouldn't be asking them to turn it back on anytime soon.

But electricity she needed. She dreaded going downstairs to the basement to turn the power on; it might have helped ease her fears if it had been an ordinary cellar, but Leonard S. Roquefort, the previous owner, had been a mortician who'd turned the rooms beneath the house into working quarters. Her father, also a mortician (although he preferred the term "undertaker"), used the same rooms and equipment. This had come with the purchase of the house, and for all she knew, those instruments and tools of the trade were probably still down there, along with the smell of formaldehyde. She didn't want to know, didn't want to have to see those things that had belonged to Father, but she needed water worse. The cellar door was right beside the telephone and she gave a shudder as she turned the knob to open it.

It creaked open, and oh, but it was dark down there!

Hurrying back to the kitchen, she fetched a candle from the cupboard, lit it with a wooden match from the holder behind the stove, and cautiously walked back to the cellar door.

The wooden steps moaned as she carefully made her way

down into the bowels of the house. The candle afforded precious little light, yet it was better than none. Halfway down, she remembered the flashlight in the car, either in the glove compartment or under the front seat, but it was too late to turn back now. Just a few more steps and she'd be there. The cellar was divided into three rooms, two of them finished: the workroom and office, but the fuse box was off to the left in the unfinished, storage room. It was a tiny, cramped space that she surmised might have once served as a root cellar. Likely, it had been here since the house was built.

Swiping at clingy strands of dusty spider web, Saxon made her way past stacks of old boxes containing God knows what. Father's magazines, perhaps? In the height of his insanity—and yes, Father was far more insane than she—he'd taken to taping dollar bills inside the pages of *Life* and *Time* magazines. On the car advertisements, always on the car advertisements. She would have gone through them for money, but Mother had beaten her to it; she'd said so in one of her few letters. That's how she bought the train ticket South. "But you're welcome to the magazines if you want them," she'd told Saxon.

Saxon didn't want them.

Finally, by groping around on the wall, Saxon located the fuse box, and pried it open with her fingers. In the candlelight, she could see the thick wire coming out of its top resembling a snake (*The Serpent!*) with a skin of heavy, black rubber cracked with age. It followed along a wooden post to disappear into the BX cable winding into the floor above. The electrical system itself was outdated, old-fashioned knob and tube, with wires strung between ceramic knobs, running along beams throughout the house.

It was dangerous and ungrounded. Saxon remembered

being lifted on more than one occasion when she'd absent-mindedly tried to turn on a light with damp fingers.

Her gloves, though, were bone dry as she pulled the main switch down. Instantly, she heard a low hum as the water pump came to life. It was an eerie sound, chugging away as the pipes filled with water, gurgling and pinging as they expanded. She turned and rushed back upstairs with her candle, not caring if it went out (which it did) before she got to the parlor. Getting out was always so much easier than going in—why was that?

She let the water run a long time to flush the rust out, and while it ran, she went back to the kitchen and removed her gloves. As always, she winced at the sight of the thick cables of bluish scars on the undersides of her wrists, those desperate, crisscrossing lines, and the unnatural smoothness of her palms. She considered slipping her gloves back on, but she couldn't work while wearing them—and besides, sometimes she had to let her skin breathe. Once, after first arriving at the hospital, she'd worn gloves for a week without taking them off, which resulted in a nasty fungal infection between her fingers.

Once the water ran clear, she freshened up in the bathroom, wetting a washcloth that she'd found in the linen closet with cold water from the tap. With a sigh, she wrung it out and ran it over her cheeks, chin, and neck. That felt better. She patted her face dry with a matching towel and hung it over the rack beside the sink. The afternoon sun cast a rich, golden glow as it flooded in from the small bathroom window, and she glanced up again at her reflection in the mirror, deciding that she looked too pale.

Back in the kitchen, she picked up her purse and rifled through it. After a moment, she found what she was looking for: her Ruby Red lipstick. *A girl isn't dressed,* she reminded herself, *unless she's wearing Ruby Red.* Or at least that's what the Revel radio commercials would have you believe.

She went back to the bathroom mirror and painstakingly applied her lipstick, thinking that there was one thing left to do: get her bedroom ready for the coming night.

The front stairs were the ones she chose to use. The back stairs, dark and narrow, had always made her feel suffocated so she avoided using them whenever possible—but the front stairs were wide, swooping down to the north end of the dining room. They were grand, the kind one might expect to find in an old, Southern mansion with polished oak steps so ample that three people could climb them together and not rub shoulders.

Saxon gritted her teeth and gripped the railing with both hands to keep herself from shaking. The stairs creaked slightly as she climbed them, grimacing at the tapestries of spider webs hanging above.

She'd nearly reached the top step when she heard the cry of what sounded like a baby. Were her ears playing tricks on her or was it real? Perhaps it was a ghost from long ago, but to her knowledge, no babies had ever been born at Roquefort Manor. This was a house of death, not life.

She paused as if frozen, straining to listen. The infant sounded like a newborn to her untrained ears and it didn't strike her as particularly healthy, but weak and pathetic. Was it possible that someone had just given birth and then fled upon her arrival, leaving their baby behind? No, that didn't make any sense at all; surely she would have seen someone, or at the very least, noticed human footprints in the dust on the floor.

"Hello?" she called out in a voice barely above a whisper. "Is anyone up there?"

Outside, the wind was picking up, becoming a full-fledged breeze, and she could hear it whipping through the tall pines in the backyard.

Stay away, they warned. *Leave, Saxon Faraday; go away.*

She turned and rushed back down the stairs, spooked, partly because she didn't like running on stairs; it was dangerous and she had a distant memory of falling. Perhaps she'd done so when she was a child? She was too upset to remember—the crying baby was just too much for her to deal with right now—if there was in fact a baby.

She stopped to listen; now all she could hear was the wind. Was she sure she'd heard the crying? No, it was probably just the wind in the trees or whipping around a corner of the house. Her nerves felt frayed, though—she'd been so sure she'd heard a baby.

Keep it up and you'll be back at the hospital, she told herself, glancing back at the stairs, and she knew she was right. There'd be plenty of time to confront the upstairs later. Right now she needed to be among people, not memories and ghosts. Friends, if she could find any.

Quickly, she grabbed her gloves, driving glasses, and purse from the countertop in the kitchen, and not bothering to lock the front door behind her, she jogged back out to the car.

2

While Saxon drove off, Leonard Roquefort remembered waking up with the axe buried in his chest, but surprisingly, the pain was gone. This was a recurring memory, one he was forced to relive over and over again. He rose to his feet with a sluggishness he'd never known in life. Something had changed; somehow the air had become thicker, soupy, almost like water, and yet he could breathe. His right lung, however, made a strange, gurgling sound whenever he exhaled . . . but dammit, he was still alive! The little minx hadn't killed him after all, had she?

He leaned against his desk and put a tentative hand to the protruding axe handle. It was slippery wet. Could he pull it out? Grunting, he tried, but the blade must have lodged between bones; his breastbone, and shoulder blade perhaps, were holding it as firm as a vise.

Damned girl. She'd been right on the verge of finding out how he'd disposed of that nuisance, Mario Delgado; he'd done it for her, *all* for her. No daughter of his was going to marry so far below her station—he simply couldn't allow it. Jacqueline was so far out of Delgado's league that they weren't even playing in the same ballpark, yet Leonard suspected that she'd mainly taken up with the boy to defy his authority.

Yes, Leonard had been trying to strangle his teenaged daughter, there was no denying that. He'd only wanted to take a few pictures of her, and she would have made a perfect subject—her torn dress, the tears streaming down her face, in the same pose on the floor as the first time he'd had to tear a dress off her. The little trollop—what did she think she was trying to do lying there, crying and teasing him like that? He'd only wanted to capture the magic of the moment—coerce her into gazing directly into his lens—he'd so wanted to capture that look!

She should have been honored: her pictures joined the dozens of others in the special folder in his desk. His other subjects had been dead, but he'd granted them immortality, caught forever in the way the light fell upon their carefully arranged limbs, their flesh so white, the cool paleness of his cold lovers. His own wife's pictures could be found in that drawer as well—the only one besides Jacqueline who was still alive—but with the power-makeup, she looked as dead as the rest. Just a little while longer and there'd be no more room for his wife's photos . . . only his lovely daughter Jacqueline would appear alive in the flash of his camera!

Alive—but for how much longer? He'd planned to kill her, too, a week, maybe more after he killed her mother. He'd do it slowly, and try to shoot the photos in a sequence of poses he'd arranged after she'd expired. This would be the *real* deal, from beginning to end, amen, and it was something that haunted his darkest dreams.

Looking down at the axe handle, he realized his ambitions for his wife and daughter would never happen. He'd been sloppy, unsuspecting. How was he to know Jacqueline was lying upon the axe, tempting him, waiting for him to come to her with his camera ready?

Leonard, come to me. . . .

The voice wasn't Jacqueline's, nor did it belong to his wife. He wasn't even sure it was female, but it had appealed to him on some shady level, sensual and full of promise. It seemed to have floated up from the root cellar, the unfinished room in the basement, but who was it—and why were they there?

He gave some thought to this. It could be the dead women; they spoke to him sometimes when he visited their photos—but no, he knew the sounds of their voices by heart. Was it a customer? He glanced down again at the axe handle sticking out of his chest. Now wasn't exactly a good time to be conducting business.

"Who's there?" he called out, stunned by the way his voice sounded, all weak and gurgled.

A friend who understands . . . I can help you, Leonard.

"Help me? How?"

You photograph the dead. I can provide you with plenty of interesting subjects. Come, talk with me.

He shifted his weight and groped around on his desk for his camera. His right arm didn't work so well; he had trouble moving it.

Leave the camera. You won't need it anymore.

"Why not? You said there were subjects. . . ."

I have everything you'll need down here. I'm in the root cellar; just take a few more steps if you can. That's right.

Leonard moved past his office door, into the cool, damp darkness where the Serpent waited.

3

Saxon drove out to her old hangout, the Reading Room at the Bar Harbor Inn. During the war, German U-boats had made their way into Frenchman Bay, and the U.S. Navy used the inn as their Observation Headquarters. The military left their mark here; she felt it as soon as she walked inside. The air felt more formal than ever, and everywhere she looked she saw the celebratory colors: red, white and blue, and decorative golden V's for Victory. The end of the War was still being observed.

If only Rob could see this place now, she thought, forcing herself to smile at strangers as she made her way into the Reading Room, the beautiful dining area that wrapped around the east side of the inn like a great curving porch. A gentleman in a tuxedo held the door open for her along with several others, and Saxon smiled a gracious thank-you as she passed through. This was the place where anyone who was *anybody* came to be seen, to socialize, to eat and drink. All her life, she'd wanted to *be* somebody. She knew how it felt to be stranded on the outer circle of the higher social classes, even though she was far from poor. She had her looks and she'd been told she had acting talent; she'd been in many high school plays. Someday, perhaps she'd find a husband here, or a movie star agent, or someone who *was* somebody, who had the means to improve her station in life. Such dreams might have been realized a long time ago, before Father's death and her own hospitalization. Now she was a woman with a past.

She wasn't about to let it get her down. Holding her head high, she gazed around at the tidy, well-placed tables and chose a smaller one in the back. It was getting late for lunch, and there were only a few patrons present. A man three tables away was smoking a cigar, the snifter of brandy near his napkin, untouched. A woman sat across from him, her back to Saxon. She was wearing a polka-dotted pillbox hat with a beaded veil, but there was something vaguely familiar about her. Saxon rested her cheek on her gloved fist as she gazed at the woman's back, observing her side profile whenever she turned. The way she tossed her head, the familiar tone of her voice, and the manner in which she lifted her stemmed glass of white wine, one pinky elegantly extended, told Saxon that she knew who this person was.

Yet, she couldn't remember her name.

It had been so long! Five years seemed like a lifetime in one's youth; she'd been seventeen when she'd been taken from Bar Harbor. Who would remember her now? Were any of her old school chums still around—or had most of them departed on the arms of husbands? Maybe some had left the region for jobs, or had joined the military as nurses? The war had changed almost everything; more women had been employed in the workforce (and in the armed forces) than ever before.

When the waitress stopped at the couple's table to leave the bill, the woman with the pillbox hat suddenly stood up to leave, turning slightly. That's when Saxon finally recognized her.

Carlotta Miller! They'd gone to school together. Carlotta's family also lived out on the Crooked Road, a little over three miles from Roquefort Manor. As Saxon stood and began to walk over to greet her old school chum, the man at the table got up, as was the custom, but he said nothing to Saxon, barely looking at her.

"Carlotta!" Saxon said, joyfully reaching out to touch her upper arm. "It's been so long; how are you?"

Carlotta turned toward her with a sniff and pulled away slightly.

"Are you feeling all right, my dear?" her gentleman friend inquired.

Frowning, she nodded. "I think so. Just a bit of a chill. It's from all the rain we've been having—makes me feel so like a mushroom."

"Good thing it's over. Perhaps I should have asked you out on a picnic instead, so you could enjoy the full effects of the sunshine?" He plucked the bill from the table and examined it.

Carlotta shook her head. "No, don't be silly, lunch here was lovely, really."

Saxon's eyes filled with tears. "Carlotta? Don't you remember me at all?"

"Then we'll have to remember to come back soon," her companion said, evidently pleased with the price he'd been charged for the meal.

"Yes, I'd enjoy that, Herrick."

"Are you ready to go?"

Carlotta nodded, smiling as she stepped away from Saxon. "You know, it's funny. I just had the strangest feeling, all of a sudden, like being young again and so unsure of myself. Do you ever get that?"

The man, Herrick, shook his head as he reached out to take her elbow. "Rarely, my dear. Are you sure you're feeling all right?"

She frowned, lifting her hand to lightly touch her forehead. "I thought so, but now I'm not so certain. I do feel quite strange, Herrick."

"Well, I'd best get you home right away."

Saxon watched the man guide her friend away from the table, slowly realizing why Carlotta had ignored her. There was a reason for the dark veil over her eyes; Carlotta was blind. It was apparent in the way she held her head, her strong grip on Herrick's arm, her steps faltering and unsteady.

She returned to her seat with a heavy heart, wondering what could have happened to cause her girlhood friend to lose her eyesight, and why her man, Herrick, had not even so much as acknowledged her presence. *Why didn't they speak to me?*

Perhaps it was because of Herrick? Maybe he knows who I am? Saxon wondered. *Perhaps he'd heard what happened to Father and he blames me? It's not right to judge me like that, without knowing me, without knowing all that transpired, but people often do, don't they? Let's not forget what happened to Gennipher York Beal out on Breakneck Island Light.*

Now that had been another tragedy, but it had happened such a long time ago, and as time went on, people forgot. Saxon remembered her mother telling about it: that awful storm, and that poor, ostracized woman. Had her baby survived? Mother didn't know, but Saxon hoped it had. If not, there was no justice left in this world.

She waited a long time for a waitress to come by and after half an hour passed, she realized that they, too, were ignoring her. Despite her dismay and shock, she held her chin high, watching people come and go; some of them were folks she remembered, but they'd merely glance in her direction without so much as a nod or a wave.

There was one, though, a young woman seated across the room, who stared at her with cold, hate-filled eyes. Saxon felt quite certain she did not know this person, but for the life of her, she couldn't fathom why the stranger seemed so angry—or why that fury was directed at her.

Had she been a friend of Father's? she wondered, feeling terribly uneasy. *Well, hell's bells. Let her think whatever she wants.* Under the simmer of the stranger's glare, Saxon decided it best to leave. Glancing back at the door as it swung shut behind her, she thought about the house waiting for her return.

I really should start cleaning my bedroom and get settled in before dark.

Dark. Just the thought of it gave her the shivers.

4

Saxon was right; the house was brooding, waiting for her, she could feel it even stronger now. She'd had no choice but to return to it. It belonged to her, and aside from the car and her clothes, it was her only possession.

Could she restore it to its former glory? Samuel D. Roquefort, III built the Manor in the late 1840s as a vacation home for him and his family when the summer heat became too oppressive in Virginia. From what Saxon had been told about the history of the house, Roquefort had originally intended to build it somewhere along the shore, but the land deal soured just before the transaction was completed, and he settled for having it built here, just beyond Hulls Cove, on Crooked Road.

There was no shore here, but from the back veranda, one could look down the hill and catch a tiny glimpse of Witch Hole Pond through the trees. She had no idea why that small body of water had such an outrageous name; everyone she'd asked in the past had no clue, either. Apart from poor Sarah Ware up in Bucksport being Maine's only legendary witch, she knew of no other women who'd been condemned for practicing the occult in the state. It was just a strange, inappropriate name for a calm, pleasant, little pond.

She stood on the back veranda, watching the sunset behind Whalesback Hill. Red sun at night, sailors' delight. After a moment, she turned away, not feeling at all delighted, and went back inside.

The lights came on easily enough, with just simple tugs on their cords, and somehow, having the house lit up made it feel more comfortable, a little less foreboding. Now it was time to tackle her old bedroom upstairs, to get it ready to sleep in.

This time, as she climbed the stairs, all Saxon could hear was the sound of her own footsteps, the dull snapping of the oak steps beneath her feet, and her own quick breath . . . and if she listened hard enough, the loud pounding of her heart. Thankfully, the wind had died down. Cobwebs welcomed her in the upper hallway, looping crazily down from the ceiling, grey and ropy-thick. She couldn't help but think it strange, how quickly the spiders had taken over after the house was empty. Perhaps they'd been here all along, waiting for a chance to lay claim to the estate, just like the Serpent was waiting for its chance? Or maybe it had called them here?

She stopped in the hallway just outside her bedroom door. She was seventeen when she'd last seen her room, that awful night they'd dragged her out of it, kicking and screaming. There had been blood, lots of it, streaming down her hands and arms, dripping from her fingertips, clotting in spots on the floor and smearing along walls—all this while Father was face-down on the cadaver table in his workroom, his head leaking precious red rivers of its own. Had her room changed? Had all the blood been cleaned up and her bedroom emptied of its contents right after she'd been taken to the hospital?

Memories were coming back to her, and she didn't like it. Pausing for a moment, she gathered up enough courage to open the door. Twisting the knob, it swung open effortlessly, and the first thing she noticed was the wallpaper. It matched the wallpaper in the front parlor and while it hadn't changed, ever the same after all these years, it still unnerved her to look at it. The pattern was that of swirling, falling leaves, burgundy and gold, but when she was a young teen, she'd begun to see things in it. Things that didn't belong—things that never should have been. Strange, gray faces: death masks, perhaps, but the features were out of proportion. It could have been an optical illusion: look at them one way and all you'd see is leaves. Look deeper and the faces would be there, staring back at you with large, black, slanted eyes and non-existent lips and noses.

But for now, all she saw were leaves and that was good. Maybe the faces had been figments of her imagination? Mother had always said hers was overactive, that she was just too *sensitive*. But once, possibly in a moment of weakness, Mother had mentioned that she, too, had noticed *something strange* in the wallpaper. Did she say that because she was afraid, even back then, that Saxon, her only daughter, was losing her mind? Or had she really seen the faces, too?

Saxon jumped when the door suddenly slammed shut behind her. Immediately, she turned and tried the knob. Yes, it opened again quite easily. It must have been the settling of the house, the way the support beams were beginning to sag. Yes, that had to be it.

Whatever it was, she didn't dare let herself think otherwise. Catching her breath, she looked around. There were no telltale bloodstains, no dark splatters on the floor and walls. The room had simply not changed, and aside from the cobwebs and dust, it was exactly the same as it had been before that awful night. Her canopy bed with its flowered, ruffled flounces stood flush against the wall near the row of windows overlooking the backyard. Her dresser sat next to it with her colognes and perfumes arranged in a neat circle on top. Across from the dresser, her closet door was open, still full of dresses that by now were two sizes too small and decidedly out of style.

Saxon approached her dresser, surprised that her fourteen-inch radio, a state-of-the-art Philco, was still here. A round mirror hung from the wall over it, and in its reflection, she watched herself reach for a bottle of perfume. She selected Pink Frosting by Jergens. It was a simple, dimestore cologne, contained in a slender bottle with a pink cloud label, but it was the first thing she'd ever bought for herself, with babysitting money she'd earned when she was fifteen. She unscrewed the dark cap and waved the bottle under her nose.

Memories flooded her mind.

They weren't all bad. The scent was that of youth, at a time when her world was new and the threat of an overseas war seemed an eternity away. Storm clouds loomed on the horizon, but she couldn't see them then. All that mattered in life was making good grades in school, and being available for the dashing Georgie Marshall, who'd take her on his bike to The West End Rexall soda fountain for a malt on Sunday afternoons. Georgie, how long had it been since she thought of him before today? Years. Was it possible it had been so long?

He'd been a handsome boy: tall, tan, and athletic. His hair was blond and his teeth straight and white. Saxon loved his smile, that bright flash, and the way his eyes lit up whenever he saw her.

He loved her, yes, but his other love was baseball; she remembered him telling about how he wanted to play professionally someday. But that was a pretty tall dream for the son of a fisherman, even though Georgie was very good at the game. In his first year of high school, he'd broken a sports record, scoring more hits during a season than any other player in the school's history. Georgie was a bright star full of promise, a high school sports star, but that's as far as fate allowed him to go. He'd drowned the summer before his junior year, a fishing accident aboard his father's boat. Taken down by a rogue wave, they'd said, boat and all. His name joined the long list of names of those who'd lost their lives at sea on the brass plaque down at the town pier.

With tears in her eyes, she screwed the cap back on the Pink Frosting and picked up a bottle that looked like a rounded heart on a ribbed pedestal. Chichi by Renoir. She didn't have to open it to remember what it smelled like. It was a special gift from Rob Carmichael, her fiancé. It was the summer of her seventeenth year and gone were the days of Georgie Marshall, his baseball games and those lovely Sunday malts. Rob was a year older than she, tall and dark-haired, a quiet, studious young man very much the opposite of the athletic Georgie, but no less kind and interesting. He'd enlisted with the Navy and was stationed at Pearl Harbor in Hawaii. She remembered when his mother had called on the telephone to tell her the bad news: the Japanese had attacked Pearl Harbor and Rob was M.I.A., presumably dead. It was the worst night of her life, and maybe that's why she imagined Mrs. Carmichael's voice on the phone today?

That was the same night Saxon had been committed to the Insane Hospital.

Did everyone assume she'd suffered a nervous breakdown upon hearing about her fiancé's death? Why wouldn't they? After all, she'd shot her father straight through the head, and then sliced her own wrists open with razor blades. "A bad spell," Mother had called it, but that was a polite way of putting it mildly. It had been the worst kind of Hell she'd ever known . . .

. . . and contrary to popular belief it had *not* started with the news about Rob. A bad brew had been simmering between Saxon and her parents long before that. Her father's iron-fisted tyranny, her mother's complete lack of esteem and willpower, these provided the building blocks for self destruction, stacked upon a foundation of addiction, obsession, and ultimate possession. Something had to give—and that something turned out to be Saxon.

She remembered her father's jeering laughter, the brutal sting of his words: "I told you what to expect from a soldier boy! Proves one thing, doesn't it, young lady. Father's always right. Always!" He peered into her face and added, "I don't suspect they'll be shipping his remains home, but if they do, I'll expect you to do his makeup."

Feeling sick, Saxon backed away from him. "Why do you say such things, Father? The man I love, the one I planned to marry, is probably dead. Can't you be decent for just once?"

She didn't step fast enough; the palm of his hand caught the side of her face in a stinging slap that brought fast tears to her eyes. "You don't *need* a husband," he growled. "You'll stay here with your mother and me—and you'll take over the business when I retire. I've got it all planned out for you."

"But I don't want to be a mortician!"

Geoffrey Faraday looked like *he'd* been slapped. "The word is *undertaker*—and you don't have a choice, girl!" He reached out and grabbed her by the arm, then whirled around to face his wife, dragging Saxon with him.

Felicia Faraday had said nothing, no words of comfort to her heartbroken daughter, not a hint of protest about her husband's behavior. Saxon had suspected for some time, but now she was sure: the woman was no more than an empty shell. The house and her husband had broken her spirit a long time ago.

"Saxon and I are going downstairs to the office for a discussion, Felicia. I expect you'll have supper ready in an hour."

Pale as tallow, her face remained expressionless as she gave a slight nod, then turned toward the kitchen. Saxon saw the fiendish gleam in her father's eyes whenever he looked at her mother—and it chilled her to the bone. Why did he look at her that way? Was he still angry about her getting sick and having to go away?

But Saxon wasn't looking at him now; she was trying to maintain balance as he dragged her through the parlor, toward the cellar door. She knew better than to scream. Dear God, screaming really set him off and that was the last thing she wanted to do. As it stood right now, he was just beginning to get worked up, so perhaps, if she kept a cool head and played her cards right, there was still a way out without taking too much damage. If there was anything she refused to become—it was a replica of her mother!

This time, she had something in her pocket of her dress to ensure that Father wouldn't go too far. His handgun. She'd taken it from his desk less than an hour earlier. Why? The answer was simple: Rob was most likely dead and she didn't want to live without him, couldn't imagine a life without him being there to share it with her. The thought of being trapped here in this house with her parents was more than she could endure; she'd take the easy way out: open mouth and apply a bullet to the back of the throat. No need to repeat if necessary.

Her father was shoving her down the stairs, jabbing her repeatedly in the small of the back. "Fix me a drink, girl," he ordered as she reached his office door.

"Gin or Absinthe, Father?"

"Gin. You know I never drink Absinthe until the weekend."

Saxon went to his desk and opened the bottom drawer, wishing the prohibition on alcohol had never been lifted. Absinthe was still illegal, here and in many countries, but like everything else, it could be had for the right price—and Father had many bootlegger friends who thought nothing of making a side trip to Bar Harbor by boat, under the cover of darkness.

She opened the gin bottle and poured two fingers into

his shot glass, careful not to let it splash. Her hands were shaking, though, her fingers trembling as if they had minds of their own. Trying not to let it show, she passed him his drink, and he downed it like water, setting the glass face down on the blotter pad beside a coffin-shaped paperweight.

"I don't want to do this," he said, his breath fiery with juniper, "but you leave me no choice. Now's the time. I'd thought your mother would be first, but I was wrong. It's you."

"First for what?" Saxon didn't like the glassy look in his eyes or the way his own hands were trembling. She watched them rise, reach out, and come to rest atop her shoulders. He had long, slender fingers like those of a concert pianist, but they were powerful; she could feel their tips digging into her flesh.

"For this," he said, his voice strangely distant. In a flash his fingers moved to her neck, her throat, and they began to squeeze.

The pressure, the pain was incredible—nearly as unconceivable as the fact that her own father was trying to choke the life from her. Pulse pounding in her ears, she struggled to get away from him, but he was stronger, his grip so firmly locked around her neck, pressing on her windpipe with his thumbs.

She couldn't breathe! Things inside her neck—bones or cartilage?—were cracking and popping, and the pain was more intense than she ever imagined. She wanted to scream, demanding to know WHY he was killing her, but the only noise coming from her throat was a strange gurgling sound.

There was one way to end this, maybe the *only* way. One of them would have to die—and it sure as hell wasn't going to be her. Keeping her eyes locked on her father's face, she reached down into her pocket and her hand closed upon the gun.

The voice, the one she sometimes heard in her head and had come to associate with the house, whispered, hissing in urgency: *Do it, Saxon! You've got nothing to lose but your life!*

She had run out of air; there wasn't much time left before she either passed out or died.

Do it, do it, do it, do it!

Lifting the gun, she never took her eyes off her father's face, not even when her trembling thumb drew back the metallic click of the hammer. She saw him blink then, his eyes widening at the sight of the gun, now at eye level.

And that's when the bullet roared out, piercing his skull, giving him the single-second lobotomy. He released Saxon and stumbled backwards—turning, his hip grazing the side of his cadaver table, flipping him onto it. He stared straight at the big light overhead, the hole in his head looking like the symbol of the Hindu third eye.

Saxon dropped the gun on his desk, and stared at her father, watching him twitch and jerk on the table. His legs wouldn't stop moving and he stank with the release of his bowels and bladder. Who would prepare him for the grave? Saxon? Not bloody likely! No, she had something important to take care of . . . and if she didn't, it would surely take care of her.

Wordlessly, she walked upstairs, past her mother who'd come out from the kitchen, wistfully twisting her apron, looking worried. "I thought I heard a loud noise," she was saying.

"It's nothing," Saxon mumbled. "Father's passed out again."

She walked upstairs and Mother didn't try to stop her.

Mother knew how Father was when he drank. Had he been drunk? Saxon wasn't at all sure, but he'd been inebriated and abusive often enough so that it didn't matter, anyway. His days were numbered and the numbers had stopped today.

In her bedroom, Saxon opened the top drawer of her dresser. Yes, they were here . . . the single-edged razor blades, each one wrapped in thick, shiny paper. She took one, sank to her knees on the floor, and tore away the paper with her teeth.

Holding one arm up, she slashed at it with the blade, first across, following the bracelets of fortune, then straight down toward the elbow. Down and deep. The blade was brand new and very sharp; she'd barely felt a thing.

This is easier than swallowing a bullet, the voice told her. She could smell the residue of gunpowder on her hand, and the odor of her blood, which was gushing good now, squirting out strong and fast. She had to be quick to get the other arm done before she lost consciousness.

Do it, do it, do it—just a couple more slices and you'll be there!

She'd just started to draw the second line when her bedroom door burst open. Saxon looked up into her mother's face and for a moment, it seemed Mother didn't recognize her.

It may have been the shock of seeing blood; there was a lot of it. Pools on the floor. Splashes on the wall. Dots of it on her face, her hair, the front of her dress. Saxon dropped the razor blade and reached for her mother, pleading in a croaking voice, not for help but to be held. To be comforted the way she had been when she was a toddler, before they moved here to Roquefort Manor.

Mother jumped backward, screaming about blood, and lunged for the door. Saxon heard her running downstairs.

Did I frighten her that much? Or is this the proof I need that she no longer loves me?

In the quietness that followed, Saxon lay down, her ear pressed to the floor. While she bled, she could hear Mother talking to someone downstairs, a one-sided conversation. Telephone, it had to be. She heard the cellar door squeak open, and moments later the shrieking began. Saxon closed her eyes, determined never to open them again.

Then they came for her, those men, picking her up, lugging her out of her bedroom. The only face she recognized was that of Joe Tuttle, Jr., her next door neighbor. No kindness there, just an urgency to get her into the back of a car. Whose car? She had no idea. Someone was making a terrible fuss about her arms, wrapping them, binding them with strips of cloth.

She felt so tired, so very weary . . . and remembered nothing else of the ride to the hospital.

Hell's bells, spells. Saxon set the perfume down, aware that tears were blurring her vision, and she dabbed at the corners of her eyes with her gloved fingertips. *Bad memories, is that all there is for me?* Turning toward the bed, she suddenly wanted to throw herself headlong onto it and release all the angst she felt inside.

But that was a luxury she couldn't afford; no way was she going to lie down on that bed with its covers so heavy with dust and the added worry that there might be spiders hiding in the folds or up under the canopy. Still, she went over to the bed and stared down at it, swallowing the hard lump in her throat.

Enough of this foolishness, Saxon Faraday. You'd do well to get your bed made up and your room cleaned of dust before nightfall. There's enough for you to do besides sulking, so get on with it.

She sighed and pulled the covers off the bed. It was too late in the day to put them into the old wringer-washer and expect them to be dry before nightfall, so she carried them downstairs and out the back door. The clothesline was gone; it used to hang between the two big apple trees and besides, she had no idea where the pins might be, so she hung the bedspread over a branch and beat the dust out of it as best she could.

By now, it was dusk and the brightest stars were starting to come into view in a darkening sky. It reminded her of a song which she started to hum, then sing, her voice carrying over the backyard: "Love me in the misty moonlight, with caresses sweeter than honey, amid the stars so bright, don't 'cha think love's funny. . . ."

"You always had such a pretty voice," she heard someone call out. "I figured by now, you'd be out West somewhere, making movies." Startled, Saxon stopped singing, stepping away from her bedspread to look around. She could hear someone walking up the backyard path, the one that led through the woods down to the carriage road and Witch Hole Pond, and she turned in that direction.

"Who's there?" she called out, then spied the long wisps of white hair and a light-colored housecoat. It was Mrs. Tuttle, her elderly neighbor: congenial, nosy, and a tad senile as Saxon best remembered.

"Why, dearie, don't you look shocked! Remember me?" she asked as she approached.

Saxon hurried over to her, delighted to finally see a friendly face. "Well, of course I do! How nice to see you again, Mrs. Tuttle. You're just the same as I remember! How have you been?"

The old woman smiled a toothless smile, her face feathered in leathery wrinkles creasing deeply at the corners of her eyes and mouth. "Oh, same as always, ornery as ever. When'd you get back home?"

"I arrived today."

Mrs. Tuttle nodded, cocking her head to one side, grinning toothlessly. "Nice to be back, isn't it?"

Saxon shrugged. "I'm not so sure about that."

"Oh? Why do you say that?"

Glancing over her shoulder at the house, she admitted in a low voice, "It's just this place, and some of the people here. So many memories—not many of them good. But I'll be all right. I'm stronger now."

Mrs. Tuttle beamed, nodding as she patted Saxon's hand. "Well, of course you'll be all right. It's so good to see you again, although I must admit, I'm a bit surprised you came back. Tell me you're not all by yourself?"

That was Mrs. Evangeline Tuttle for you. Saxon figured it was her way of snooping around, trying to find out if she'd brought home a husband or beau.

She looked away and folded her arms in defense. "No, I'm alone. Figured I may as well get this place tidied up a bit. No one else is going to do it, that's for sure."

Mrs. Tuttle shot her a knowing look. "I can appreciate that. Sometimes, the only way to get a job done right is to do it yourself." Suddenly, her hand fell away from Saxon's hand, and confusion knit her furrowed brow. "It rained for such a long time, didn't it? Now that the rain's finally stopped, I can go for walks in the evening. Helps to keep the arthritis at bay. I just wish Old Joe would come with me."

Old Joe? Oh no, the poor dear really had lost touch. "It's getting awfully dark, Mrs. Tuttle. Why don't I walk you home?"

The old woman nodded. "That'd be real nice, dearie.

You can tell me all you've been up to since you've been gone, and I can fill you in on the latest gossip."

Saxon smiled and took her frail arm. For her part, there wasn't much to tell and she really didn't want to talk about her hospital stay; Mrs. Tuttle was set on bending her ears about news that was older than dirt, anyway, stuff she'd heard all about when she was younger. She half-listened to the old woman ramble on, then asked: "Did you happen to know Jacqueline Roquefort?"

At this, Mrs. Tuttle stiffened, nearly stopping in her tracks. "Why, of course, I knew her; years ago, she was my neighbor, too. Pretty little thing, she and her family lived in your house before your folks moved in. I make a special point to know all my neighbors. Why?"

"Just wondering what you could tell me about her."

"T'was a pure tragedy, what happened to her. I saw it coming—her father was drinking too much, doping himself up all the time. Oh, he tried to hide it, but everyone knew and nobody said a word. I think it was because of the kind of man Leonard was, you know. Prejudiced to a fault, absolutely no sense of humor, a teetotaler who'd spend his days with the dead and his nights in the cups." She swallowed and Saxon could hear the dry click in her throat.

"He was one of the few morticians in town, and everybody respected him for that. But I knew as soon as Jacqueline took up with that Italian boy that she was headed for trouble with her father." She tapped her chin with a gnarled finger, thinking. "The boy, his last name was Delgado if I remember right. Nice family, hard workers." She paused and added, "But you can only say so much, you know. I tried to warn the two of them, but they were young and in love. I doubt they wanted an old woman's opinion, anyway."

"I suppose."

The old woman turned, glanced back at Roquefort Manor, and Saxon thought she saw something like a shadow cross over her face. Apprehension, perhaps? "Any reason why you'd ask me about Jacqueline?"

Saxon shook her head. "No, not really. I was just curious." She didn't want to explain that she'd befriended Jacqueline during her stay at the hospital . . . that Jacqueline had died; she'd taken her own life just before Saxon's release. Did Mrs. Tuttle know about Jacqueline's suicide? Probably not, and there was no reason to upset her. They stopped in back of Mrs. Tuttle's house, a small, yellow cape surrounded by gardens. "Would you like me to walk you in?"

Mrs. Tuttle waved a liver-spotted hand. "Thank you, dearie, but no. I can find my way from here just fine. Old Joe's waiting up for me. Nice to have you back in town, honey."

"Uh, thank you." *Old Joe? There she goes again.* Saxon managed to cover her sudden puzzlement with a smile. "Have a good night, Mrs. Tuttle."

"Same to you, dearie."

She watched her neighbor walk up to her back door, open it, and go inside. *How very strange,* she thought, *that she'd mention Old Joe walking with her, waiting up for her.* Joe Tuttle, Sr. had died more than ten years ago.

The old girl isn't that far from the grave herself, she added. *Why she was ancient when I was just a mere slip of a girl. She may be a tad senile, but she's one smart cookie, sharper than she lets on. But why did she say that? Does she really believe Old Joe is at home?*

Saxon glanced back over her shoulder as she made her way to her own backyard. The outside light at the Tuttles' had darkened, and she sighed, walking toward her own backyard. *Well, this is the first time in five years I've ever really been alone,* she thought as she tugged her bedspread down from the tree, then carried it inside and up over the stairs.

There were linens in the upper hallway closet which had been packed in bags to keep the moths out and Saxon found some pillowcases to match. She turned on the radio and let it play while she remade her bed. Everything had changed in the past five years, including the music . . . everything except for this room. When she was finished making her bed, she lay down across it, thoroughly exhausted.

Pulling off her gloves, she put them on the nightstand. *I must be getting older,* she decided. *I never used to poop out so easy. Must be the long drive home—and the stress I've been under.*

She half-listened to the "Fibber McGee & Molly" show and Johnson's Wax commercials and relaxed, letting her mind drift.

. . . *why'd I come back here?*

. . . *had no choice . . . nowhere else to go . . .*

. . . *spooky, old house . . .*

. . . *spooky, old Mrs. Tuttle . . .*

. . . *so quiet here . . . just not used to it . . .*

. . . *so very, very tired. . . .*

Before she could get back up to undress for the night, Saxon Faraday fell asleep.

5

Sometime in the night, gloomy, minor-key music of a pipe organ woke her with a start, and she sat bolt upright in bed.

After wiping the sweat from her face with her hands, she reached over to turn on the light with trembling fingers.

Instantly, she was zapped. Not bitten hard enough to numb her from her fingertips to elbow, but hard enough to make her whole hand tingle.

Damn! She'd forgotten about the wiring, forgotten that her hands were gloveless and damp, forgotten momentarily where she was. The lamp came on, but her hand smarted with pins and needles as if it had been slapped. She'd been dreaming that something was chasing her through the woods, and now this awful scary music must have made her think that whatever was after her had to be huge and horrible. No wonder she was having a nightmare!

While her dream was imaginary and surreal, the music was not, and it took her a second to realize it was coming from the radio. CBS was playing *Phantom of the Opera* as a midnight special. Shaking her head, Saxon got up and, using a tissue as a barrier between her fingers and the knob, she shut the radio off.

That's when she heard something scarier than the music.

The crying of a baby. Again, it started low, like a kitten's mew, then gradually got louder, more demanding and desperate. Saxon looked around her room in fear. Everything seemed different somehow, turning almost misty. The wallpaper with its swirling leaves (*faces!*) had faded to nearly grey, and the tiles on the floor became transparent, revealing the rough oak planks beneath. She smelled a horrible stench, like that of rotten eggs, causing her to gag.

Her mind raced in frantic circles. *What's happening? What's that smell? Where's the sound of the crying baby coming from and why is it here?*

Heart pounding, she stood still by her dresser and listened. The pitiful crying seemed to be wafting down from above. But the attic stopped over her parents' old bedroom; there was nothing over hers—at least no room that she was aware of. She doubted there was even enough space up there to move about in—if so, it would be tiny, cramped, and confined.

The baby's cries grew progressively weaker, more pathetic. Just then, a shrill scream pierced the air, like that of a frightened woman. Heavy footsteps followed, then a sudden, loud crash, like that of a door being kicked in.

Saxon began pacing around her room, wringing her hands, her heart racing with worry. *Who's making all that noise? I want to leave,* she thought, *but I'm too afraid! Why are there people in my house? What are they doing here and why are they all so upset? And what of that poor little baby?*

She felt like cowering at the booming sounds of men shouting. One of them, the clearest, yelled, "Run—don't worry 'bout me!" And another, meaner-sounding voice screamed, "Stop, nigger-bitch!" The woman shrieked again, and Saxon heard the sound of footsteps racing down steps and padding into the hallway past her bedroom. Despite her panic, Saxon hurried to her door and opened it just a crack to take a look, ready to spring back and slam it shut at the first sign of immediate danger.

Danger was on its way, though; she could hear it coming in the heavy, rushing footsteps as they approached, then before she had time to shut the door, she saw, oh God, she saw . . .

. . . a big, raw-boned man with flame-red hair and a bushy beard. He was running down the hall, the sleeves and tail of his long buckskin coat flapping out behind him like sinister wings. His eyes were full of hatred; his thick lips were curled back in an evil snarl, revealing crooked, yellowed teeth.

"Don't you run from me," he bellowed. "Don't you dare run from me again!"

Another voice echoed down from above, "Please, Mister, please don't hurt her! Take me instead!"

A new voice, what sounded like a young man, screamed up from downstairs, "Don't let me die this way! Let me out! Let me—"

Saxon shut her door and sank to her knees, listening as the big red-haired man ran past her bedroom. She gripped her head in her hands and began to rock. "Stop it," she sobbed. "All of you, just stop it right now!"

Just then, a shotgun blast shook the whole house. Saxon clutched her chest in utter terror, her mind racing: *Someone's been shot! Murdered! Oh dear God, someone's in my house with a gun!* It reminded her so much of what happened with her father, and she had to bite her bottom lip to keep from screaming.

The din slowly faded, as if perhaps the people making all that noise had heard her pleas. Even the baby upstairs stopped wailing and a terrible thought occurred to her:

They know I'm here and now they're going to get me!

She looked up through a blur of fear, but the mist in the room was dissipating, the wallpaper returning to normal. All seemed quiet now throughout the house.

"Now that was *not* my imagination," she whispered in a small, stubborn voice, trying to convince herself that she was right. Her legs wobbled as she stood up. At the hospital, they'd called such episodes "auditory hallucinations," but the doctors were wrong. Sometimes these things were real.

Jacqueline knew they were real, too. She'd lived here before Saxon and she'd heard and seen the same sort of things. Saxon had almost begun to believe the psychiatrists, to question her own sanity, when, thankfully, she'd met Jacqueline.

Jacqueline Roquefort was another patient at the Hospital for the Insane. She was there because she, too, had killed her father and was deemed too incompetent to withstand trial. Labeled schizophrenic by the doctors, she was doomed to live out the rest of her days in the confines of the women's ward of Wing Three.

If Saxon and Jacqueline had had the same physicians and psychiatrists, they might have never been allowed to develop such a close friendship, but the hospital was crowded, the staff overworked, resources and budgets stretched as thin as possible. Because of this, patient records and case histories were seldom, if ever, compared.

It was unsettling for the two friends to learn that they'd both grown up in the *same* house—but they were also quite relieved. They'd each seen and heard similar things, and they shared these experiences with one another in whispered conversations, their heads bowed over rudimentary games of Old Maid and Chinese Checkers.

Perhaps this was the best form of therapy: Each woman's fears were confirmed and neither was a solitary prisoner of them any longer.

Saxon had been surprised to learn that Jacqueline, like herself, hadn't killed her father in cold-blooded murder; she'd hacked him to death with an axe in self-defense, maintaining that she'd had no choice—it was either him or her.

Of course, the doctors at the hospital were convinced otherwise, that Jacqueline had done it because her father disapproved of her beau. The boy had mysteriously disappeared around the time of Leonard Roquefort's murder, and it was supposed that Jacqueline and her beau were in on the murder together. The doctors begged her to reveal the boy's whereabouts, even going so far as to promise to release her if she told.

Jacqueline honestly didn't know and that sealed her fate.

"I could tell you what Father was like after the house got to him," Jacqueline had said to Saxon, "but I doubt you'd believe me. No one else does."

Saxon remembered reaching out to grasp her friend's hands. Her skin was so thin it was nearly transparent, very pink, and it felt fevered, hot to the touch. "I'll believe you," she'd promised. "Whatever you want to tell me, I'll know it's true. I think the same sort of thing must have happened to my father."

Jacqueline had glanced around the room, rabbit-nervous, and lowered her voice to a mere whisper. "It was that house. That's where it started. I was sixteen when we moved in—and I noticed certain things . . . like the people in the wallpaper and—"

"The faces!" Saxon blurted, then she lowered her voice to a hushed whisper. "I've seen them in my bedroom wallpaper lots of times."

Jacqueline knit her brows. "I suppose you heard things at night, too?"

"Yes. Shuffling around. Sounded like it was coming from upstairs."

"Did you ever see the red-haired man?"

Saxon shook her head. "What red-haired man?"

Jacqueline gave her a chilled look. "Oh, you'd know it if you saw him. Big, scary guy. You know what?"

"What?"

"I believe he was a ghost. I think there's a lot of ghosts at Roquefort Manor."

Saxon frowned as she picked up a shiny black marble

from the game board and squeezed it in her fingers. "Makes sense when you think of all the corpses our fathers moved through there."

Jacqueline nodded. "Roquefort Manor is a lightning rod for the dead. And you know, I think that even though Father claimed he didn't believe in ghosts, he could hear them, too. That house was affecting him in the strangest ways."

Saxon leaned forward, still gripping her marble. "Can you talk about it?"

Jacqueline hugged herself and as she did, the table jerked and some of the marbles on the game board rolled out of position. "Sorry," she murmured. "I didn't mean to ruin our game."

One of the orderlies glanced over in their direction, then went back to reading his dime-store novel.

"Think nothing of it," Saxon told her in a soft voice. "Are you sure you want to tell me about your father? If you don't, I'll understand. It must be a very deep wound for you."

Jacqueline shot her a hard look. "Deep? Heck, no. It happened almost forty years ago; it's an old scar." She cleared her throat and added, "It was a subtle change with my father. He was never what one would call a friendly sort. Maybe it was his job, I don't know, but he was a very skilled mortician. Trained in Boston. Outside of his work, he had a wife to see that he ate three meals a day and he had his camera."

Saxon cocked her head. "Oh, his hobby was photography? I suppose that provided a good outlet for someone who had to deal with death so much."

Jacqueline gave a nervous laugh. "I wouldn't call it *good,* my dear. He took pictures of dead people, the ones he embalmed. Mostly, he did it for the families of the deceased—a last photo type of service. The wealthy were the ones who requested it be done. They kept such photographs in special books. Dead books. The poor rarely asked for photographs, though, unless it was done for a very young person. Father had a wonderful way of making the corpses appear asleep. 'Trick of light,' he'd called it. He was a wonderful artist."

Saxon exhaled with a low whistle. "Even so, no wonder he was so somber all the time." Her own father had been a mortician, but she'd never known him to take pictures of corpses.

Jacqueline continued, "But after a year or so of living at Roquefort Manor, Father began acting strangely. Taking pictures of dead folks wasn't all he'd do with his camera. I found *other* photographs in his desk—the ones he didn't let the families see. All of them were of dead women. He'd disrobed them and positioned them in very indecent poses. It was disgusting. Horrible."

"Why? Why'd he do it?"

Jacqueline shrugged. "I don't know. Something inside of him must have snapped; whatever was in our house was getting to him . . . but at some point, he grew tired with that particular hobby and moved onto a new subject: me."

Shocked, Saxon covered her mouth with her hand. "How terrible!"

Jacqueline lifted a brow. "Ah, but he was crafty. Slow and careful. You see, Father was a calculating sort. Mother knew all about it, too, or at least I think she did. The photos of the dead women in his desk disappeared right after I killed him, and I think *she* was the one who hid them. Maybe she destroyed them to protect his reputation. I don't know. At any rate, there would have been a huge scandal if those photos were made public."

"When did he start taking pictures of you?"

Jacqueline sighed. "My sixteenth summer. I remember I'd bought a dress. Oh, Saxon, you should have seen it—it was glorious! I'd saved my allowance all summer just so I could buy it. Ordered it special from Spiegel's, just like a rich girl. I planned to wear it to the Autumn Ball at The Tall Pines, you know, the Penns' Estate."

Saxon nodded; she knew the place. The Penns had been famous for their annual Autumn Balls, the last hurrah at summer's end. These affairs always made the front page of local newspapers, as well as several that were not so local, like *The Boston Courier*, and *The New England Press*. They'd hire a full orchestra and invite nearly everyone on the island, rich or poor. For six hours, everybody would mingle over fancy drinks and take turns on the dance floor as if there were no class differences at all, as if they did more than rarely rub shoulders the rest of the year. Then after it was over, the poor went back to being poor and the rich went back to being rich, busying themselves with moving away for the winter.

"I so wanted to impress Mario Delgado with that dress," Jacqueline added.

"Mario Delgado?"

Jacqueline blushed even pinker. "My secret beau. If Father knew about us, Lordy, he'd have raised the roof. You see, we were very much in love. I wish you could have seen him, Saxon. He was drop-dead gorgeous. Those eyes of his, those dark curls . . ."

"Why didn't your father like him?"

Jacqueline gave her a wry look. "Oh, he liked him just fine. The Delgado family worked for us. His mother did our laundry; his father was our groundskeeper. They were Italians, plain working-class folks, and while Father felt they were good enough to work for him, they were not the kind of people he wished to socialize with. Certainly not good enough for his daughter, and there wasn't anything Mario could have done to merit Father's approval when it came to courting me."

"That must have been so hard for you."

Jacqueline nodded. "Oh, indeed it was, for both of us. We knew if we ever were caught alone together that Father would fire his family. He'd make them move away—and where would they go? They didn't have any money."

"What happened to your dress?"

Jacqueline sniffed but her eyes became steely, cold. "Father demanded that I take it off and destroy it. He said no daughter of his was going anywhere 'gussied up like a floozy.' "

Saxon looked shocked. "Hell's bells, what kind of dress did you buy?"

At this, Jacqueline sighed. "Oh, it was an evening gown of silk georgette, inlaid with glass beads and faux pearls, a lovely thing, really, in complementing shades of peach. The skirt had one of those tulip patterns."

"It must have been simply beautiful."

"Oh, it was. You can imagine my dismay when Father ordered me to destroy it. It wasn't any different than what the other girls my age were wearing, and I told him so. That's when he said the other girls had fools for fathers, and he ranted on about young people having no rules at home: no discipline, responsibility, or sense of direction."

"God, that sounds like my father. So what happened?"

"Mother tried to stop him. She'd been sitting on the davenport doing some embroidery and she got up to grab him by the arm, to make him stop picking on me. You see, she liked my dress very much and was proud of me for saving up the money for it." Jacqueline's voice caught in her throat. "That's when Father slapped her. I'd never seen him raise a hand to her before. Mother just stood there afterwards, perfectly still, holding her hand to her cheek in shock. Then she spun away and ran from the room . . . and Father destroyed the dress with me still in it. The beads, they scattered everywhere. Months later, I was still finding them in the front parlor whenever I swept the floor."

"And what of Mario Delgado?"

Jacqueline shrugged. "He and his family went to the Autumn Ball, where he waited for me but I never showed up. The next day I told him what had happened. Father had taken pictures of me with my dress all ripped up and Mario wanted to kill him. I don't know why Father did what he did, but I think that was the first sign that the house was getting to him, turning him into a monster, if you know what I mean."

"Please tell me he didn't . . . that your father didn't, well, spoil you?"

To Saxon's relief, Jacqueline shook her head. "No, and I never realized why he didn't until the winter of that year . . . I was too *alive* for him."

Too alive? "I'm afraid I don't understand."

Jacqueline sighed and her shoulders slumped. "Father was in love with the dead. There's a name for it, I think. Necrophilia. I know that sounds crazy, but I realized it one night when I found Mother taking an ice-cold bath."

Saxon's face revealed her shock. "My mother was doing the same thing! Taking cold baths, my God."

Tensing, Jacqueline nodded. "They were doing it for their husbands, I think. It's what they wanted. What the house *wanted* them to want, if that makes any sense. Mother would lie there in a tub full of ice water until she began to shiver and her lips would turn blue, then she'd powder herself from head to toe with talc. She'd hurry to bed before she warmed up. She never said why she was doing it, but I knew it was the only way Father could get aroused. I suspect she played the part of a corpse, pretending to be dead, while he had his way with her."

Saxon shuddered. "How utterly bizarre . . . I couldn't imagine doing that for any man."

Leaning forward, Jacqueline whispered, "I don't think the house gave our mothers a choice. It was sickening them, too—"

Just then, one of the orderlies blew his whistle. "Okay, ladies, time to tidy up and go back to your rooms." Dutifully, Saxon helped Jacqueline put the game back in its box. "I'm so sorry for what you had to go through," she whispered.

"Don't be," her friend told her. "I'm better off here than I ever was at Roquefort Manor."

Better off? Saxon thought about the conversation with Jacqueline as she crept downstairs. There was no use in trying to sleep now. She turned on the lights in the house as she walked through, wondering if she was going to run into another ghost, but all was quiet, as if nothing at all supernatural had happened. She went out the back door and onto the veranda to gaze up at the night sky. The moon was almost full and Witch Hole Pond reflected its silvery light like a mirror, glittery slits through the tall, dark pines.

Sitting down on the top step, she placed her elbows on her knees and rested her chin in her hands. She could smell the rich scent of newly-opened sea roses, probably wafting on the breeze from the long-abandoned gardens.

Okay, she thought, *so Roquefort Manor really is haunted. It's not all in my head. But what can I do about it? If I tell anyone or ask for help, they'll ship me right back to the mental hospital faster than I can say, "Jack Sprat." Nobody believes in ghosts anymore, do they? I mean, outside of novels by Lovecraft or Poe and pulp magazines, ghosts just don't exist. Besides, there's something more than a ghost here. Something that's pulling them to this place and anchoring them down. It's the Serpent, and I don't know how I know it, but I do. I don't think it's an actual snake, but more like a metaphor, so I call it the Serpent, because it's so crafty.*

But what does it want with the ghosts? And if it's holding them here, why can't I sense my father's ghost? Or the ghost of Jacqueline's father? It just doesn't make any sense. After all, they were both killed in this house—and according to the stories, doesn't a violent death almost guarantee a haunting?

But what about that poor baby? And what's with the woman and those men upstairs? Why are they chasing her? And what about the young man downstairs, pleading for his freedom or perhaps his life?

What does it all mean?

Oh, why am I the lucky one who gets to sort this whole mess out? Didn't I fight hard enough for my sanity? I didn't ask for this! Maybe I should just pack up and go, leave the whole works behind. The house is in shambles, anyway.

"Go ahead, Saxon, take the easy way out." The voice sounded dark and silky, fluid as the night and full of malice.

She was so startled to hear it that she nearly fell off the steps, but she managed to turn around and look up at the house. Although deep in her heart, she knew the answer, she still had to ask, her voice faltering, "Who said that? Who's there?"

No one answered. In the distance, she could hear the mocking laughter of a loon out on Witch Hole Pond.

I've heard that voice before, she thought, hugging her arms to her chest. It had been ages ago, when she'd held a razor blade between her shaking fingers. She'd listened to the voice then, heeding those dreadful, mellow instructions: *Do it, Saxon! Here's the gun. It's loaded and ready. Here he comes now. He's so very angry. This time he'll leave worse scars than the last time. Aim carefully, girl. That's it, go for the brain. Now squeeze the trigger. . . .*

And that horrible, final command moments later: *Do it, Saxon! It will only hurt a little; then you'll fall asleep and it'll all be over. No more punishment, no more pain. They're going to come and get you soon . . . take you away so they can hurt you some more. Maybe even kill you for shooting your father. That's a good girl, pick up that razor blade. No, don't slice across—you need to cut the long way to make it count. Yes, yes! See, the pain isn't that bad, is it? You've endured far worse than that. Remember those beatings with his leather belt? And what he did to your hands? It's all over now. . . .*

But she knew better; it was *far* from over.

"You're the Serpent!" she said, angry spittle flying from her mouth. "Whatever you are, I will defeat you. You may have won a battle or two, I'll give you that, but you haven't won the war. You'll never win because I'm going to find a way to end this. You'll never hurt another family again."

But exactly what was the Serpent? Did it exist only in her mind—or was it a mere circumstance of misfortune visited upon two families living in the same house, decades apart? *No,* she reasoned, *it's something very real and very evil. And it's in my house and it spoke to me.*

She reached for the railing beside the steps and, clinging to it, she forced herself up the stairs. Her legs felt like lead, her knees jelly, and her heart was thumping way up high in her throat. She didn't want to be here—and it wanted her to leave. She could feel its negative energy enveloping her, prickling the hairs on her arms and on the nape of her neck.

The Serpent's like a parasite, she thought. *It feeds off anyone who lives here. If I can't defeat it, it's bound to sicken others. I have to stop it because I won't live forever.*

But was the Serpent a ghost?

No. Ghosts were neither good nor evil; they just are. *Probably most of them don't even realize they're dead,* she thought. But something else was here, something capable of charging her house with negative energy, something capable of trapping the dead and driving the living insane. *Maybe, if I balance out the negative energy by providing some sort of positive polarity, I can destroy the Serpent?*

The Serpent. That was her name for it, although she knew it wasn't its true name. It wasn't the Devil, not in the sense of the Biblical Satan, but she was quite sure they were closely related, cut from similar cloth. Was it a demon? Maybe. But why was it here, in her house? How long had it been here? What did it plan to do?

Lower lip trembling, she lifted her chin as she reached the top step. *In order to destroy the Serpent, I must first understand it. How's that saying go? Know thy enemy. I need to find out why it stays here and what it intends to do. Only then will I know how to defeat it. But where do I begin?*

By the time she reached the back door, Saxon knew where to start.

CHAPTER TWO

1

Evangeline Tuttle lived next door in a small cape, painted canary yellow with forest green trim. Flowerbeds sprawled across her front lawn, dappled with various-sized bushes: Japanese yew, snowball, forsythia, and lilacs in purple and white. Her tea roses were the envy of her friends and neighbors—no one knew her secret for growing such luscious blooms: American beauty, Lincoln, Peace, Black Magick; they were gorgeous to the eyes and heavenly to the nostrils.

It was after 9 a.m. when Saxon Faraday made her way over the narrow garden path to the Tuttle house. She hadn't expected to sleep in so late, but with so little rest the night before, she forgave herself the transgression.

In the daylight, everything seemed and felt back to normal. Certainly, the house was a wreck but it didn't appear to harbor the surreal ugliness she'd experienced the night before. Still, there was something about it, the knowledge, perhaps, that she knew the Serpent was somewhere inside, coiled, lying dormant . . . waiting . . . waiting for what? Night? Biding its time until she fell asleep to start terrorizing her all over again?

She didn't want to give it that chance. Mrs. Tuttle would know the history of Roquefort Manor, and she might even know about the Serpent. She was one of the oldest people in town, and she made it her business to know everyone and everything. Fortunately, for Saxon's sake, she probably wouldn't mind sharing her knowledge.

Saxon stopped for a moment to examine Mrs. Tuttle's flowerbeds. Something wasn't right; they looked a bit unkempt and weedy, and she sighed, remembering their former beauty. Well, Mrs. Tuttle was getting up in age, and she did mention she had arthritis, so Saxon made a mental note to offer her neighbor some help with the gardening.

That's when she heard the voices. Both were male and coming from the front of the house. Leaving the garden path, Saxon spotted a man and a teenaged boy, and she approached them with a smile. They were Mrs. Tuttle's son and grandson, Joe, Jr. and Clement, an odd pair; Joe, Jr. was the silent type. He never waved, but if you caught him on a really good day, he might give a slight nod of his head to acknowledge your presence. His son, Clement, was friendly by far. He had Down Syndrome and a slight speech impediment. Usually the happy one, despite his challenges, you could count on Clem for a wave and a smile.

They were raking lawn clippings and when Saxon called out a greeting, Clement gave her a friendly wave of his hand. He was a big, sandy-haired kid with so many freckles it looked as if he'd been dipped instead of sprinkled. The ones on his cheeks and nose ran together so much it was difficult to distinguish where one freckle stopped and another began. His eyes, bright blue, were slanted slightly upwards and outwards, giving him a distinctive, Oriental look.

He grinned and waved at Saxon as soon as he saw her, while his father merely glanced up and, apparently choosing to ignore her, continued to rake the lawn.

"Hi," Clement said with a wide grin. His teeth were big for his mouth, rabbit-like incisors that reminded Saxon somewhat of shovels.

"Hey there, Clem," she said, returning his smile. "I need to talk to your grandmother. Is she home?"

His smile dropped instantly and Saxon wondered if something was wrong. "Grammie's sweeping," he told her.

Saxon frowned, trying to understand. "She's doing housework? Is that it?"

Clement shook his head and turned away; Saxon could sense his frustration. "Sweeping." He laid his head on his folded hands and closed his eyes, making a soft, snoring sound.

"Oh, sleeping? I understand."

When Clement turned to face her again, his eyes were so bright they were nearly wet. "Yes! Sweeping!"

Saxon held up one hand, smiling. "Well, I'll come back later when she's awake." She couldn't help but notice that every time Clement spoke, his father would shoot him a sidelong glance, one eyebrow raised. He'd never really hidden the fact that his son was a major disappointment to him, and it upset Saxon because there wasn't a thing she could do about it. Children were a blessing, even if they weren't perfectly made; they were always perfect in God's eyes. Because Clement had Down Syndrome, he wasn't expected to live a very long and healthy life; he'd be doing well to make it to age twenty or twenty-five. His grandmother even mentioned in the past that it was a miracle that he'd survived birth.

Saxon couldn't help but think about this as she smiled back at Clem, and if she could have, she would have adopted him. But that was impossible; she had no husband. Plus she'd been in a mental hospital for the past five years. As much as she loved kids, though, she felt she'd never be blessed with motherhood, adoptive or biological. Rob's death at Pearl Harbor had killed that dream for her. There'd never be another Rob, or another Georgie either, for that matter.

She shot a glare at Joe, Jr. but it softened into a smile when she glanced back at Clement. "I'm glad to see you're helping your grammie. You're such a good help to her. See you later, Clem."

"Bye-bye," he said with another wave. Saxon watched him twist his ball cap around so the visor hung down in the back, then she walked away without so much as a word to Clem's father. Joe, Jr. made her so mad she could almost spit—treating Clement like he was sub-human—how dare he? What gave him that right? Old Mrs. Tuttle tried her best to make up for her son's ill treatment of the boy; Saxon had seen it time and time again . . . the way she'd scoop him into her arms and hug him, telling him he was so special to her. She never made him feel sad or call him awful names like Joe, Jr. sometimes did.

Saxon pondered this as she made her way back to her house. Was Joe, Jr. bitter because his son had been born less than perfect? Or was it because Clement's mother had left them both shortly after giving birth? She'd never known Joe's wife at all, had never even seen her for that matter. Supposedly, she'd hailed from some small town north of Bangor, the daughter of a lumberjack, so it was said. No one really knew why she left her husband and newborn son, except maybe Joe, Jr.—and he wasn't talking. Oh, there was plenty of speculation: that maybe she had a lover somewhere up from whence she'd come or that she had some kind of dreadful disease having to do with the baby blues. All anyone knew was that she'd left and never returned and eventually Joe, Jr. and Clement moved in with the elder Tuttles.

One look at Roquefort Manor was enough to tell Saxon that she wasn't ready to go inside yet and tackle the monstrous job of cleanup. The day was too new, too bright and pretty, to be stuck in the house, so she took the side path leading down to Witch Hole Pond.

For some reason, she felt her blood surge with a passion for living, her soul brimming with spirituality, as if all events of the day would be tinged with some sort of sacred overlay, as if every event seemed significant in some way. It was a connectedness she'd never felt before. Intense, that was a good way of describing it.

She didn't know exactly what she was going to do once she got to the pond, maybe just sit on a rock by the water and think. The path she walked was smooth but narrow, with thick, tangled vegetation on both sides. A dragonfly with iridescent wings zipped on ahead of her, causing her to smile. She'd always liked dragonflies, despite what people said about them sewing up people's mouths. Devil's darning needles, that's what they were sometimes called. Saxon figured some people just didn't know how many bad bugs they ate. Once, she'd seen one grab a moose fly right out of the air and devour it in mid-flight.

She could smell the pond now—that wet, warm, fresh-water scent—as the footpath led down the hill and eventually merged with a carriage road. The philanthropist, John D. Rockefeller, had designed these roads. Of firmly packed, crushed grey stone, they intersected, winding and looping throughout much of Acadia National Park. Built especially for horse-drawn carriages, they were a standard sixteen feet wide, ideal for strolling and biking. Saxon knew them well; apart from the last five years, she'd walked them all her life.

Leaves rustled in the breeze, reminding her of the times when she and Georgie would "go down to the Witch Hole" for a swim in those long, languid days of bike rides and Sunday malts. She was sure if she imagined hard enough, she could almost see him zipping by on his cherry red

Schwinn DX, and the blur of those white-walled tires. He'd be laughing as he sped downhill, hair whipped back, feet resting coolly on the pedals, not pressing the brakes.

Then he was gone and the view of Witch Hole took his place. It hadn't changed much since she'd last seen it, except the water level had receded some, making her pebbly beach a little larger than before. Saxon wasn't alone with her observations; there was another woman here, one with skin as dark and sleek as wet auto tires, her hair covered with a twisted cloth wound atop her head. She was knee-deep in the water and turned to look at Saxon as she approached.

Saxon gave her a friendly wave. "Hey there," she called out. She wasn't used to seeing black folks around here. Oh, sure, they'd come up with the rich people for the summer, always as cooks, chambermaids, and butlers. The few she'd met, Hannah Somerby, the Gayelords' cook, and old Mr. John Jacks, the Yorks' hired man, were fine people in her book. What struck her most was their passion, their zest for life. The stories they told could make you laugh until tears ran down your cheeks and you had stitches in your belly. Their scary tales, though, could induce nightmares that would last for weeks.

"Well, hello," the black woman called back as she lifted something out of the water. Saxon saw it was some sort of cloth she was washing.

"Anything I can do to help?" she asked, feeling it would be rude to sit down without offering a hand.

Smiling, the black woman shook her head, and Saxon was impressed by the stark whiteness of her teeth. She was strikingly handsome, not fat and not thin, maybe a few years older than Saxon but not by much. "I do my own washing," she called back with a chuckle. "I always know it's clean if I do it m'self."

Saxon kicked off her shoes and pulled off her stockings. She left them on the bank by a rock as she waded into the water. "Ooh," she said. "Nice and warm, isn't it?"

"You call this warm?" The woman gave a melodic chuckle. "This is colder than Corby Pond gets in January, that's for sure."

"Corby Pond. Never heard of it. Where's that?"

The black woman looked up and stopped rubbing the wet material in her hands. Her eyes were dark and beautifully shaped, accented by long, thick lashes. Her nose was wide but pretty, perfect for her face, her lips, a natural dark red. It was only then that Saxon noticed her belly. The woman was pregnant, heavily so.

"Georgia," she murmured, her smile dropping. "Corby Pond's way back in Georgia." From her expression, it was apparent that this was some sort of secret, although Saxon couldn't imagine why.

"Is that where you're from?"

"Yes, Ma'am. But you won't tell no one, will you?"

Now it was Saxon's turn to chuckle. "I won't say a word. I didn't know it was a crime to be from Georgia."

"You wouldn't."

"My name's Saxon Faraday," she said, not really knowing how to take the woman's last reply. "What's yours?"

"I'm Suki," she said, picking up the cloth and wringing it out again. Saxon saw then how strong her arms were, all muscle, long and lean. "Suki Freemont."

"That's a pretty name," Saxon told her. She was about to say something else, maybe ask her when her baby was due, when a bunch of boys, four in number, came racing down out of the woods, hollering and whooping, heading for the beach.

"Uh oh, we's got trouble now," Suki muttered, tucking her laundry under her arm.

Before Saxon could ask why, one of them pointed and yelled, "There's the black witch! Let's get her!"

"You boys best leave me be," Suki shouted back at them. "I'm leaving now. Lemme go in peace."

"How 'bout a piece of this?" The ringleader picked up a rock and flung it at Suki. It hit the water, splashing both women. "What you think you're doing, polluting our pond?"

"It's not *your* pond," Saxon shouted back, brandishing her fists. "It belongs to the Park Service. Leave her alone or I'll see to it that your parents find out you've been harassing a lady."

The boys laughed and it sounded hateful and cruel. "So the black witch has a white wench. Maybe we should stone both of them? They'd make pretty good pickerel bait."

"You throw another rock and I'll zap ya's wid da Voodoo hex," Suki warned, accenting her words with a heavy Georgian twang. She raised a hand, two fingers making a perfect V. "You don't wants to be messing wid me."

The boys were picking up more rocks from the beach when Suki pointed at a tree near the water's edge. There was a loud and sudden crack and a thick bough came crashing down, nearly landing on the ringleader. "Damn you, bitch!" he called out, then he screamed in pain, dancing about, swatting at the air.

The fallen branch held a paper nest and the wasps were none too pleased about being disturbed. Naturally, the boys were the nearest targets and they soon sent them sprinting back into the woods.

Saxon laughed, watching them go, seeing the humor and

poetic justice in such big, strong bullies brought low by tiny insects, but Suki didn't crack a smile. "What's wrong?" Saxon asked, as she gained her composure.

"They got for what they deserved," she said, wading laboriously out of the water. "But they'll be back. Their kind never learns."

"How'd you do it?" Saxon asked, her voice nervous.

"Ah, so you think it was Voodoo, too?" Suki flashed her another terrific smile. "It only *looked* that way. That branch's been loose for a long time. Might have been struck by lightning a while back. I saw it was going to fall just then, but it happened too fast to warn those bad chilluns."

Despite her smile, Saxon had the distinct feeling Suki wasn't being exactly forthright or, if she was, she wasn't telling her the *entire* truth about what had just transpired. What if the boys were right? What if she was a witch?

"I did no Voodoo," she said, as if in answer to Saxon's thoughts. "But I do believe everything makes full circle. You do bad, you get bad in return. You do good, and good comes back to you. Not always, not every time, but that's how the odds is stacked. I think you probably believe that, too." She sighed, wringing the water from her laundry. "Odds could'a been stacked better for me, though. I must'a done something wrong, somewhere along the way. I'd leave here today if only I could."

"Where would you go?" Saxon asked, struggling to keep up with her.

"Canada, that's where we was headed, when my man, Stevie, got himself sick, laid up with some kind of fever. So we's here until he gets better."

"Where are you staying?"

Suki tilted her head toward the path leading toward Roquefort Manor and the Crooked Road. "Up there a ways. 'Spose to be a secret, though. The fewer folks who knows, the better."

"I live up there," Saxon told her. "Perhaps we could visit each other?"

Suki shook her head. "You kidding? You're white! Blacks and whites don't mix, Miss Saxon. Only times they do is if the blacks is *working* for the whites."

"But we're 'mixing,' aren't we?" Saxon maintained.

At this, Suki threw her an amused glance, almost smiling, and she started for the path. "You's an exception, lady. The world would be a better place if there were more folks like you, no doubt 'bout that."

Saxon stopped at the spot where her shoes and stockings were lying on the beach. "I do hope to see you again," she called out.

"I hope so, too." With a nod of her head, she disappeared up the path, barefooted, with her wet laundry tucked under her arm, dripping, leaving spatters in the dust.

Saxon sighed and sat down to pull her stockings and shoes on. *Now I have three friends,* she thought. *Mrs. Tuttle, her grandson Clement, and Suki. How about that? Not bad for my second day back home.*

She wondered why Suki and her man, Stevie, were going to Canada—and why they had to keep it a secret—and if the bough had really fallen from the tree under its own power.

2

Saxon didn't get as much done on the house as she'd planned; it was just too overwhelming a task for one person.

She thought about offering a job to Suki, when and if she ever saw her again. She wouldn't be able to pay much in terms of money, but she had a closet full of clothes that would fit Suki better than herself, after the baby was born, of course.

She spent the day sweeping and dusting, and tackling the cobwebs along the ceilings with a broom wrapped in an old, woolen cloth.

Long about dusk, old Mrs. Tuttle appeared in the backyard, on her nightly stroll, and Saxon invited her to come sit for a spell on the porch. Earlier she'd brought out a couple of wicker chairs and a small table. It wasn't much, but at least it was a place to relax. Mrs. Tuttle took her up on the offer—and the chance to chat.

First, Saxon asked her about Suki, but the older woman had no idea who she was talking about.

"Everyone would know if there was a darkie 'round here," she told her. "Chances are, your friend works for some of the rich folks and was feeding you a line—or she stowed away with them when they moved up for the summer and has cooked up a grand plan of sneaking off to Canada."

"I don't think she was lying to me about that," Saxon said, then she told her about the boys at the pond and the branch full of wasps and her doubts that Suki hadn't caused it to happen.

"Ooh, sounds like you've seen the ghost of the Witch Hole," Mrs. Tuttle whispered, looking more than a bit uncomfortable. "Back when I was a youngster, there was a story about a witch around these parts. I don't remember it very well, but as I recall it had something to do with wasps."

Saxon laughed. "Now that's silly. Suki isn't a ghost—she

was just as real as me—and she's no witch, either. At least, I don't *think* she's a witch. It was probably just a strange coincidence. Another thing I wanted to ask you, though . . . what can you tell me about the history of Roquefort Manor?"

Mrs. Tuttle sighed, relaxing in her chair, leaning back, looking up at the first stars of twilight. "Oh, dearie. Where do you want me to start? You know, that house was built long before I was born."

"Do you know who built it?"

Mrs. Tuttle scratched her head with bent fingers, and Saxon could see her hair was thinning, poor thing. "Well, let's see," she said, "that would have been Samuel D. Roquefort. He was from Virginia, if I remember correctly. Made a mint in the cotton business and owned several textile companies down South."

Saxon leaned forward. "I know he was before your time, but do you remember hearing anything about him? Anything at all?"

Mrs. Tuttle nodded. "Yes, one thing sticks in my mind: he was an adamant abolitionist, which everyone thought strange because he owned several cotton plantations. But according to his son, Leonard, the old man paid his slaves regular wages, treating them just like hired hands. Gave them all their freedom papers, too, providing they attend church on a regular basis. He was a bit eccentric, but a very good-hearted man," she added.

"How'd you know that?"

Smiling, Mrs. Tuttle replied, "Well, when my mother was a young woman, before she met my father, she used to work as a summer cook for the Roquefort family when they'd vacation here. I remember her telling about it some." Mrs. Tuttle reached out and patted her knee. "You know,

Mama always thought it strange. 'All that food,' she'd say, 'and only the three of them to eat it: Mr. and Mrs. Roquefort and their son, Leonard.' She had no idea where the leftovers were going because there never were any—and the Roqueforts were thin people. Picky eaters, not the type who'd pack away a dozen or so eggs for breakfast, along with two or three pounds of bacon." She chuckled before continuing.

"Mama always complained of rats in the attic. Not that she ever saw one, mind you—she'd have fainted dead away if she'd ever seen a rat. But she swore she could *hear* them up there, scurrying around. Even after she got old and lost her mind, she began to imagine there were rats like that in *our* attic, too." Mrs. Tuttle shook her head in pity. "This one time, I recall, Mama was having one of her spells—that's what we called them, spells—she grabbed me by the sleeve and demanded to know if I'd been feeding the rats upstairs. Of course, I told her I wouldn't feed a rat if it wore a halo and sang *Ave Maria*, but she swore that she knew *someone* was feeding them. At night, always at night, and the poor thing was scared to death they were going to chew their way down through the ceiling and land on her bed."

"How terrible!"

Mrs. Tuttle nodded and gave her a concerned look. "You haven't noticed signs of rats in your house, have you, dearie?"

Saxon shook her head. "Just mice and the occasional squirrel."

"Ah, varmints." The old woman looked around, as if suddenly realizing something important. "Oh my, it's getting late, isn't it? I really have to get back home to Joe. He's not feeling well and I don't like leaving him home alone when he gets the collywobbles."

"Joe, Jr.?" Saxon thought he seemed fine when she'd seen him earlier that day. Aloof and mean, but nonetheless healthy.

Mrs. Tuttle chuckled as she struggled to her feet. "No, Joe Jr.'s fit as a fiddle. It's his father I worry about. His stomach isn't doing so well these days. That's what he gets for spending his youth treating his stomach like an iron gut, eating all those rich, greasy foods. It's catching up with him now."

Saxon trembled. It was hard to hear her talk about Joe, Sr. as if he were still alive, although maybe in her mind, he was. But was she that far gone? She'd seemed fairly coherent until now. Was that how senility worked? In fits and starts? Fine one minute and gone the next?

She offered to walk Mrs. Tuttle home, but the older woman wouldn't hear of it. "No, dearie, you get settled in for the night. I'll be just fine. Bye now."

Saxon lifted her hand in a wave she wasn't sure Mrs. Tuttle even saw, then she turned and went inside.

Wonder what's going to happen tonight? she wondered. *I should check out the cellar before I go to bed, I know I should. Maybe if I do, they'll leave me alone?*

But I don't want to! It's dark and it smells bad—and there have been so many dead people in the workroom over the years. Maybe some of them are down there, still? Maybe their ghosts are waiting for me? If so, I'm outnumbered and I know it.

But why?

Because Roquefort Manor is a lightning rod for the dead.

Saxon shivered.

3

1850

Recollections rose from the warm, dank root cellar as fodder for ghosts—and one in particular, because this memory belonged to him. He now recalled his death, and the seductive way that voice had fallen so sweetly on his ears the first time he'd heard it speak:

Come to me, be mine, Gerard. . . .

He'd opened his eyes, expecting to still feel the fiery agony deep inside his chest, and yet, there was nothing. No excruciating pain, no shortness of breath, like there had been only moments ago. He'd stared upward at the night sky, a black blanket studded with stars, and he realized how very still and beautiful it was. It reminded him of home.

And yet that voice, floating down to him, more demanding now, more urgent: *I need you!*

Gerard Wendell Beaumont listened, trying to place the voice. No, it wasn't anyone he knew, he was quite sure of that . . . but it was the same voice he'd heard in his dreams and sometimes in nightmares warning him of perils and occasionally forcing him into danger. Not being particularly pious, it was the closest thing he knew to be God.

"Am I dead?" he'd asked, sitting up to look around. No one answered, but off in the distance, he could hear the sounds of lamentation and the heavy clanging of chains. Where did Adam Walker go? Where were those two slaves? He'd remembered Walker had taken the woman out into the water—and he was afraid he might try to drown her. Not that Beaumont particularly cared a whit about her life, but as a bounty hunter, he was in this for the money. He'd been hired to return them to Silas d'Mornay of West Atlanta, Georgia, where he'd be paid for his services, and from there, he'd move onto the next job.

He wasn't a well-loved man; many people had hated him, despising his line of work, refusing to even consider it as a necessary evil. Escaped slaves weren't the only ones he tracked down; there were outlaws and fugitives of justice, runaway wives, and the occasional whore who'd skipped town with her madam's pocketbook. Gerard Wendell Beaumont called himself a hunter by trade. A *manhunter.*

It was an easy enough occupation, once the signs were interpreted correctly (and everyone always left behind signs, no matter how good they were at hiding them). And while he had to admit there was no such thing as a clean getaway, he was well aware that the Underground Railroad was becoming increasingly clever at helping slaves escape the South. It forced Beaumont and other hunters like him to rely on connections, people like Adam Walker, from whom information could be purchased for a mere pittance.

Did he harbor one ounce of compassion for the individuals (and sometimes the families) he returned to slavedom? Nope. He'd believed he had the good fortune of being born white and free, so the turmoil and tribulations of others was of no cause for great concern to him. As long as he was paid for his efforts, and paid well, he could sleep with himself at night. He couldn't sleep now, though. That voice, that awful, sweet-sounding, seductive voice beckoning still:

Come to me now. . . .

In the milky moonlight, he'd turned to get up and was surprised to find that he'd been sitting on someone. One of the slaves? No. As he'd stood up and turned, sheer horror spread across his face as he recognized the buckskin coat, the long breeches. Those well-worn boots. The crimson beard flowing down over the barrel-shaped chest—and that gaping hole where more crimson flowed, spreading its sticky wet stain.

What in Hell's tavern was going on here?

Damned if he don't look just like me! Beaumont thought, leaning over the body for a closer look. Reaching out a finger, he'd gingerly touched the buckskin coat and his finger sunk right *into* it, clean out of sight, as if it hadn't been comprised of anything more substantial than fog.

Well, it was him, all right; he was pretty certain of that, but how he'd gotten *outside* of himself, he couldn't quite figure it out. *So where's the glorious afterlife they're always preaching about?* he wondered. He'd always figured that if *they* were right; after dying he'd probably find himself on the receiving end of a sharp poker . . . being prodded by a horny ol' demon into some fiery furnace. Heaven with its choirs of angels sitting around on clouds didn't much appeal to him, anyway.

Better to lead in Hell than to serve in Heaven. Who'd said that? Was it his mind or was it that voice, the one he kept hearing, asking him to come. Come where? He'd glanced down again at his body lying there on the bank of some weedy, little no-count pond way up in the wilds of Maine. He'd never been this far north before and he didn't care for it much. It was too cold, too foggy, too far away from everything else, and too long a journey on horseback. He'd never had the belly—or the sea legs—for traveling by ship.

Gerard, I need you. I have a job for you.

Who said that? Gerard looked around but the only other person here was his carcass, and that was well beyond the talking stage. "A job for me?" he asked. "What kind of job?"

There was a path leading up from the gravelly shore and joining a wider road.

Yes, my good man, that's the way. . . .

Beaumont had followed the sound of the voice and when it drew him into the woods, to a footpath leading to a black house on a hilltop; he never looked back, never questioned the almost magnetic lure or authority in that voice.

Even when it brought him down into the root cellar.

4

With all the lights on, the cellar wasn't quite so unnerving; the floors in the finished rooms were tiled, black and white, in a checkerboard pattern. The walls were painted stark white, mildly reflecting the light, and yes, Father's tilted cadaver table was still there, dead center in the room, with its heavy glass top, now thick with dust. Cobwebbed rows of shelves behind the table boasted various, multi-colored bottles of serum-colored embalming fluids labeled "Cavity Fluid" and "Mack Necropsin," among many others. Formaldehyde and phenol, methanol, distilled water, and some whose labels were so old that the ink had faded clean away. Disinfectant, deodorizers, the shelves were well stocked. Saxon didn't bother to read them—she knew what most of them were and how they were to be used.

On this side of the cadaver table, black rubber tubes led to stained, wide-mouth gallon jars, the aspirating bottles for blood and other body fluids. A black, medical cabinet stood in the corner. Saxon knew it stored yards of gauze and bags of cotton batting, heavy thread, bee's wax, an embalming kit containing the surgical tools of the trade, and the makeup kit: the tinting creams and flesh pigments, the drying powders and wound fillers. The aspirating pump was in the opposite corner, its chrome dull from years of use.

She turned from the doorway for a moment, gathering her courage. The room still stank of formaldehyde and its heavy odor stung her nostrils. No, she'd not find any answers here today. She wasn't at all sure she could handle it if she *did* find some answers in this room.

But her father's office was another matter entirely. This was where he kept the records of whom he embalmed, the names, the dates, and where they'd been buried. Many of the records stored in the file cabinets had belonged to Leonard Roquefort. Would she find anything there?

It seemed a good a place to start as any. She seated herself at her father's desk, perhaps in the very chair where he'd sat down and plotted her murder five years ago. Shivering, she tried to concentrate on the task at hand, trying to push the vile, black thoughts from her mind. It did her little good; knowing that her own father hated her enough to kill her was always at the back of her thoughts . . . and over time, it had woven itself into the core of her personality, poisoning and tainting it with statements such as: *I'll never be loved. Never be quite good enough. How can I ever trust another man? How could a man ever trust me, after what I did to my own father?* Yes, there had been Georgie, and then Rob, but they loved her *before* her father tried to take her life, and mercifully, they'd died before she'd taken his.

Her father's desk was a heavy, roll-top monstrosity of red oak, beautifully crafted and ornate, with silver corners and handles. She blew some dust away and attempted to lift the cover.

It was jammed. She tried again, grunting with effort,

then gave up. It was worse than jammed; it was locked.

"Damn!" She gave a frustrated yelp and pushed the chair away from the desk. Where was the key? Likely, long gone by now. Hidden away in some secret, forgotten place—or thrown away because Mother had no idea what it belonged to. But Saxon was determined, knowing there was some reason she had to get into that desk. Something important was in there: a clue, perhaps, to help unravel the riddle of what was infesting her house—and how to get rid of it.

It. The Serpent. She'd thought about it a lot, trying to fathom what it could be. It seemed to her that whatever being the Serpent was, it was a force to be reckoned with. It was capable of possession, she was quite sure. Certainly, it must have possessed Jacqueline Roquefort's father, Leonard, before his death. Yes, certainly, the man had done terrible things in life: wife-beating and photographic perversions involving the corpses of women (as well as his own living daughter), but even so, Leonard wasn't entirely wicked; indeed, he hadn't started out that way. Before moving to Eden, Maine, he'd been one of the most highly skilled morticians in the state, a good businessman, a decent provider. He was educated, well spoken and well read. How did he become possessed?

Was it a slow siege or did it happen overnight? Saxon reasoned that it must have come on slow and steady, subtle at first then growing stronger as time went by until it consumed him entirely, leaving nothing but the outer core, a shadow of the man he'd once been.

That's how it had happened with Father.

He hadn't been inherently evil, no, he'd been *influenced.* Maybe the Serpent came to him one night while he'd been relaxing, sipping his gin? Perhaps it appeared in the form of the green fairy while he swallowed glass after glass of absinthe? It must have been mighty seductive, likely promising him great power and riches. Hinting to him that his wife really didn't love him, that she planned to leave him, and that his daughter was a bad seed. No doubt, it had permitted him some time to stew in these dark thoughts, then when it knew it had enough influence, it started dropping suggestions . . . and at some point, Father listened. At any point in this downward spiral did the words of his number one bootlegger, the one he called "Old Chief," return to haunt him?

"Beware, good man—the green fairy will become your queen if you let her," he'd always say, pocketing the money and passing the bottle.

How Geoffrey Faraday had laughed at that; Saxon remembered him joking about it. No female was going to rule over him; he'd made it very clear to his wife and daughter, but in the end, the green fairy won, and her mission accomplished, she seceded her throne to another tyrant. Saxon figured that's how it must have happened.

Father's desk was his throne, an antique monstrosity of well-worn wood decorated with silver latches and handles now tarnished black. The ornate edges were now a dull ebony, cold and smooth. Saxon wanted so badly to get into those drawers, to investigate the cubbyholes behind the writing area, but she really didn't want to break the top of the desk to do it. She sat back in her chair, legs crossed at her ankles, chewing thoughtfully on the thumb of her glove. Did it really matter if she broke into the desk? It was hers now; she could do with it as she pleased. Still, breaking into it would make her feel profane and dirty, as if she were violating some great law, a sacrilege for which there never could be any forgiveness. *Father would kill me if he knew what I'm thinking,* she thought. But did it matter? He *had* tried to kill her and he was dead; there was nothing he could do about it now. Unless, of course, he was a ghost.

Now that was a cheery thought. No, she had to take the risk.

There must be something here. Contemplating, she pressed her lips together, adding, *Something that will help me understand what I have to do. I'm sorry, Father, maybe you're right; maybe I really am a bad girl like you said, but I feel I don't have any choice about this.* Turning in his chair, she got up and hurried into the small, unfinished room with the breaker box. Several tools leaned up against the wall, garden tools mostly, old rakes and shovels. She selected a heavy, iron bar suitable for prying, and this she brought back to the office, working its flattened end into the crack between the top of the desk and the edge of the roll-top.

Jamming it in, she pushed down on the bar with all her weight, using it as a lever, and winced at the sound of the wood cracking. Then there was a louder metallic snap and the lock was broken. She put the bar down and gently lifted the roll-top.

It was a man's desk, a mortician's desk, sporting an ashtray, an old inkwell, fountain pens, stacks of yellowed papers at each corner, and a large, leather blotter in its center. Over the musty scent, she could still smell her father's lingering presence: the spicy cologne he'd worn, the rich tobacco he'd smoked in his pipe, and she knew if she closed her eyes, she could almost picture his face in her mind.

She didn't want to see him now and hardly dared blink as she rummaged through the things in his desk, first pulling out the flat middle drawer. More instruments of his trade were here: unopened boxes of syringes, needles, and razor blades. . . .

Razor blades?!

. . . and that small whisper at the back of her mind came back to haunt her: *Do it, Saxon, do it now! You can do it right this time—no one's here to save you!*

Shuddering, she slammed the drawer shut and opened another to its right. This one was deep, packed with the files of her father's embalming records, invoices from pharmaceutical companies, and not much more.

The drawer beneath it contained a half-empty bottle of Absinthe, the liquid inside green and thick. She remembered the ritual Father used when he drank it, sprinkling droplets of water onto a sugar cube, filtering down into the glass, making the green liquor turn milky and opaque. And she remembered the monster he'd become whenever he drank his fill of it.

There's got to be something I'm missing, she reasoned, shutting the drawer. The back of the desktop was lined with small cubbyholes; one by one, she pulled out their contents: receipts and bills. In the last one, far in the corner, she found a small leather book, its cover unmarked. It was a journal filled with entries written in spidery handwriting. Opening it, she began to read:

June 18, 1940

Today I write my last will and testament. Having dealt with death so much over the past twenty years, I must question if I am experiencing a feeling of impending doom because my work is catching up with me. Or can it be something else? This mind-numbing bottle I've climbed into for relief and respite? It's claiming me, eating me alive, killing me slowly, I can feel its hooks, and yet I cannot break free. The best I can do is know that my wife and daughter will be well taken care of, provided for, after my demise. This, I know, is the right thing to do. Snake has told me to tie up any loose ends and this is the final one.

Snake? Who the heck was Snake? Was he referring to the Serpent? Saxon bit her lower lip to keep from trembling as she continued to read:

June 20, 1940

My last will and testament completed, Snake and I have come to terms with his occupancy. Now I shall learn his secrets and why things around here are changing. My wife, surely she thinks me mad, spending all my time down here, conversing with someone she cannot see. She has come to despise this house and quite honestly, I don't know why. It angers me; I've given up so much to be able to purchase this home for her. We chose to buy it together, she and I, to build a life here. Now she wants to leave and she's threatened to take Saxon with her. God help me, she's repeating past behavior. What to do about her? I need another drink.

Saxon flipped ahead to the last page, the day before her father's death.

December 9, 1941

I cannot let them go! Felicia, damn her, has already begun to pack. The woman is insane. Last time she left, I could see her reason. I didn't like it but I understood. Now I don't understand at all. I'm quite certain Saxon doesn't know of her plans. Does my daughter have the strength to fight her crazy, iron-willed mother? Nae, of course not. I've been too harsh with the child, I know, but she's soft, her spirit is far too pliant. When her mother tells her to pack her belongings, she will do so, no questions asked. Saxon cannot recognize her mother's flights of fancy for what they are. She dreams of marrying that soldier boy two years from now. Foolish girl, doesn't she know there's a war in Europe and we'll soon be yanked into it? Soldier boys have a bad habit of dying young. I've tried to warn my daughter time and again of this, but she doesn't listen. In her eyes, I am a drunk, an old meanie who doesn't want her to be happy. She may be right; I know it in this sober hour. Maybe it's for the best that both mother and daughter to die by my hand, dispatched quickly, painlessly. I have the means to do the deed, and although it will certainly break my heart, I know it's the right thing to do. The only *thing I can do to stop them. Snake has told me it needs eight souls, a number that will outdo God's perfect seven. It has six now: the Snake, the Necrophiliac, the Heartbroken, the Embalmed, the Hanged, and the Hunter. It needs two more: the Deranged and the Impure. I'm certain that must be Felicia the Deranged and Saxon the Impure. I shall be honored to provide this ultimate sacrifice and reap my promised rewards. If only there were . . .*

Her father's handwriting tapered off, growing fainter as if running out of ink, but there it was, the proof in black and white that she truly wasn't insane. Father was the crazy one! *If only I'd known about this journal,* she thought, *before . . . before my arrest, before Father tried to kill me that awful night.* She now realized her mother sensed something was wrong, and she'd wanted to take her away, possibly to her native Florida. *But Father never would have allowed that,* Saxon reasoned. *That's why he wanted to kill us—to keep us from leaving so he could carry out his evil plan, his al-*

legiance to the one he called "Snake."

But what was his strategy? What could it be that was so strong that it would drive him to drink to excess and make him believe he should kill his family?

From reading the journal, Saxon understood that someone named Snake was behind all this trouble. Snake . . . Serpent, names too close in nature to be a coincidence. How had she always known its name was Serpent? Did it come to her in a dream—or in a nightmare? Was it because the town's original name was Eden, hence the name "Serpent" made sense as the perfect name for the Evil that resided here? No, it had to be something more than that, but what?

She spent the remainder of the night at the desk in the cellar, reading her father's journal page by page, not wanting to miss a word. Much of it sounded rational; her father had always been a thinking man, but the closer she got to the end, the harder it became to read. These may have been the irrational rantings of a drunk, but Saxon knew it was more. Much more, and it scared her deeply.

When she was finished reading, she knew where she had to go.

5

The Jesup Memorial Library stood in the heart of Bar Harbor, an impressive, gray, granite building, two stories high. As a girl, Saxon had been here many times, escaping to the coolness of its aisles, always looking for a book to lose herself in. She'd always loved the great authors, Mark Twain and Rudyard Kipling, and as she approached the library now, she wondered if Miss Geddy still worked here, the pleasant, quiet woman who loved books as much as Saxon did. Whenever Saxon had returned a book with a due date several weeks passed, Miss Geddy would simply smile, whispering that it was like a lost child returning home. She never charged her a late fee, either.

"You're a reader. That book was being read and loved," she'd say, "and that's good enough for me."

But Miss Geddy wasn't there today. No one was; the library was completely empty, devoid of visitors. Saxon thought it strange that the doors weren't locked; she had the whole building to herself. She milled around the front desk for a moment, hoping someone would show up, but when they didn't, she decided to browse on her own.

She'd come looking for something in particular: old periodicals, newspapers that might mention Roquefort Manor or a man named Snake. Moving along the towering aisles of bookshelves, she located the large stacks of newsprint, divided by years into large, cardboard binders with old fashioned, marbleized covers. *May as well start at the very beginning,* she decided, running one gloved finger along the spines. The year 1859 stood out apart from the rest, poking out slightly, not flush with the others. Saxon had remembered, according to Mrs. Tuttle, that Roquefort Manor had been built in the 1840s, and she shrugged. There had to be a reason why this year, 1859, was sticking out, as if daring her to take it down from the shelf.

She hadn't expected it to be so heavy and she grunted as she pulled it down, a sound echoing through the silent library. She half expected Miss Geddy to come around the corner, her slim forefinger pressed to her lips, reminding her to be quiet.

Or something worse, like that awful man she'd bumped

into a few years ago. She'd just come around the corner, past the periodicals, and they'd nearly collided head-on. Although she'd never seen him before, she knew something about him just was off.

It wasn't because of his milky, blue eyes or the way his dry skin was flaking, peeling on his face and hands—lots of older folks had cataracts and dermatitis—it was more in the way he'd looked at her . . . like he could see right through her, as if she were nothing more than a ghost.

His stark-white hair had wisped out crazily from his dandruffy scalp, moving about as if blown by a breeze. But all the windows and doors were closed; it was January, after all. And she'd stood there as if the soles of her boots had suddenly taken root to the floor.

His eyes—they'd been so full of anger, rage . . . and an alarming vacancy.

Only when he'd leaned forward and hissed in her face, did she move, jumping backward, knocking into a bookshelf . . . then he'd turned the corner and was gone.

What had he said to her? *The Serpent shall awaken to crawl through Eden!*

Shaken, Saxon had peeked around the corner of the bookcase to see where he'd gone, but he was nowhere in sight—and that was impossible, for he had to be in the foyer near the front desk.

But only Miss Geddy was there, sitting back, slowly indexing library cards.

Saxon blinked, wondering if she'd seen a ghost. Moments later, when she'd described the old man, Miss Geddy gave her a strange look. "Sounds like you saw Henry," she'd said, careful to whisper. "He was the librarian here," she'd added, "some thirty years ago."

Saxon could feel her heart beat way up high in her

throat. "Well, I think something's wrong with him," she'd said, trying to keep her voice steady.

Miss Geddy only shook her head. "You're right. Something *was* wrong with him; he turned senile shortly before passing away. But that was at least ten years back."

Eyes steady, filled with all the seriousness a thirteen-year-old girl could muster, Saxon had said simply, "Then I've just seen his ghost."

Miss Geddy had rewarded her with a little nod. "Sounds like it. He looks fierce, I know, but he'll do you no harm."

"Why's he here? Why isn't he in Heaven?"

Pursing her lips, Miss Geddy had taken Saxon by the hand and led her over to a bookcase filled with a number of religious-type books and she'd pulled one out from the highest shelf. It was an old book, bound in leather, with very fine typeset on thin, yellowed pages. "I'm not one to preach, but this should tell you everything you need to know," she'd said, placing the book in Saxon's hands.

Its title read: *Book of Riddles: Mysteries of the World and Universe Explained.* The author was anonymous.

Saxon had taken the book home and spent the next three weeks reading it. Far from easy to understand and often cryptic, she was able to glean from it a few solid answers: Ghosts were described as earth-bound spirits unable to let go of their past lives or trapped here by the violence of their deaths. Spirits, however, were often free to come and go, to visit the living and drawn to the places they'd frequented in life. Everything, physical and spiritual, and everyone, was somehow tied together, completing some kind of complex web that wove on into infinity . . . and God had put it all into motion. And what of God? According to this book, He was the God of all life, of all people, living and dead—and He went by many, many names and He had so many different faces that it was impossible for one person to understand or recognize all of them.

Saxon couldn't begin to comprehend all the author was trying to convey within those crackled pages, but this she knew for certain: She'd seen a ghost.

No ghosts now, though; she was alone with this binder in an empty library. She carried it to a nearby table and opened it. The pages were yellowed with age and quite delicate; she turned them with great care, her eyes scanning the columns for any mention of Roquefort Manor.

Half an hour passed, the clock on the opposite wall softly ticking the time away, the only sound in the room except for her breathing and the crackle of the pages as she turned them. She was well into October when she found something of interest.

The headlines blared in bold print: **MURDER AT ROQUEFORT MANOR!** Right below, in smaller print, the by-line: **Two dead: one woman, one man.** Saxon knit her brows, as she bent down over the paper to read the article:

> ***October 17, 1850***—*On Tuesday, October 15, a double homicide occurred at Roquefort Manor on the Crooked Road. Samuel D. Roquefort, III, estate owner, was not home at the time and is not available for comment. Sheriff John Handy reported that the body of a Negro woman was retrieved from a small pond, not far from the estate grounds. According to local coroner, Arthur Wells, her death was due to drowning. On the banks of the pond, the body of a man identified as a bounty hunter from Kentucky, Gerard Wendell Beaumont, was found, shot to death. A search of the estate resulted in the apprehension of Stephen Freemont, a Negro, allegedly from Georgia,*

who identified the dead woman as his common-law wife. According to Freemont, he and his wife had run away from tobacco plantation owner, Silas d'Mornay of W. Atlanta, and were planning to flee to Canada when Beaumont located them. Freemont has pled guilty to shooting the bounty hunter and awaits trial in a cell in the Sheriff's office.

Saxon had held her breath while she read; now she let it out in a sob. Could Suki be the ghost of that poor, drowned woman? That would explain a lot . . . but not everything. She'd seemed so *alive* yesterday at the pond. Weren't ghosts supposed to look like specters? All hazy and white, speaking in wavering, eerie tones? The red-haired man in her hallway, now that had been a ghost for certain—could it have been the spirit of Gerard Wendell Beaumont, the bounty hunter? No mention was made of a baby, though, and Saxon felt sick at heart. They hadn't even known she was pregnant and had just given birth—or if they did know, it wasn't mentioned in the article.

But what happened to Suki's man, Stephen Freemont? Stevie, Suki had called him. Had he been set free? Surely, someone must have realized he'd likely been defending his wife and child, trying to prevent them from being forced back into slavery.

Saxon carefully scanned the next two weeks of newsprint and her heart fell. According to the paper, some men (no names mentioned) had broken into the Sheriff's office on Halloween night . . . a lynch mob comprised of angry men dressed in white sheets and carrying burning crosses. Having never seen anything so terrifying, no one dared stop them when they came riding into town that awful night. They'd taken Stephen out and hung him from a tree near the town dump. It was assumed his body was disposed of in the cranberry bog near the dumpsite. A search was conducted but proved fruitless. The article did mention that Suki had been buried in an unmarked pauper's grave.

Apparently, Roquefort Manor had been one of the 130 refuges, known as "stations" in Maine's section of the Underground Railroad that led to New Brunswick, Canada.

While not an actual railroad, nor literally underground, this route to freedom became "incorporated" in 1804, after General Thomas Boudes, a Revolutionary War veteran, aided in the escape of a slave, whom he refused to surrender to authorities. The wheels that set the railroad in motion had been started by a Pennsylvanian Quaker, teenager Isaac T. Hopper, in 1787, but it took a network of persons with similar convictions, like those of Boudes, to turn it into the powerhouse it would become.

Although the first draft of the Declaration of Independence contained a clause banning slavery, the institution of slavedom existed in the United States for 250 years, from colonial days to the very end of the Civil War.

An estimated 30,000 to 300,000 escaped slaves "rode" the Underground Railroad to freedom in the nineteenth century. Philadelphia was one of the first "stops" on the way to New York, Vermont, Massachusetts, New Hampshire, Maine, and finally Canada, where the government refused to return slaves to the United States. Canada became the prime destination after the Compromise Bill passed in 1850, ordering the return of runaway slaves in the North to their former "masters." By this time, ex-slaves endured the added dangers of being tracked by bounty hunters.

By good health and fortune in terms of food, shelter, and clement weather, a runaway from the South could make it to Canada in roughly two months on foot. For those less strong or lucky, the trek might have lasted a year or more. Some ex-slaves traveled as many as 560 miles before attaining precious freedom.

Those who made it to Canada enjoyed freedoms they had only dreamt of before. Here, they were able to vote and own land. They were not denied educations. They could marry and raise families without the fear of seeing them torn apart to be sold on auction blocks. Even so, there were many difficult challenges to face: the winters this far North were dreadfully cold, unlike those in the mild climate of the South. Land had to be purchased, homes had to be built, and the refugees had to find jobs to support themselves and their families. It wasn't easy, but at least they were free.

Harriet Beecher Stowe had written *Uncle Tom's Cabin* from her home in Brunswick, Maine. First published as a serial in the *National Era* in 1851, and later as a book, it lit the fires of abolition across the United States and Europe and became the object of violent hatred in the deep South. While her house was not directly linked to the Underground Railroad, her writing most certainly was.

Maine homes serving as stations in the railroad included the Holyoke House in Brewer, where Penobscot Indians guided ex-slaves to Canada. It was said that Joshua Chamberlain grew up next door to the Holyoke House.

Eastport, Maine, served as sister site for the Brewer/Bangor Underground Railroad. A station on the St. Croix River had been built and the Passamaquoddy Indians who lived there communicated regularly with the Penobscot Tribe of the Brewer/Bangor area. Native Americans used the 100-Mile Trail to guide many runaway slaves to Canada.

Saxon could only guess that Roquefort Manor served as a station for those coming North by sea . . . and the scurrying of rats Mrs. Tuttle's mother had been so frightened of were likely the sounds made by the runaways who'd been hidden away in the upstairs of the manor.

But there were so many loose ends: nothing to explain the pleading voice of the young man in the cellar nor the identification of the person her father called Snake.

I need to go further back, Saxon decided as she closed the 1859 binder. *Maybe back to the very beginning? When the house was built.*

Because she had no idea what year Roquefort Manor had come into existence, she began pouring through 1840, then 1841 and 1842. In 1844, she found it—in the Properties section, a sale of land, warrantee deed, to Samuel D. Roquefort, III of Virginia.

In 1845, she found another article of interest: a deadly accident had occurred in the middle of April that year during the construction of Roquefort Manor. A bricklayer by the name of Claude Trank Viperstadt had been struck by lightning while working on the roof, laying bricks for the chimney. Witnesses reported that it was a natural phenomenon, an act of God. Not a cloud in the sky that hot, humid day, just a low, gray fog hanging just offshore. . . .

Saxon stopped reading, her breath caught in her throat. That name, Viperstadt. Viper. The Serpent. Snake. Could it be him? If so, that would have to mean the Serpent had been human and was now no more than a ghost. An ugly, angry ghost, yes, but at least it wasn't a demon!

She read on. Not much was mentioned about Claude Trank Viperstadt, except that he was an immigrant from Eastern Europe with no known relatives, his age approximately thirty-seven. In the next day's issue, she found another article about him.

Evidently, he had raped and tortured several women

since moving to Maine. Police found articles of the missing women's clothing in his bungalow, along with handcuffs, blindfolds, whips, and various other items of bizarre, sexual deviation. Instruments had been used; human hairs were found clinging to blindfolds, bits of torn skin lined the insides of iron manacles. Lipstick was discovered, smeared along the handle of a bullwhip. Viperstadt's surviving victims remained unknown; no woman in her right mind would dare go public with such an accusation; even though she might be innocent of wrongdoing, she'd be labeled a harlot for life.

How had he killed his victims? Guessing was easy enough: by torture likely, but no one would ever know for sure. Their gravesites were never found.

Just his name gave Saxon chills. Viperstadt, the Snake. The Serpent. *At least now I know what he is and how he came to be in my house,* she thought. *He was the first person to die there.* She remembered the spirits in the order according to her father's journal: the Necrophiliac, the Heartbroken, the Embalmed, the Hanged, the Hunter, and the Deranged. It made sense that Snake had to be Viperstadt a.k.a. the Serpent. . . .

Taking a slip of paper from the table, Saxon made a list of the spirits and what person she assumed went to each name.

The Necrophiliac would likely be Jacqueline Roquefort's father, Leonard, who seemed so morbidly in love with the dead. The Heartbroken, no doubt, was Suki, and The Hanged was her man, Stephen. The Hunter was probably the bounty hunter, Gerard Wendell Beaumont, and the Deranged, Saxon felt certain, was her own father. If Viperstadt was the Serpent, then who was the Embalmed?

She believed firmly that every house had a spirit. Most

were benevolent, but some were bad. Evil from the get-go. What if, when Roquefort Manor was being built, the Evil had absorbed Viperstadt's spirit into itself? Upon death, had he become *something else,* being fully melded with the manor? Perhaps it was a better fate than the one awaiting him in Hell? If so, he was still obsessed with rape and torture, and even now, for what was rape but rampant penetration, and possession?

But what did Snake want with the souls he'd captured? What could he be using them for? Saxon shivered, knowing she was the first and only one to figure out this mystery.

Now if she could only determine why he needed eight souls and what he planned to do once he had them. . . .

6

Back at Roquefort Manor, Saxon found her mother's Ouija board in one of the downstairs closets. Felicia had used it sometimes as a parlor game with her friends, and Saxon could remember lying in bed some nights, listening to her mother's laughter as she read aloud what the board was saying. It sounded silly and harmless: "Wash your feet," Saxon recalled Mother reading over her giggles. "And dry between your toes." Or, "Feed the cat leftover SPAM." Silly stuff like that, which made little or no sense. Some nights, Father would come up from his office in the basement, bringing his bottle with him, and there'd be more laughter as the night wore on.

The box containing the Ouija board was yellowed and dusty; mice had chewed away one of the corners but the contents were still intact. The board itself was constructed of cardboard, painted tan with black letters and numbers, while the planchette was some sort of light wood. Saxon removed the board from the box and laid it on the kitchen table. She set the planchette in the center of the board and placed her fingers upon it, closing her eyes.

"Who are you?" she asked, her voice soft, figuring this whole idea was nothing more than a lesson in futility. What stupid answers would it give, if any? "Who are you and what do you want from me?"

Nothing happened, so she repeated her question. When she opened her eyes, the candles she'd lit began to flicker, even though no window was open.

"Are you here?"

The planchette moved under her fingers, a fluttery-type of sensation, then it glided over to **YES**. Saxon could feel her heart pounding against her sternum.

"Who are you?"

Again, the fluttery movement, then the planchette took off so quickly she could barely keep her fingers on it, spelling: **M . . . U . . . R . . . M . . . U . . . R**.

"Your real name is Viperstadt, isn't it?"

The planchette moved to **NO**.

"What is your real name?" Saxon asked, barely able to mask her nervousness.

M . . . U . . . R . . . M . . . U . . . R. The planchette raced to the letters.

"What are you?"

M . . . U . . . R . . . M . . . U . . . R.

"Murmur? What's a Murmur?"

I. . . . A . . . M. . . . M . . . U . . . R . . . M . . . U . . . R.

Saxon waited but the planchette stopped. *I'm not asking the right questions*, she thought. Then she had another idea. "What do you do?"

The planchette fluttered again. **A . . . B . . . S . . . O . . . R . . . B**.

"Absorb? What do you absorb?"

S . . . O . . . U . . . L . . . S.

"Why?"

P . . . O . . . W . . . E . . . R.

"How many souls do you have?"

The planchette sped over the numbers and stopped on 7. Then it glided to the letters, spelling out: **N . . . E . . . E . . . D**, then back to numbers, resting on **8**.

"Eight? Why do you need eight souls?"

C . . . O . . . M . . . P . . . L . . . E . . . T . . . E. . . . P . . . O . . . W . . . E . . . R.

Seven, Saxon knew, was a Biblical number: God rested on the seventh day, deeming it holy; there were seven deadly sins, seven seals of Revelation, Joshua marched around Jericho seven times, there were seven gates of Hell. She didn't think the number eight had any arcane meaning. Was this entity playing games with her? "So what happens when you get complete power?"

She watched the planchette spell out a sentence that chilled her blood:

I. . . . B . . . E . . . C . . . O . . . M . . . E. . . . A . . . E . . . L . . . I . . . M.

Frowning, puzzled, she asked, "What's Aelim?"

G . . . O . . . D.

Oh no, this wasn't good; there was no way it could be her mind playing tricks on her, she was sure of that now. Whatever this thing that called itself a Murmur was, it had to be some kind of demon or devil. Perhaps even Satan himself. But why here? Why in Eden, Maine?

She tried to keep her voice steady. "So who are the seven souls in your possession now?"

S . . . N . . . A . . . K . . . E.

N . . . E . . . C . . . R . . . O . . . P . . . H . . . I . . . L . . . I . . . A . . . C.

H . . . E . . . A . . . R . . . T . . . B . . . R . . . O . . . K . . . E . . . N.

H . . . A . . . N . . . G . . . E . . . D.

E . . . M . . . B . . . A . . . L . . . M . . . E . . . D.

H . . . U . . . N . . . T . . . E . . . R.

D . . . E . . . R . . . A . . . N . . . G . . . E . . . D.

Just like in my father's journal, she thought, wryly. "And who's the eighth?"

Y . . . O . . . U.

Immediately, her back stiffened and the hairs on the nape of her neck prickled. Surely, this thing was playing games, trying to frighten her. Either that, or it was her own paranoia running rampant. "Why me?"

I . . . M . . . P . . . U . . . R . . . E.

Saxon shook her head in disbelief. She knew she wasn't impure; she was still a virgin, but there was little use in arguing about it. *Let it think what it wants,* she decided. *I'm not going to play its little game.* "So what about Suki and Stevie's baby?" she asked. "Why don't you have it?"

The planchette paused, vibrating slightly before moving across the letters: **L . . . O . . . S . . . T**. On the **T**, it suddenly picked up momentum, skittering across the board, spelling out: **H . . . E . . . A . . . R . . . T . . . B . . . R . . . O . . . K . . . E . . . N. . . . W . . . A . . . N . . . T. . . . B . . . A . . . B . . . Y.**

"Suki? Is that you?"

B . . . A . . . B . . . Y. . . . G . . . O . . . N . . . E.

"Am I speaking to Suki?"

NO.

"Is Suki there?"

A . . . B . . . S . . . O . . . R . . . B . . . E . . . D.

Saxon shivered, reckoning that whatever she was dealing with, she probably couldn't outwit it. "I want you to leave," she said, her voice as firm as she could make it. "Go back to the place from whence you came and cause harm no more. Release the souls in your captivity so that they may find peace."

The planchette flew out from under her fingers and landed on **NO**.

"I command you to leave in the name of the Father, the Son, and Holy Ghost!"

The candle flickered again and went out as if snuffed, pinched between invisible fingertips; at the same moment, Saxon felt something brush across her legs. It was icy cold and scaly but it moved like an animal, a squirrel perhaps but not much larger; she could hear the scraping of feet on the linoleum. Then came a loud crack, the sound of something breaking. Glass maybe? Trying not to scream, she arose and turned on the light.

The creature was gone but the planchette was broken, each half lying over the word **NO**.

Is it really gone? she wondered, her hand on her chest, trying to calm her racing heart. The planchette jiggled slightly as she stood there looking down at it. Crying out, she scooped up the board, pinning the broken planchette between the two halves, and carried it to the stove. Lifting the cover on the stovetop with one hand, she jammed the whole works into the firebox, and with a shiver of revulsion, she tried to light a match with trembling, gloved fingers.

The third match took and she lit a fire, then quickly set the lid cover back on the stove. She stepped away as the pain in her palms raged a blistering scream of remembrance:

Daddy, please, I'll never do it again!

Give me your hands, Saxon.

No, please, oh please! It's so hot! Oh-God-Oh-God-Oh-God-my hands—they're burning up—hurts so bad!

You'll never do it again, will you, child?

Screeching inside my head . . . fire . . . pain . . . blisters . . . blood. The stovetop had been cherry red then, its belly stuffed with ash and birch. Mama called this a "biscuit fire," the highest temperature attainable for a woodstove.

She could feel the flesh of her palms cooking, swelling, rising like biscuit dough, and the stretching of her skin as blisters burst open. The sizzle of blood droplets on the stovetop. Father's vise-like grip on her wrists.

After her punishment, she'd run outside and thrust her injured hands into the snow, where they steamed and pulsed, red raw meat with shreds of blackened skin hanging from her palms. It hurt too much to do anything but scream.

When Mother saw her hands, she cried as she covered them with salve and promised Saxon that they'd leave Father. But after he told Mother what she'd done, Mother didn't talk about leaving anymore, and Saxon knew that day would never arrive; things would just continue to get worse until Father killed her. Or Mother. Or both of them.

She'd been thirteen at the time.

When Christmas vacation ended, Saxon wore gloves to school and never took them off, no matter how much Georgie begged her to. She couldn't let him see the terrible burns that branded her, nor could she allow him to see the scars on her soul. Only one person (other than her parents) would ever know what happened to her hands and why—not the psychiatrists, nor the doctors and psychoanalysts—only Rob Carmichael knew. He'd promised Saxon he'd marry her as soon as he could. He'd take her away from Father's awful temper, where she'd never have to fear his terrible wrath again.

Thinking about Rob, a tear broke free from the corner of her eye and rolled down her cheek. *Dammit, Rob, why'd you have to die?* She struggled to keep her composure, but her heart ached for the love she'd lost. She swiped at her cheek with a gloved finger, then reached up and shut the damper on the stove. Mother's spirit board was gone now, reduced to ashes.

Saxon walked upstairs, listening, concentrating for any strange sounds coming from the house, but all remained quiet. *Perhaps I made it go away,* she thought, barely daring to hope against logic. *Is it even possible to make such a terrible thing leave? Do I have that kind of power?* She felt drained, lethargic, as if her legs were dead weights not wanting to move.

I just need some sleep, she told herself as she flopped down on her bed and shut her eyes. *Just a few precious hours of peace.*

7

Sleep was a long time coming. Saxon kept thinking about the things the Ouija board had told her. Had it spelled out the truth? Yes, she thought so. *Something here is absorbing souls,* she'd sensed it all along. The Murmur, the Serpent, said it planned to become Aelim—in other words, God—as soon as it absorbed her soul, and she was determined not to let that happen.

So what are you going to do to stop it? a voice asked.

Saxon bolted upright in bed, clutching her covers in her fists. "Who's there?" The room was dark, mightily so, making it impossible to see the intruder.

Saxon, honey, it's me. I can't stay here very long; I'm not strong enough. It's sleeping right now, so this is my only chance.

She blinked in disbelief, recognizing the voice. It couldn't possibly be—and yet it was. "Rob? Is that really you?"

Yes, hon, it's me.

"B-but you're dead. . . ."

It's okay, Saxon. Death's another dimension in the time-space continuum. The Serpent is weak right now, resting; otherwise I wouldn't have been able to break through to talk to you. It spent a lot of energy communicating with you tonight.

Saxon couldn't keep from shivering. "Can I see you, Rob? Please let me see you!"

Shh, darling. It's better that you don't. Not yet, anyway. I haven't much time and there are things I need to show you, to protect you.

"But—"

Hush, now, love. Lie still and relax. Close your eyes. I'm right here beside you. Can you feel me?

Saxon reached out, wanting so much to believe he'd really come back to her. It was his voice, soft and deep, so full of youth and hope. Through her gloves, she felt how cold he'd become and it made her sad.

"I can feel you, Rob," she whispered, tears squeezing out from her closed eyes.

I can feel you, too. Now I'm going to show you some things in your mind. Pictures, like movies. Things that happened here. Not easy to watch, I know, but if it can save your life, your soul, then I need you to see. Understand?

She nodded, trusting him, and behind closed lids, she strained to see.

★ ★ ★ ★ ★

At first, all was black, then it slowly faded to gray, images coming into view like from a black-and-white film, grainy and choppy.

She recognized her kitchen, the way it might have looked in the 1800s. A polished plank floor, a bigger stove, an old-fashioned icebox in the corner. The table was smaller but heavier, and two men were seated at it, drinking rum. Money was exchanged between them and they were shaking hands.

The man at the right is Adam Walker, Rob whispered. *The other one is Gerard Wendell Beaumont.*

"The caretaker and the bounty hunter?"

Yes. Do you see what's transpired?

"They look like they've made some sort of deal."

That's right. Beaumont gave Walker some money in return for the runaway slaves. Now watch closely.

Saxon saw both men get up from their chairs. Beaumont was a rugged man with wild red hair. He had a chain coiled in his hands, a chain with heavy, iron shackles on the ends. Walker led him to the back stairs and grinned, watching him go up as he pocketed the money.

She heard Beaumont's footsteps and the steps creaking beneath them. Moments later, from overhead, distressed screams filled the air and the sounds of running feet pounded across the floor, followed by more screaming. In horror, she watched Suki scramble down the front stairs. The frightened woman slipped once, fell, and kept on running, clutching a stomach heavily laden with child. She made it to the front door, flung it open, and ran out into the night.

Walker followed, toting a shotgun in one hand and a lantern in the other. Upstairs, a terrible fight broke out; Saxon could hear men's voices, loud and angry. Then the sound of something—or someone—being dragged across the floor. Now she could see Beaumont at the top of the stairs yanking a black man with him in chains.

Saxon knew this was Stevie. He struggled, pleading for Beaumont to let his wife go. *Take me instead,* he kept urging, but Beaumont wasn't listening.

I came for two niggers, Beaumont said with a snarl. *Getting three just sweetens the bargain. Now get moving.*

Saxon watched him drag Stevie down the stairs, forcing him to take two steps at a time. They went out the front door and in the distance, she could see the light of Adam Walker's lantern swinging to and fro as he raced after Suki.

Better call out to her, ya black bastard. Tell her to come back. Beaumont wrapped a section of chain around Stevie's neck, threatening to choke him if he didn't comply.

Run, Suki!

You'll pay for that, big boy, Walker said, raising his gun and striking Stevie across the cheek with its butt. Dazed, the poor man was dragged by Beaumont, who was following Walker out behind the house, down the path that led to the pond. It didn't take them long to catch up with Suki, who was already knee-deep in the water, scared out of her wits, splashing frantically as she tried to run, wading away from them; but now in the throes of labor, she couldn't get very far or move very fast.

She heard Beaumont's shout that he had her man, threatening to kill him if she didn't turn around and come back. But she couldn't; she knew what would happen: *they're gonna kill us anyway.* She panted, glancing over her shoulder, and saw Adam Walker set his lantern and gun down on the bank. He began wading in after her.

It didn't take him long to catch up. He grabbed her by her nightshift, knocking her off balance and they tumbled into the water. Suki came up first, scratching and digging at his face and neck, trying to escape. Despite Beaumont's shouts, urging him to drag her back to shore, Adam wanted some kind of sick revenge. Suki was screaming that the baby was coming, that it was *falling* out of her, but he dragged her farther and farther out to where the pond deepened.

On the bank of the pond, Stevie was struggling, but his illness had left him weak. His left foot had become severely infected after becoming entangled in barbed wire in a field in North Carolina. Dogs—bloodhounds—had been chasing them then, their baying growing ever close, and behind them, lawmen on horseback. Suki grabbed him, half-carrying, half-dragging him across that meadow and into a creek where they managed to hide while their predators, human and canine, scouted the surrounding area.

The water had been murky, full of snakes and leeches, and more than a bit stagnant. He and Suki had breathed through reeds, letting their bodies sink, unseen by their would-be captors. How long had they stayed underwater, feeling the occasional water moccasin glide over their skin? Hours, likely, for the sun had set and the moon began to rise before they dared to emerge.

Going into water that deep, snakes or no, had been a brave decision for Suki, and Stevie's pride in her had grown that day . . . as did his fear for her at this moment.

She can't swim! She's having a baby! he screamed at their captors, lunging against his chains.

The movement caught Beaumont by surprise, pulling him off his feet, and away from the gun Walker had left behind. Stevie saw his chance in an instant; it was their only hope.

He scrambled to reach for the shotgun, and Beaumont was upon him, one knee placed between his shoulder blades, a section of chain looped around his neck and drawn up tight.

Stevie's hand closed around the gun.

Drop it, Beaumont growled, tightening the chain, cutting off all breath.

In a burst of adrenaline, Stevie raised his arm, lifting the gun, its barrel facing backwards, right at Beaumont. He pulled the trigger with his thumb and the night exploded.

Beaumont fell away from Stevie, clutching his chest.

I did it! Damn, I really did it!

He dropped the gun and grappled through Beaumont's pockets, searching desperately for a key. The key, the one that would release his shackles. He couldn't find it and kept looking up, his eyes full of fear and anger, watching Walker in the water with his wife.

Did he dare try to shoot Walker?

What if he hit Suki by mistake?

He couldn't take that chance. Where was the key? It had to be here! Giving up, he began walking toward the water, dragging Beaumont along with him. He had to save her—she was quickly losing the fight with Walker, who was holding her by the shoulders, forcing her head underwater.

Stevie struggled to wade out to Walker, but underwater, the rocks were slippery. His bum foot, the one he'd nearly lost to infection, didn't move well at all. He couldn't have done worse if he'd had a brick on the end of his leg instead of that foot.

Before he could reach Suki, the splashing stopped, and Walker held something up over his head, hooting with glee, and in this horrible picture, Saxon heard what sounded like the weak cry of a baby.

"He took her baby," she whispered in shock. "My God, he took Suki's baby!"

That's not all he did, Rob told her. *Look.*

The scene by the pond darkened into obscurity and another took its place.

Saxon recognized the cellar. It didn't look the same; the rooms weren't yet finished, lined with earth. On a workbench illuminated by a single lantern, a tiny baby cried out, pitifully wailing. Its wet, umbilical cord dangled from its heaving stomach, and a man stood in the shadows, his head covered by a heavy cloak.

I present you with sacrifice, he said, and Saxon recognized the voice as that of Adam Walker. *Blood and water, flesh and wine. May the Serpent partake of my humble offering.*

Something inside the earth moved, something big and twisting, locked in another dimension, barely seen except for its movements, which could be felt in the heavy air.

It's too pure! Saxon heard a voice hiss. *Take it away—you failure, you miserable worm!*

Walker cried out in dismay, but in apparent fear, for he scooped up the newborn, and the scene darkened once more.

"What happened to Suki's baby?" Saxon whispered to Rob.

I have no way of knowing, he told her. *All I'm sure of is that he lived—and he's living still. He's not in this realm. It's up to you to locate him. If Suki and Stevie know where their baby is, they may find the strength to break away from their confines. But look now.*

Saxon squeezed her eyes tightly, her hands gripping the bedcovers, not sure she really wanted to see more of what Rob was trying to show her, and knowing at the same time that she had to. This was *her* house now; it was her obligation to stop the madness.

She saw the cellar again, only this time, it had changed again. Now the walls and floors were finished. The office and desk were there, in exactly the same place as they were now. She could hear muffled sobs coming from the workroom. Only this wasn't her father's room, not yet. Those weren't his things on the desk. That wasn't his coat and hat hanging on a hook by the door. The picture seemed to somehow focus on the sounds floating in from the workroom and her gaze followed . . .

. . . settling upon a young man with black hair. He'd been strapped to the cooling board, a thick wooden plank where the dead were laid out to await the fading of rigor mortis so they could be re-positioned for their wakes and funerals. Only this boy wasn't dead; he struggled against the leather constraints, his eyes bulging with terror. Even through the gag in his mouth, Saxon could hear his moans and screams.

The mortician was back too, gathering up his syringe and the fluid jars, along with the thick rubber tubes that fit into their tops.

"But he's alive!" Saxon cried out. "That poor boy—he's about to be embalmed!"

Shh, pay attention, Rob said.

The mortician turned toward the boy, snarling. *You won't ever see my daughter again, now will you?* he asked in a strangely excited voice, a little too high, a bit too fast. Although Saxon couldn't see his face clearly, she knew he had to be Jacqueline's father, Leonard. She wanted to make him stop this senseless torture, yet she knew he wasn't able to hear or see her. This had already happened; it was locked into the past, and like a movie being played, there was no way she could change it. The script had been written many years before.

She squirmed in horror as Leonard pushed the thick needle into Mario Delgado's jugular vein. Blood squirted rhythmically down the rubber tube into a large, glass, aspirating bottle, a terrible thing to witness. As the blood ebbed from the boy's body, Leonard busied himself by pumping formaldehyde into the veins in Mario's arms and legs. It must have burned horribly beyond description. Mario's eyes glazed over, as his resistance grew steadily weaker; his eyes filled with the knowledge, the gradual acceptance, of his demise just before they rolled upward. His body convulsed once, twice, then a third time, stretching at the leather confines, then dropped limply to the cooling board. His color was white, mottled with bluish-grey.

Leonard stood back, looking down at him, hands tightly clasped. *For you, my dark lord,* he said in a low voice that sounded barely human. *A sacrifice for you. The Embalmed One.* He looked around, nervously tapping his chin, then went over to the wall that separated the office from the workroom. He'd had bricks brought in yesterday for just this reason: he'd build a new wall, using Mario Delgado's corpse for insulation.

Saxon watched as Leonard stuffed Mario's corpse behind the wall, and as the last brick was placed, she heard a rattle and a hiss, like that of a snake.

★ ★ ★ ★ ★

"That's the Serpent," she whispered to Rob.

It is indeed.

"So Mario is the voice I've been hearing in the basement. He's a trapped soul."

He's been absorbed, Rob told her. *But while the Serpent is not of this world, it is still a snake, a reptile; thus it must regurgitate much of what it digests in order to molt. I'm showing you these things because the Serpent is about to expel the contents of its stomach unto the world. When it sheds its old skin and takes its new form, it will be unstoppable. It will be a god. It's up to you to make sure that doesn't happen.*

Saxon sat up, clutching her pillow to her chest, her heart pounding. "What are you saying? I don't know how to stop it! I'm scared to death of it! Why do I have to do this alone?"

You won't be alone, my darling. Suki and Stevie's child will join you in the battle.

Saxon opened her eyes to the darkness of her bedroom. "But how will I find their baby?"

Much time has passed; he's not a child anymore. But someone else will join you, too, one who will always be a child.

"A child? Who?"

Saxon felt Rob's weight shift on the bed, even though she could not see him. *You will know when it's time, but I must leave now before the Serpent stirs again,* he told her.

"But I don't want you to leave!" She reached out and grabbed at the spot where she thought he was. It felt colder than ice. "Please, please, don't leave me!"

Shh, love. His voice was against her ear now, his breath frozen. *Stop the Serpent and I'll come back for you, I promise. If you fail, all will be lost: past, present, and future. Remember the things I have shown you tonight and arm yourself with this knowledge. You must stop it before it fully awakes.*

"How much time do I have?"

It will molt in autumn. That's as much as I know.

She turned her face, brushing the air with her lips. "I love you so much, Rob."

And I you. Be brave, darling.

All at once, he was gone. Saxon fell back on her pillow, touching her face with gloved fingers, and she stayed awake for a long time afterwards, pondering the horrors Rob had shown her. It was a scary time for her, alone in this house with the powers that be.

8

The world was changing. Saxon's days were spent listening to the radio. Strange things were happening, events that frightened, worried, and confused her; she'd witnessed some of it with her own two eyes.

For instance, on the afternoon of July 3rd, she'd been sitting outside on the veranda, taking a reprieve from the housecleaning and the constant thinking about what to do about the Serpent, when she heard a strange, distant, roaring noise. Was it a car? No, it couldn't be, unless something was wrong with its engine. A boat, maybe? She lived too far from the ocean to hear boats except on the stillest of days when there was no breeze at all. Wind ruffled now through her hair and she looked around, then turned her eyes upward, shielding her vision from the sun with her hand. That's where the noise was coming from.

Something was up there, a group of objects—not birds or airplanes—moving across the blue sky. Airplanes didn't fly that way and neither did birds; these things (she had no idea of what to call them) moved more like flies zipping around. Or bumblebees. But they were much bigger. They had to be some sort of strange flying machines she'd never seen before, and she figured that perhaps the Air Force had invented a new type of plane. That had to be it; there was no other explanation.

She gave it no more thought until July 8th.

That was the day the radio news declared that spacemen had landed, or crashed rather, in an obscure, ranching town in New Mexico. The newsmen called the spacemen's ship a "flying saucer" but for reasons unknown, the story was quickly recanted. The Air Force was now saying it was a weather balloon.

But what about the bodies they'd said they'd found? she wondered. *And if there had been a weather balloon, what could have knocked it down out of the sky?* The men from outer space, there had been four or five of them, and according to the reports, one had survived the crash—but where was he now? According to the news, they were dummies, mannequins, which had been tested with the weather balloon.

None of it was making much sense, but everyone on the radio was talking about it.

When Saxon heard a description of the spacemen, her heart skipped a beat. According to an eyewitness, they only had four fingers on each hand. They were short, like children, but with grey skin and slits for mouths, hardly any noses at all, and large, black, slanted eyes. "They kind'a looked reptilian to me," one man said in an excited voice, muffled by shuffling in the background.

Reptilian! Slitted mouths and big, black eyes—why, they sounded like the faces she'd seen for years in her bedroom wallpaper. Not ghosts, but *spacemen!* Saxon thought about this, trying to rationalize it. Could the faces in the wallpaper have been a sign? If so, what did it all mean? Was the arrival of the spacemen somehow linked to the Serpent? She began watching the sky avidly now, wondering if she, too, would see another flying spacecraft, fearful that one would land nearby. But the skies over Maine were quiet.

Abnormally quiet, for it hadn't rained since June and although it was a nice reprieve from the soggy spring, this was unusual weather. Dampness had always been keen to follow the Gulf Stream, dumping rain and fog on the Maine coast . . . but not this summer.

So, could it have been weather balloons she'd seen that day, zipping about the sky? *No,* she reasoned, *balloons float. They don't zip and zag around.* She might not have believed the reports so strongly if she hadn't seen those strange flying machines for herself. Intuition told her that the spacemen and the Serpent were somehow connected, that there was a linking explanation for both of them, and slowly she began drawing her own conclusions to what it all meant.

Although she believed Rob had really visited her and had truly shown her the terrible past of Roquefort Manor, she had to prove it to herself, if only to maintain her sanity.

And she had to begin in the basement.

Starting with the wall behind her father's old roll-top desk. Saxon noticed the bricks were different there than the ones used in the other walls throughout the basement. Their color was slightly redder, the mortar that held them in place a shade or two lighter. Could this be the same wall Rob had shown her? The place where young Mario Delgado had been entombed?

She picked up a hammer and hit the wall with it.

It *sounded* hollow, but not enough to convince her, so she hit it again.

This time, the brick she'd struck broke in half and was dislodged. One more strike and the halves fell away, leaving behind a hole. She hit the wall again and broke another brick, then another. Now she could tell that *something* was back there in that space, something that had once been organic.

The smell was musty and slightly sweet; Saxon recognized it at once as the odor of death. Still, she couldn't leave it at that—she had to see if that poor, young boy was back there.

After pulling the desk away from the wall (a monstrous task in itself), she tackled the wall with a determined attack, breaking away brick by brick until at last she made a hole big enough to shine her flashlight into.

And there, not two feet back, the remains of Mario Delgado stood propped, still strapped to the plank upon which he'd been murdered. The embalming fluids had proven effective; he hadn't decayed as much as one might suppose after almost fifty years. His was a pitiful, waxy corpse, his eyes shrunken, his curly, black hair covered in a veil of cobwebs. The mice and rats had been at him, too, from the looks of it.

Saxon broke down more of the wall, then pulled him out, plank and all. She dragged him into the workroom and lifted the plank, one end at a time, onto her father's cadaver table. It was a distasteful task set before her, but she had to do it, if only out of human decency—and because of her love for her friend, Jacqueline.

She thought of notifying the police about finding the body, but decided not to. They'd try to push charges against her for murder, just like they did before. Only this time, they'd throw her in jail, she was sure of it. They'd wanted to lock her up behind bars before, but the judge wouldn't allow it. He'd said she was too young, that she'd suffered a mental breakdown—and was so upset she apparently didn't know what she was doing when she shot her father.

She knew, oh, she knew, but there was no way she could tell anyone.

And at the end of the trial, she'd gotten the bars anyway, imprisoned with a whole bunch of strangers, most of whom were truly crazy. There was no way she'd be going back there, either.

So she cleaned Mario's body the best she could, dressed him in one of her father's suits, and applied makeup just the way her father had taught her to do. His mouth was a problem—the gag had misshapen his lips, pressing them against his teeth, but she sewed them together with white floss and after a little lip color; he didn't look quite so bad.

She buried him that afternoon in the garden in her backyard, and felt terrible that she couldn't have given him a proper burial with a coffin and a nice service. But at least this way, she was sure he could rest in peace.

It took her a long time to gather up enough courage to go back down to the basement to clean up the mess of broken bricks in the basement. She didn't want to do it; she *had* to. What if someone saw the bricks and the hole in the wall, and began asking questions? What would she say? That she'd decided to try some remodeling? Not with the rest of her house in such sorry shape—starting a project in the basement would hardly seem convincing.

But it was here that she found a small, metal box on the floor in the same space where Mario's body had been hidden. She carried it out to her father's desk and sat down, gazing at it.

What's in it? Do I really dare to open it?

She knew she had to. Whatever was contained in that box couldn't be any worse than the horrors she knew to be part of Roquefort Manor. It was heavy, made of steel, with strong latches on one side. Using a screwdriver for leverage, she pulled them up, then slowly opened the lid of the box.

And gasped. Here were the photographs Leonard Roquefort had taken. His secret collection. There was no need for her to look through them to know—the picture on top of the stack was proof enough.

She felt terrible for the dead woman in the photo, sickened by what had been done to her body.

Quickly, she shut the lid.

I can't do this alone, she decided, *I can't fight this Evil by myself. I need help. Mrs. Tuttle will know who to ask.*

9

October 15, 1850

Suki rose to the water's surface, gasping for air. Through the blur of her tears, she could see her newborn baby, held high in Adam Walker's hands, and with the last of her strength she reached for the child. Her fingertips could almost touch him . . . but she was too weak. She fell back.

Walker ignored her and turned toward Stevie who'd come out into the water, dragging the dead man along behind.

"Stop right there, darkie, or I'll drown the git."

Stevie stopped, the look on his face utterly devastated. It frightened her to see him that way.

"You drownt my wife," he said, his voice low and full of sorrow.

"Wife?" Walker's jeering laughter sounded like the cackle of an insane man. "So the Black man don't even know he's an animal—and animals don't marry. They *breed.* That was the sole purpose of your Black Betty, now weren't it? Breeding stock." He sneered, lowering the infant to his chest. "No big loss. But this little fellow, now I wager he'll fetch a pretty price at the auctions."

Stevie growled, nostrils flaring, but he didn't dare move toward Walker; Suki could see the battle going on, written in the lines of his face. He wanted to kill Walker, she could tell, and he was angry enough to do it, but on the other hand, he didn't want his baby—their baby—harmed in the process.

"You turn around right now," Walker was saying, "and get out of the water, else I drop your git."

Suki watched the murderous cloud pass over Stevie's eyes, replaced by grim apprehension. He turned and began to wade out of the pond. Walker followed from a distance, reaching down with one hand for the chain attaching Beaumont's corpse to Stevie.

At the water's edge, he ordered Stevie to halt in his tracks, promising again to harm the child if he so much as moved. Suki continued trying to reach for her baby, but to no avail. Her hands kept going through Walker, through her child, as if both were made of nothing more substantial than vapor, and she didn't understand why.

Walker moved past Stevie and picked up the gun. Aiming it with one hand, he fired and a shot rang out. Suki watched the bullet leave the barrel of the shotgun, moving as if in slow motion, spinning as it traveled through the air; she'd reached, trying to snatch it in her fist, but it went straight through her fingers and continued on its course deep into Stevie's left shin.

He collapsed, hands wrapped around his leg, and his screaming frightened her more than seeing the gush of blood seeping from between his fingers. It was the sound of a wounded animal in unbridled pain. It was also the sound of rage, dark and twisted, no longer human.

She ran to him, brushing her hands over his face, wishing with all her heart that she could make him well. She'd come so far with healing his foot, but that had taken months.

Stevie looked past her, gasping, eyes narrowed in hatred as he watched Adam Walker move away from the banks of the pond. He didn't say a word; he didn't have to. Suki knew what he was concerned for the baby, and she knew what she had to do.

She just didn't want to leave him.

Go, my beloved. Go save our baby.

She blinked, rising to her feet. This was strange; they were communicating, not by voice but by pure thought. *I'll save our child; then I'll come back to you.*

His head dropped as he shuddered in pain, and she reached out to touch the top of his head, but he gave no indication he'd felt her presence. Turning, she picked her way over the beach toward the path where Walker had gone with her newborn. She could hear the cries of their baby, and shuddered to think of its fate in the rough hands of that bastard.

The path was dark; she followed the sound of her child's cries, muted by the dry rustle of leaves. Crossing the densely pebbled carriage road, she pursued Walker to another path, this one twisting uphill toward a tall house. Frosty moonlight glistened on the shingles of its steep-peaked roof. This was the "station" where she and Stevie had been staying these past few months, and until tonight it had been a safe place.

Now she saw it in an entirely different light.

It was a Death House. Why hadn't she known it before?

Walker was crossing the backyard, headed for the cellar bulkhead with her baby in his arms. It didn't take her long to catch up with him. She had no idea how to stop him, but she knew she had to try.

Heartbroken mother . . . I can ease your suffering.

Startled, Suki looked around. Who'd said that? It certainly wasn't Walker; that wasn't his voice and she doubted he even knew such kind words.

Who are you? she asked with her mind.

A friend who sees much.

A friend? If you're a friend, then why didn't you help us?

Walker was taking her baby down into the cellar and Suki hastened to keep up with him. She could hear her infant's feeble cry and it tore at her heart.

That's my girl, come down here and let me bid you comfort.

The cellar steps were wide, heavy planks of wood, and she sought for balance by holding a palm to the rock wall as she stepped downward.

Walker was doing something to her baby. His lantern light cast crazy shadows on the walls as he placed the newborn on a bench, and bent on stopping him, Suki stepped forward—

—and something caught her from behind. Something big and strong, with arms like iron. Twisting about, she found herself looking into the grinning, red face of Beaumont, the bounty hunter Stevie had just killed.

"NOOO!" she screamed, clawing, kicking, struggling to get away from the beast.

Snarling, he picked her up and carried her into another room, away from her baby, away from her murderer, away from everything she'd ever known to be true and sane . . .

. . . into the heart of darkness, the great belly of the Serpent.

10

October 31, 1850

Stevie stared up at the sorry corpse hanging slack from the thick bough. It was hard to believe that was his body up there, beaten and broken, as saggy and limp as the poppets his mother used to stitch together from old socks for him and his sister to play with.

Only the body up there was no toy. It had once belonged to a man who refused to be anyone's slave anymore, who'd seen the chance to ride the freedom train and had taken it. That body had also belonged to a woman, a beautiful dark woman with skin as soft as silk, who knew how to ignite the flames of his passion. He'd been hers and hers alone. Surprisingly, though, he felt no physical pain. Sorrow, yes, and anger . . . but the pinching in his neck was gone, as was the pain in his left leg and foot. He looked around for Suki.

She was dead now, as he was dead. The white brute-bastard had drowned her while she was giving birth. Stevie scanned the faces of those who'd thrown back the white hoods of their costumes, laughing, congratulating one another on their success. No, Suki's murderer was not among them.

He'd never seen these men before but he knew who they were. Their sheet-like robes fluttered in the brisk breeze, and flames danced on the crosses they carried, these prophets of prejudice and hateful intolerance.

Hanged Man, you want revenge?

The sound of the voice caused Stevie to jump and look about. Who'd said that? Certainly not any of these sheet-draped cowards!

You want to be with your wife? Come, Hanged Man. There's a place for you here beside her. A place where you can grow the seeds of vengeance and reap its rewards.

Well, now. That didn't sound half bad.

He remembered the way they'd broken into the jail, dragging him outside, taking him to this lonesome place of broken glass, twisted heaps of rusted iron, piles of rags. A dumpsite. Here, they'd beaten him, breaking several ribs and teeth while showing him what happens to "nigger boys who dare murder white men."

He'd tried fighting back, but there were so many of them—and his bum foot and the bullet in his shin put him at great disadvantage. Toward the last of it, all he'd been able to do was hold his arms in front of his face as a shield. He felt himself being lifted onto the back of a horse, and when he felt the noose tighten around his neck, he knew, oh Lord, he knew what they were planning to do to him.

He'd prayed it wouldn't be a slow torture like some of the Southern executions were known to be. Victims doused in lamp oil and set afire as they were being hung, those had been among the worst. Stevie figured it was done to terrorize other slaves. When this happened, it was next to impossible to identify the victims; therefore, they could never be properly buried. How could they go to Heaven if nobody could see their faces? How would anyone know their names?

Was he going to Heaven? Stevie didn't rightly know. He couldn't hear a choir of angels singing "Glory!"—all he saw were these men in white, some seated on horseback, some standing there beside trash heaps, grinning, watching his body swing on the end of that thick hemp rope.

Come to me now and I'll give you all you need.

"Who are you?"

A god to some, a devil to others, depending on the point of view. Those on the receiving end say I'm evil, but those on the giving end know my benevolence. Your woman is here and she's coming to realize I am divine.

"You've got Suki with you?" Stevie's heart quickened.

Yes. She's calling out to you. Can you hear her?

He strained to listen for any sounds over those of horses breathing, of their riders chuckling, the leathery squeaking of their saddles, and the roar of fire from those flaming crosses.

Stevie! I need you—I'm so scared!

"Suki?" Stevie turned around.

That's right, my good fellow. Just follow the sound of her voice while we talk, you and I. We're going to be great friends, I think.

Stevie began to walk along the side of the road, toward Roquefort Manor. He never looked back.

11

"I have flowers for Grammie," Clem told Saxon as he stepped off the front porch of the Tuttle house. She noticed he was neatly dressed, sporting dungarees held up by fire engine red suspenders. In his hand, he held a bouquet of dried wildflowers: purple lupine and brown-eyed Susans. The roses that grew wild along the shores and roadsides were long gone now; it had been a poor summer for them, and the lupines had taken to seed early; Clem had been lucky to find a few good flowers. Although it was still warm and uncommonly dry, summer was well on its way out.

"It's okay, I can come back later," she said with a smile. "You're looking mighty spruced up today, Clem."

The boy beamed, his slanted eyes twinkling. "Flowers for Grammie, then I go visit Mr. Moses. He's my teacher. You wanna come meet him?"

Saxon paused for a moment, thinking. Did she know a Mr. Moses? No, the name didn't ring a bell. She could have come up with a million excuses not to go with Clem, but something told her she should. She'd always liked the boy and had spent little time with him since returning home. Besides, something deep inside her hinted that Clem could lead her to an answer. She had a feeling today just might be the day.

"Sure, I'll come along. I'm looking forward to a visit with your Grammie."

He gave her an odd look, but then again, he was prone to giving people odd looks. She knew he was a lot sharper than folks gave him credit for; he often had a very good reason for those odd looks.

"Where does Mr. Moses live?" Saxon asked as she walked with him toward the old stone barn. Across the field, she could see Fair Acres, the Whitney farm with its huge barn and gable-roofed farmhouse sitting atop Prosperity Hill on Norway Drive. They were now at the crossroads, both literally and figuratively; Saxon could feel certain changes in the air.

Clem pointed straight down the Crooked Road. "Mr.

Moses lives at the old folks' home just yonder. His bedroom is blue. Mr. Moses says they want to paint it white but he won't let them. He likes the color blue. Do you like the color blue, too?"

Saxon nodded, quickening pace to keep up with him. "I love that color," she said. "The shade the sky is today, that's my favorite."

Clem smiled. "Mine, too."

She couldn't help but notice the tinderbox dryness in the air and the dust they kicked up just by walking. "Awfully dry, isn't it?"

Nodding, Clem replied, "Our well's gone dry. Dad's garden died, everything in it. Grammie's roses died, too."

Saxon frowned. "That's a shame. She was so proud of those roses."

"Did your water dry up, too?"

She turned to face him. "Why, I don't know. I haven't checked it for a while. I guess I should."

"Funny thing. No frogs, no mosquitoes around."

"It's because of the drought," she told him.

They chitchatted as they ambled along the dusty road, talking mostly about Mr. Moses teaching Clem how to read and write and cipher numbers. Between topics, they listened to the constant chirping of crickets in the dry, dead grass, and the calls of birds from the pines which were beginning to yellow from lack of rain. It was a golden, lazy day, but to Saxon, it was a stroll in Eden, despite the drought. She needed the sunshine and the company to relax, a brief reprieve from the stressful situation at her house.

Clem stopped and turned toward a footpath cutting through a meadow.

"Hey, where are you going?" Saxon called out to him.

"Gotta give Grammie the flowers."

She cocked her head, watching him go, her brows knit. Now he wasn't making any sense at all, for the path he'd taken led to a little family graveyard, shared by the Tuttles and Fernalds. Was Mrs. Tuttle up there, visiting old Joe's grave? She thought it very possible; the old lady had moments of clear thinking despite suffering a senility that came and went. With a sigh, she followed Clem up the narrow path.

The grass crunched and broke beneath her feet. Leaves had changed their colors early and many of them had fallen to the ground, even though it was the middle of October. *So very dry,* she observed. *It's as if the earth is burning up. I bet that under the grass, the dirt is as dry as powder.*

It wasn't far to the small cluster of graves, surrounded by a rusty iron fence. Clem pushed the squeaky gate open and went inside to pick his way through the headstones. Solemnly, he knelt at a grave at the far end of the lot. Not wanting to invade his privacy, Saxon watched him from a respectful distance as he laid the flowers in front of a relatively new stone.

A long moment passed; Clem had taken off his ball cap and held it reverently over his heart, head bowed. Then he looked up and called, waving for Saxon to join him. She came, a bit hesitantly, puzzled by his actions. He'd said he was taking flowers to his grandmother—but where was she?

As she came to a stop at Clem's side, her breath caught in her throat when she saw the words carved in that white marble stone: *Evangeline Tuttle, beloved mother. Born June 14, 1861. Died September 5, 1945.* She took a quick step back, shaking her head, bewildered.

No! How could this be? She'd seen and spoken to Mrs. Tuttle on many occasions since she'd returned home. This had to be some kind of mistake! Clem looked over his shoulder at her and she noticed fresh tears welling in his eyes.

"I—I don't understand," she stammered. "I had no idea Evangeline died."

Clem shook his head with a sad smile. "Grammie's sweeping. She sweeps here now with God and His angels."

Now some of it was beginning to make sense. Sweeping. Sleeping. Yet, there was more that did not make any sense at all.

"What happened? How'd she die?"

Clem stood up and put his cap back on. "She got sick. Real bad sick. Doc couldn't do nothing. Then she went to sweep."

Saxon felt faint and reached out to him for support. "I don't know what's happening, Clem. I thought she was alive; I really did. I'm so very sorry . . ." Just then, the whole world shifted, growing dimmer. She felt herself quickly weaken, unable to stay upright, and her words trailed off as she collapsed to the ground.

"Miss Saxon? Gorry, Miss Saxon, you okay?" She could hear his voice, but he sounded a million miles away.

"Miss Saxon, please wake up, please."

Her eyelids fluttered then opened, squinting in the sunlight. "Clem? My God, what happened?"

"I think you fainted, Miss Saxon. Are you OK?"

She nodded, leaning up on an elbow. "I'm just really shocked. I didn't expect your grammie to be here." How could she tell him she'd been seeing Evangeline, had been walking and talking with her? Clem straightened up and offered her his hand, and she accepted his help as she rose to her feet.

"Do you believe in ghosts?" she asked. It was a quiet

question, not meant to frighten him.

Clem shrugged. "I 'spose I do, Miss Saxon. I see 'em sometimes but they don't scare me like they used to when I was a kid. You gonna be OK now?"

She pressed her lips together for a moment, then answered, "Yes. I believe so. Can I tell you something, Clem?"

"Anything. You're my friend."

She gazed into his eyes and squeezed his arm. "I think I've been seeing ghosts, too. But I'm afraid. I don't know what to do about it."

Clem returned a puzzled look and looked around. "Do you see them now? Are they here with us?"

She shook her head. "No, they're in my house."

"I know."

"You do? Have you seen them, too?"

He stared at his shoes. "There's always been ghosts in your house. Even when you was gone, they was there. I still see them in the windows sometimes. Some are bad and some are good. But it's the Serpent that scares me the most." He looked up, his gaze meeting hers. "That one scares me real bad."

Saxon let go of his arm and hugged hers to her stomach. "My God, you know it by name! How did you know that?"

"I just know. It's something like a big snake, only it's not really a snake, and it keeps the ghosts inside."

She felt faint again and grasped his shoulder for support. "I'm scared to death. I need to find a way to get rid of it, but I have no idea how."

"I dunno." He scratched his head for a second, looking puzzled, then Saxon saw his eyes light up. She figured something must have fired in his brain: an idea, or an inkling of an idea. "Maybe Mr. Moses knows," he added.

"He's awfully smart; he knows all kinds of stuff."

She raised an eyebrow, aware of the goosebumps on her arms. "You think he'll believe us?"

"Yes. He sees ghosts, too."

Together, they left the little graveyard and walked back to the Crooked Road. Clem took Saxon's hand and placed it in the crook of his arm. Kane's Rest Home lay just beyond the next meadow, a low, white building with grey shutters and trim. Neat and well kept, it was home to twenty-three of Bar Harbor's senior citizens. A wooden ramp with a sturdy hand railing led to the front door, which Clem opened for Saxon with a gentlemanly flourish.

She thanked him and went inside. "This way," he told her, leading the way past a busy parlor full of old folks, many of them playing card games or knitting, and down a well-lit hall. He stopped at the door numbered three and rapped lightly.

"Mr. Moses, you home?"

"Clem, c'mon in," she heard a voice call from within.

He opened the door again for Saxon and she walked in. She gave a friendly smile to the man sitting on the bed in his blue room. His skin was dusky black and very wrinkled, in contrast to his teeth and hair which were as white as virgin wool. He smiled back broadly and pushed his dentures into place with his fingers.

"Howdy, Clem! Ready for another lesson? You don't want to get behind the grind. Hey, I see you've brought a friend today."

Clem nodded, closing the door behind him. "This is Miss Saxon Faraday. She lives right next door to me at Roquefort Manor."

Saxon went over to Moses, extending her hand. "I'm very pleased to meet you, Mr. Moses."

He took her hand in his, marveling at the softness of her touch. His eyes met hers, and his sparkled with delight. "Very nice to meet you, too, Miss Faraday. My name's Mr. Brady, actually, but you can call me Moses, or Mr. Moses if you like. Just don't call me late for dinner." He laughed at his joke and Saxon joined him.

Clem gave them both a puzzled look. "We need to tell you something. The Serpent's in Miss Saxon's house."

Saxon felt Moses shiver, then he dropped her hand. "W—What did you just say?"

Clem faltered and looked down at his shoes again. "The Serpent," he whispered, "it's in her house. She's been seeing ghosts, too, but she knows the Serpent is there."

Moses sat back with a dumbfounded look and tugged a white handkerchief from his pocket. He mopped his brow with it. "Lord Almighty, I never thought I'd see the day . . ." he murmured. He turned his eyes to Saxon, his gaze nervous, unsettled. "How do you know about the Serpent? Have you seen it?"

She pulled away from his stare and glanced over at Clem. "Maybe this wasn't such a good idea. I don't want to bother anyone with my troubles."

At this, Moses reached out and grabbed her wrist. "Listen! You ain't bothering me, young lady. I'm just a little shocked is all. It's been almost ninety years since I'd last heard anyone refer to it by that name. The Serpent. I thought I was the only one still left around here who knew what it was." He cast a long, deep look at Saxon. "Tell me, truthfully, is it strong?"

Saxon nodded.

"I was afraid of that."

"Clem's right; I've seen ghosts, but I haven't seen the Serpent. I only know it's there," she admitted. "It's much stronger than it was before. It's going to molt this fall."

Moses cleared his throat. "How do you know its name?"

Saxon gave him an unfaltering gaze. "I've always thought of it as 'the Serpent.' Ever since I was a little girl," she said. "I don't know why. Maybe a Biblical play on words since Bar Harbor used to be Eden?"

Moses frowned. "It's no play on words, believe me."

"If you don't mind me asking, Moses, how old are you?"

He cast her a sad smile. "Ninety-seven."

"Then you could tell me what's going on, couldn't you? Surely, there must be things you know, things you've seen or heard over the years?" Her voice trailed off and she glanced over at Clem, but he was busy browsing through a *National Geographic* atop Moses' dresser. "I already know Roquefort Manor is haunted with several ghosts, not just the Serpent," she added in a whisper, "so please don't feel you'd need to mince words with me."

His eyes widened. "You don't mind living there?"

Saxon gave a sarcastic sigh. "You kidding? I hate it! I'm scared out of my wits half the time."

"So why do you stay?"

"Because it's mine. I have no other place to go."

"And you say your last name is Faraday?"

Saxon nodded. "My father, Geoffrey, was an undertaker. Maybe you knew him?"

At this, Moses shook his head. "No, but I knew Leonard Roquefort, the undertaker before him."

Jacqueline's father! At this, Saxon smiled hesitantly. "I knew I could learn a lot from you, Moses."

"We could learn a lot from each other," he told her, but the sparkle in his eyes was replaced with something else. Saxon recognized it as trepidation.

"Can you help me get rid of the Serpent and the

ghosts?" she asked, unable to hold the question back any longer. "Just tell me how and I'll do it."

Moses shook his grizzled head. "The Serpent is a powerful entity, maybe the strongest enemy mankind has ever known. And old, perhaps even older than the Earth itself. One of the ancient gods, maybe even one of the original *sons* of God, no blasphemy intended. I don't know a better way of how to explain what it is. All I'm sure of right now is that you can't defeat it alone. No one can."

"It's going to wake up," she said. "Something terrible will happen once it sheds its skin."

Moses sat forward, rubbing at his temples. "Dear God, no, it mustn't wake up. We can't allow that to happen. Ever."

It means to destroy all of us, Saxon thought miserably. She knew Moses knew it, too.

"It wants to lay the entire world to waste," he remarked as if he'd read her mind.

"Can you help me?" she asked, taking his hand in both of hers. "Please. I need to know what to do."

Moses Brady put on a brave face, but Saxon wasn't sure if it was only for her benefit. "If it's waking up, we haven't got much time to act," he told her. "Best we go right now and confront the thing. It's now or never. What do you say, Clem?"

Clem looked up. "We're going to fight it?"

Moses waved his hand and reached for his cane. "I don't think we have a choice. We might stand a chance at defeating it while it's still weak . . . but if we wait until it wakes up and sheds its skin, we're all doomed." Rising to his feet, the joints in his hips and knees cracked audibly.

Saxon reached out to help him. "Maybe this isn't such a good idea."

But Moses shook his head, frowning. "It's the *best* idea I've heard in a long time. We have to stop it from waking up if we can. Now let's get going." He lifted a grey fedora from his dresser and put it on his head. Leaning on his cane for support, he glanced over at Clem and Saxon. "You young folks lead the way."

Before they turned to leave, Saxon admitted she was scared.

Moses nodded. "Me, too."

CHAPTER THREE

Moses trusted the staff would let him go out on this venture, and they did, treating him as always like a favored pet. He noticed that they all said hello and smiled at Clem, but none of them spoke a word to Saxon. He knew why, even though she didn't, so he held her hand ever so gently as they walked out the front door. He could sense her sadness, her alienation, and wished he knew the right words to comfort her. He didn't want to cause her any distress just because she was different.

Still, it wasn't anybody's fault. They hadn't been through what Saxon had been through; they couldn't possibly know—and no one could begrudge them for that.

Everyone liked him, though; Moses was quite aware of this but attributed it to the fact that he was unique, too, but in a different way than Saxon. He was sort of a novelty, as much a part of town as it was a part of him. As far as he knew, he'd been born here, a foster son, an orphan.

They'd found him on an October evening in 1850. Alton and Elvie Brady were taking their twilight stroll, a habit they'd embraced as newlyweds and carried through until 1892, when Elvie contracted polio and became confined to a wheelchair.

Who were Moses' biological parents and why had they left him on a park bench, wrapped up in that burlap sack, still wet from birth, his umbilical cord crudely tied? No one knew. But the Bradys adopted him and raised him as their own. Over the years, he realized they'd taken on a difficult task and he respected them for it. Back then, they were a young, white couple with a black son, in an age where blacks and whites didn't usually mix socially. Not that prejudice ran rampant in the Northeast, but there were always those looks and whispers. The arched glances from a handful of people who'd chosen to ignore Moses altogether. But Alton and Elvie didn't care; God had provided them with a healthy baby. Who were they to question His judgment?

They proved to be loving parents to him, their only child. His earliest memory was of resting in the crook of Elvie's arm while she read to him. She loved the classics, books by Victor Hugo, Irving Washington, Nathaniel Hawthorn, and Herman Melville, and Moses came to love them, too, if only by osmosis. Later would come Twain, Kipling, and Poe, but that would be long after he'd learned to read on his own.

Because of his love for reading, Moses had often entertained the thought of becoming a writer. This pleased his mother greatly, but it was not to be. The war had started between the North and South. The Union wanted to free the Southern slaves, and Moses begged his parents to let him enlist, believing this was a fight for *his* people. It would have been next to impossible for him to do nothing while others fought and died for the cause.

Naturally, Alton and Elvie were dead set against sending Moses off to war. He was only twelve years old, but the 20th Regiment of Infantry, Maine Volunteers, had need of a drummer boy, and Moses knew how to play the drum. Finally, in the early summer of 1863, they relented. No one could have guessed the war would have lasted this long; it had to end soon. He gave his parents a solemn vow that he wouldn't be sent to the front lines.

Hence, he joined up, was issued a blue uniform, and was given a United States regulation drum, bigger, fancier, and sturdier than his homemade one. He left his parents at the train station in Ellsworth, and in her tearful goodbye, Elvie handed him a box of stamps and made him promise to write home. Moses said he would, as often as he could.

No one warned him, though, how heavy his drum would become during those long, dusty marches, or how tired his arms, shoulders, and legs would get. Thankfully, the cherries made life bearable.

They grew wild along the roadsides in Pennsylvania and were sweet and juicy, unlike Maine's bitter chokecherries. For the rest of his life, whenever Moses had a dessert containing cherries, be it ice cream, cheesecake, or jubilee, he'd be reminded of those long marches, so proud to wear his uniform and play his drum. The acrid smell of black powder would come floating back to him, and he'd remember the thunder of cannons, the long billows of grey smoke that trailed over the battlefields like ground fog. He'd recall the almost paralyzing fear that gripped him when the bullets flew so close he could feel the air of them rushing past, kissing his skin. He'd never forget the sounds made by dying men or how the faces of the dead ones remained frozen in agony, forever etched into his memory. And how many ghosts he'd seen after a field was cleared, the dead and wounded hauled away in wagons. These were things he never wrote about in his letters home.

Still he knew his mother fretted about him getting hurt or worse, but he never entertained such worries. Red Feather, an old Wabanaki woman who lived down in Otter's Creek, had assured him when he was five that he was a "Protected Soul." She said she could see a "glow" inside him, a gift from the Great Spirit, and then she made a prediction: Moses would do battle using his gift as both shield and weapon—and this would please the Great Spirit. When she passed away a few years later, she left him her cane, a staff of ash wood, carved with tribal symbols. He didn't understand their meaning—but perhaps it wasn't for him to know. Red Feather wanted him to pass it onto someone else, who would need it when he was done using it.

He hadn't taken her cane to war, reasoning that the Civil War was probably not the battle she had spoken of. He'd know when the time came for him to use it and pass it on.

Aside from the cane, the "glow" was hard to explain; Moses thought of it as a sort of a second sight . . . more a keen intuition than hearing, touching, and seeing, but sometimes, when it came on real strong, it was a lot like sight, sound, and touch. Years later, he would describe it as a radio wave that few people could tune into. Usually the signal was weak, but once in a while it could allow him to hear and see things that other people couldn't.

Like dead folks. Ghosts, trapped spirits. He didn't mind seeing them, but occasionally the signal would come from something else, something so malignant and hateful he'd feel his insides shrivel at the very thought of it.

He'd first sensed that terrible signal in Eden, a year before he left to go to war. He and his pals had been playing a modified game of baseball along the Crooked Road, tossing the ball back and forth, then taking turns cracking it with a homemade bat. It was a safe game to play in the road those days before the motor car claimed rule of the road.

As long as he lived, he'd never forget that day in October, when the air had taken on a brittle crispness fat with the promise of a coming winter. The leaves had turned already, red, brown, and gold, and they rustled in the breeze as the boys passed beneath them.

Moses had the bat and when Billy Wallace tossed him

the ball, he leaned into the swing with all his might. It made a loud crack as oak made contact with the ball, sending it airborne, flying between those two marble lions that served as gatepost sentries to Roquefort Manor. The boys watched in awe as the ball touched down once, then bounced high and rolled to a stop near the bushes beside the driveway.

At first, no one said a word; then Billy spoke up. "You go get it, Moses. It's your ball, anyway."

Moses looked over at Billy, then up at the house on the hill with uncertainty. None of the kids he knew liked that house much. It was a Death House, a black house, the only one like it in town. A few years back, the caretaker, a man named Walker, had killed himself there, and now it was unoccupied, left alone to brave the elements. Its lack of human care gave it a foreboding spookiness, pre-labeling it "haunted."

"No, that's okay," Moses told Billy. "It's just a dumb ol' ball. I got another one at home."

"You chicken, Brady?" Ken Wells asked. "You're afraid of Death House?"

No, Moses Brady wasn't a chicken, but truth was, he was very much afraid of that house. None of the boys felt very comfortable about it, standing there between those two, fierce, marble lions, having that house glare down at them, taunting them: *Come hither, young men, I'll play games with you . . . and I'll win. I always win.*

Could anyone else hear that? Moses didn't know, but he swallowed the growing lump in his throat and put on his bravest face, lifting his chin with defiance. "Heck, no. That place don't scare me one bit. Ain't like it's gonna reach out and grab me."

"Prove it," Billy said.

Moses gave him a challenging look. "Why don't you?"

Billy shrugged. "You first."

Now Moses had had enough; he knew if he didn't do anything, they were going to start calling him a baby, a scaredy cat, and he wasn't about to let *that* happen, so he threw his arms up in the air. "Well, I dare to walk straight up to the porch. I ain't scared of Death House." He eyed his pals suspiciously. Were *they* scaredy cats? Proof was in the pudding. "Anyone coming with me?" he asked.

Billy said he would and Ken agreed too, then lastly, Joe Tuttle, the most reluctant of the group. It was a long, uphill hike and they had every opportunity to turn back, but they wouldn't, they couldn't—the challenge was on. As the boys crept closer, Moses sensed something—the most powerful *glow* he'd ever experienced. It wasn't the pallid, ghostly vapor of a semi-transparent dead person . . . nor was it a distant voice from beyond the grave.

The air had suddenly grown thin, and it was in this change that Moses sensed something liken unto an odor, if it could be described as such. It wasn't exactly something he could smell with his nose but rather something that fired every nerve in his body all at once, and the message was clear, booming like thunder, smelling strangely of black powder, camphor, and hot metal: *Danger!* it seemed to tell him. *Stay away! Stay away!*

In midst of the words (or rather the *feelings* of words), Moses could make out disturbing noises: human cries, shrieks of rage, anguish and torment. Ghosts were in Death House, he was sure of that, but something else was here as well, something deep and hidden, something primeval that was not of this world but beyond, something that was *keeping* the ghosts here.

Apparently unaware of the danger, Billy bolted up and bounded onto the porch. He stood there a moment, peering into the nearest window, when the voice came floating again to Moses:

Little man, I know you can feel my presence. Don't even think for a second you can walk away from a confrontation with me. I am everything you've ever been afraid of and everything you will ever fear: your darkest nightmares, your deepest terrors, the worst death you can imagine. I have a special place waiting for you down here in the ground, with someone who has a special message for you, my boy.

The terrible voice fell silent and another took its place, female and husky, full of urgency: *Beware the Serpent; it's after souls to eat, the endless feast infernal!*

The woman's voice died out, replaced again by the terrible one:

Go away, little man, and don't come back!

The color in his cheeks took on an ashy hue, and Moses fell to his knees, clutching his chest. Ken and Joe rushed over. "Hey, what's wrong with you?"

Raising a thin, shaking hand, Moses pointed at the house where Billy stood, transfixed, staring at a window, mouth hanging slack, a long line of drool dripping from each corner of his mouth. "G—get Billy away from there," he managed to say, panting, unable to catch his breath.

The other boys raced over and dragged Billy off the porch. He looked as if someone had just walked over his grave; he couldn't even speak for several minutes, then slowly, he wiped his hand across his chin.

"What I saw . . ." he said, swallowing, rapidly blinking his eyes.

"What? What'd ya see? Here, clean yourself up." Ken handed Billy a handkerchief.

". . . something awful in there . . . blood coming up through the floor. I thought it was water, that maybe the basement was flooded . . . but it was gurgling . . . and I knew it was blood—it was so red and bubbly. There was something else in there, too. A snake, I think. Like a rattlesnake. Oh, I know they don't live 'round here, but I swear I heard it rattle. And out of the blood on the floor, a man stood up. He wasn't there before. His eyes, oh God, his eyes were glowing . . ." Billy looked up with tears in his own. "He had blood all over him, too. Buckskin clothes. You guys think I'm making this up, don'cha?"

"I dunno," Joe said, "but Moses saw something, right?"

Moses scratched his head, shrugging. "I didn't really *see* anything; I just felt it—and it felt real bad." He got up and brushed the grass off his knees. "I think we'd better get out of here."

"We gonna tell anybody about this?" Billy asked, his voice still shaky.

Each boy shook his head solemnly and as they walked back to the road, their ball forgotten. Moses was the only one who looked back over his shoulder at the house. Something terrible lived there, not in the house but in the ground *beneath* it. He'd felt its eyes upon him and no amount of lye soap and hot water could ever scrub that awful feeling away. It was as if his flesh had been peeled back and his bones laid open bare. Whatever it was, it wanted to hurt him and his friends . . . but something stopped it, preventing it from doing so. Moses had detected a note of fear in the thing—but why would such a creature be scared of a kid? Why him?

He thought long and hard about Red Feather's words over the decades that followed. She was long dead now, part of the Great Spirit, living in the happy hunting grounds in the sky. Was this why he'd been kept alive these past ninety-seven years? To fight a final battle with the Serpent under Roquefort Manor? Why now? It would have been much easier when he was younger, when his bones were strong, his feet sure, his heart steady.

He wondered if this might be the day of his death.

He couldn't help his suspicions. Did the Serpent send this woman with Clem, the grandson of a boyhood friend, to coax him out there, seeing that he was a weak, old man? *The good is gone,* he thought. *Wouldn't take much to do me in. Bones all brittle, joints full of rust, I'm all used up.* He half-listened to the pair walking on ahead of him; no, they didn't sound like they were up to something—and besides, he trusted Clem. The boy had a good heart. He'd had a rough life, physically abandoned by his Ma, emotionally abandoned by his father, and having to deal with that syndrome he had. Moses didn't know what had happened to Joe, Jr. to make him behave so indifferently toward his son; this grieved him deeply but there was little he could do about it.

The woman, Saxon, though, now she was an enigma. Moses sensed there was something unique about her, a hard inner core hidden beneath a fragile, almost ethereal quality. He'd known it when he touched her hand and he'd vowed to keep her secret to himself. The fact that Clem had befriended her both amazed and amused him. Clem had the gift, too, but Moses had known that for quite some time. He surmised that the good Lord was prone to give something special to those who lacked insulation in their attics.

Did Saxon or Clem know anything about what they were about to face in the battle that lie ahead? Moses wasn't sure, but he suspected the woman suspected a little something. *She knows more than she lets on,* he decided. Women were experts at secrets, keeping them as well as making them. He loved the fairer sex in general, how they made the world a nicer place, but for him, only one had captured his heart. Thoughts of her filtered into his mind like falling rose petals.

He'd met Glory Jackson in 1880, when he was thirty. She worked as a maid for the Vanderbilt family, joining them at their summer cottage, and that's where he'd met her. Never had he seen a creature so fair, so full of life. She was out watering the roses in the yard, singing in a husky, almost sensual alto voice, when he spotted her and something deep inside him told him he'd best go over and make her acquaintance. For him, it was love at first sight; he was badly smitten, but as fate would have it, their romance was short-lived. Glory died of scarlet fever a year after their wedding.

After that, she'd come to him once, in spirit, in 1900, to offer comfort after the death of his child. John hadn't been hers; Moses had adopted him in 1895 when he'd shown up at the school where Moses taught. No parents, the boy had been left there on the front steps, a white, autistic child of seven or eight.

That had been Moses' job; he worked with mentally handicapped children. After he'd received his degree, it was the only teaching job he could find—and he'd grown to love it. In 1916, St. Edward's Convent was built, and he'd been invited to teach there.

But the day John drowned in Witch Hole Pond left a mark on Moses. He remembered carrying his child's body up the hill to Roquefort Manor and how a young Leonard Roquefort had been so helpful, taken care of everything: the embalming, the funeral arrangements, the works. In his grief, he'd almost forgotten about that autumn day in 1860 when that house (or whatever lived there) had nearly scared the pants off him and his friends.

Yet, it reminded him, didn't it? Subtly, sneaking into his

vision, those strange faces swirling in the parlor wallpaper. He only saw them for a brief moment, a flash in time, but whether it was an optical illusion or real, he could never truly be sure. He'd felt the pain, though, the agony that house contained, and he had the distinct feeling that whatever was there, it wanted him to leave.

When he returned to Roquefort Manor in 1910, to pay his respects to Maryanna Roquefort, he felt it still. It was a hard time; Leonard had been murdered by his teenaged daughter, a heinous crime, hacked to death with an axe. He'd heard they'd shipped the girl up to the mental hospital in Bangor. Maryanna was in a terrible state of affairs; she'd just lost her husband and child, and wasn't making much sense at all, raving on about how Roquefort Manor was under a curse. She said it played a part in the Underground Railroad, and surmised a Voodoo hex had been put on the house and all its inhabitants.

That got Moses to thinking. What if it was true? Not the curse, but the other part. If Roquefort Manor had been a way station in the Underground Railroad, could *his* parents have been some of the slaves it sheltered? Made sense all right, the timing would have been perfect. But why had his folks left him here? Didn't they want him?

In 1911, he began searching for his biological parents.

And came up empty-handed.

Leads were practically nonexistent then, and those who knew about the Underground Railroad didn't have much to say about the slaves they'd helped. No records kept, no names remembered.

There'd been one hint, an old article in the local paper mentioning a black couple, a woman drowned, a man hung, and a murder down at Witch Hole Pond, but it wasn't exactly a lead; it was more like chasing shadows. Moses, however, felt fairly certain that Roquefort Manor held the key to his background. If only the walls could talk.

Well, perhaps they could. He remembered that horrible voice and those faces in the wallpaper while he was arranging for John's funeral . . . and what Billy had said years ago about blood coming up through the floor. Was the house trying to tell him something then? Or was it only trying to frighten him away?

It wouldn't succeed this time; he couldn't let it. An old warrior, Moses was sure he was about to go to war with the dark forces that resided there. He'd met battles before: one of the hardest had been at Little Round Top, where he'd abandoned his drum and picked up a rifle, following direct orders from Colonel Chamberlain. What he'd seen that grey day in July—the horrors of battle, soldiers racing uphill, gunfire ringing through the trees and out from behind rocks, the acrid smell of gunpowder in the smoke-filled air, the screams of the dying, the blood—dear God, red had been the color of the day under those dismal clouds.

How many men had been killed? Moses couldn't be sure. How many had *he* killed? None. One of the soldiers he'd tried to fire at was a boy armed with a bayonet, no older than himself. A moment's hesitation, then Moses pulled the trigger. Nothing happened; the gun was jammed. Then, as he watched, the boy fell, dropping his weapon, and Moses wondered who'd killed him; it was such a chaotic, frantic battle, the bullet could have come from anywhere, even from the boy's own side. Hours later, when it was all over, Moses found the soldier boy draped like a discarded doll over a rock. He reached out to touch him with trembling hands and as he did, the boy opened his eyes, looking straight at him.

"Hey, darkie," he grunted through bloodied, broken teeth.

Moses jumped back, tripped, and landed on his backside. The soldier boy's eyes were shut now and he knew they'd not really been open. Not physically, anyway. The boy was dead, his blood drying on the rock, turning crusty black.

At this point, Moses burst into tears. For almost any other person, it could have been a release from the stress of battle, or homesickness, or weariness, or hunger, but not for him. They were coming to him now, the dead on that hillside. Coming because they *knew* he could hear and see them, and all of them were talking so loudly, calling out to him; he could hardly make out what any of them were trying to say.

It wasn't scary or startling, like it had been with the first dead boy; it was sad and frustrating. There was nothing he could say or do to help them; they were beyond *listening*. Trapped in an eternity of marching onward, seeking, ever searching for the doorway into the Great Hereafter.

He could smell them: the bitter sting of black powder, the salty tang of spilt blood wafting in the air like that of old pennies, the pungent odor of their sweat and fear.

"You're dead," he shouted. "Go to Heaven—that's where you all belong now!"

The nearest soldier fell to his knees. His was a terrible wound; he'd taken a bayonet in the guts and his intestines spilled down over his thighs. "My fiancé," he uttered, "I must find her—promised her I'd return."

Another soldier pushed him aside, reaching out to grab his arm. "Where's the son of a bitch who shot me? Tell me where he is!"

Beside him, another was begging for his mother to help

him. Half of his face was missing.

Moses clapped his grimy hands over his ears and rocked back and forth on his haunches, weeping openly, his tears making streaks down his dusty cheeks. "Go away," he sobbed. "Leave me alone. . . ."

That's when he felt a strong hand on his shoulder and looked up into the face of Colonel Chamberlain. The Colonel was a quiet, thoughtful man and Moses admired him greatly.

"You all right, Son?" he asked.

Moses nodded, swiping at his tears with the back of his sleeve.

The Colonel gazed about the hillside with a quiet expression. "Well, it had to be done; there was no other way. Come up the hill and get something to eat."

Moses rose to his feet, saluting the Colonel, and made his way back up the hill, leaving the dead behind. Their faces, their voices, would haunt his dreams for the rest of his life, but he'd never return to Pennsylvania, to Gettysburg, to the place where cherries grew by the roadsides and where he was quite sure the dead still roamed the fields and hills.

Back then, the Confederates had been the enemy; now he was facing a greater challenge, something he knew that wasn't even human. Not even halfway there, and Moses was feeling the rusty grind in his joints, paining him, slowing him down, but his spirit was strong even though his body was weak. He had his wits about him and he hoped to hell he had the guts to follow it through to the end.

CHAPTER FOUR

Clem Tuttle had a rough life from the very start; the survival rate of a Down's baby hovered between twenty and twenty-five percent, and somehow, he'd beaten the odds. Abandoned by his mother and raised by a father who made it clear he had little use for him, the only person who made life bearable was his grandmother, Evangeline.

She saw to it that he got an education—she wasn't about to let Joe, Jr. put him in an institution. "Clem can learn," she'd insisted. "It just takes him a little longer than most children, but he can do it." He was seven when he started first grade, a year older than his classmates.

Most of his peers were kind to him (Clem was friendly and outgoing), but there was always a handful of schoolyard bullies who did their best to make his life a living hell. Their name-calling and jeers stung him deeply, but he tried not to let it show, just like when his father called him a retard when he didn't do something right.

The teachers were nice to him, though, and always allowed him extra time to complete his assignments. Even so, as the years progressed, it became harder and harder for Clem to keep up with his studies. He got as far as fifth grade and that's when Evangeline decided it was time he needed a private tutor.

She hired Moses Brady, a black teacher from St. Edward's Convent, who'd recently retired and was living at the old folks' home down the road. Moses proved to be the most patient of mentors; he and Clem developed a close relationship. It seemed Moses needed Clem as much as Clem needed him, and in a way, Moses became a surrogate parent to the boy. When Evangeline went to her grave just after Clem turned thirteen, it could be said she'd died content, knowing that someone loved him almost as much as she did.

Although he was now sixteen years old, Clem knew something was wrong inside his brain. His father called him "slow," and yes, that was a good part of it; he wanted to learn so badly: to read grownup books, not little kid stories. He was no longer content at just looking at illustrations in magazines—he wanted to read the articles, too, and to cipher numbers and count out change quickly, to remember important things like who the current president was, or all the names of the states in the whole country. But none of this came easy to him. Moses was helping him with reading—and he was already up to fourth grade level . . . yet, no matter how hard he applied himself, he just couldn't seem to progress any further. It was all very frustrating.

And then there was his speech impediment, that maddening lisp that sometimes made his L's sound like W's, especially when preceded by an S. SL always came out as SW. *Baby talk,* his father called it. That was one reason why the bullies teased him mercilessly, but the other was his slanted eyes and his round, moonlike face . . . and the fact that the teachers at school coddled him somewhat, giving him extra time and praising him whenever he did well.

Maybe things might have been different if his mother had stuck around long enough to raise him. Clem thought about her a lot, especially after Grammie died.

Would she have been nice to me? he often wondered. *Or would she have been like my father?* He might have been able to reach a decision, if only he could have seen a picture of her. The eyes tell so much, he knew that, but he had no idea what she looked like—or even what her real name was.

His father's name was Joe, just like his father before him, but in those rare conversations, his mother was only known as *that woman.* No name, no identity. She may as well have been dead.

Clem felt fairly certain, though, that his mother was still alive. This was another matter of contention between him and his father. Clem could see and talk with spirits—and Joe, Jr. couldn't.

Dead people were everywhere, always zoning in on Clem because they *knew* he could see them. Most were just passing through, and that was fine because they were usually the ones who left him alone. There were others, though, who tormented him . . . asking, sometimes begging, for him to do certain things for them. Things they should have done when they were alive.

Like that fisherman who drowned a couple years back. He'd show up in Clem's bedroom, pleading with him to tell his wife that he still loved her, despite the fact that she was ignoring him. Clem tried to explain that he couldn't lie—that the mariner was dead, buried up on Summit Hill, but he wasn't terribly articulate about it—and apparently this was something this ghost didn't want to hear. That's when things got ugly; the fisherman no longer appeared anymore as a spirit, but began appearing to him as a kelp-draped wraith, a visage of white, waterlogged flesh with a missing nose and black caverns for eyes, scaring the crap out of Clem every chance he got.

Over time, he learned to ignore it and the visitations became less frequent. That's not to say others stopped coming. Heck, he couldn't even take a stroll down the road without having to stop and talk to a dead person. There were so many of them walking the roads, troubled souls trying to remember where they lived or who they were in life . . . searching, always searching for a way home.

How did they become lost? Clem thought he knew.

Some had died in accidents and, like the fisherman, had no inkling that they were dead. Others had passed away in their sleep or in comas and they'd woken up *outside* of their bodies, unable to comprehend what had happened to them. Then there were the ones who'd been murdered; some of them resided at Roquefort Manor, and Clem shuddered just thinking about them. Most of the others he'd been able to help . . . but not the souls owned by the Serpent.

Of course, his father didn't know about any of this. He just thought Clem was acting strange, foolishly talking to himself like an imbecile, another of his pet names. When he'd tried to explain what was going on, Joe, Jr. accused him of reading too many comic books.

But Grammie knew and she loved him anyway. When they'd go for walks together, she'd stop and wait for him while he conversed with the dead. Once, she'd asked Clem if he ever saw old Joe, her husband, his grandfather, but no, Grampa Joe had gone straight to Heaven. When he'd told her that, she'd sobbed with relief.

Clem remembered asking Grammie that when she died, if she'd not go right straight to Heaven like Grampa had done. He wanted her to stay with him for a while, until he was ready to let her go, and it comforted him to know she'd done that.

Saxon had seen her, too . . . when she fainted in the graveyard and told him she'd seen Grammie, he believed her. He wasn't sure what to do for Saxon when she fainted—if only he'd been born with a clearer mind, he might have known. He'd wanted to cry, he felt so frustrated, but then Grammie whispered in his ear, telling him to take Saxon to Mr. Moses. He couldn't see her anymore;

he could only hear her voice sometimes, because she was on her way to Heaven. She missed Grampa Joe real bad.

Before Grammie left, though, she warned him about the Serpent. Yes, Clem knew Roquefort Manor was full of trapped souls and he'd sensed something else there as well . . . but thanks to Grammie, he now had a name for it.

He didn't know what the Serpent was or how it got here; all he knew was that it was made of ice and fire. The bad kind of fire. Chaotic fire. Not like the fire in the stove or like the flame at the end of a match, but a sort of wildfire, the kind that burned down whole forests and sometimes towns and houses and people, too. God had made the Serpent with that kind of fire, but the Serpent hadn't been born bad . . . he'd *become* bad after a long time.

Even now Clem could feel that fire raging.

CHAPTER FIVE

1

In its underground den, the Serpent stirred, uncoiling itself, bristling and relaxing its body. Its dreams were fading now and reality was beginning to set in. It suspected people were coming, coming with the intent to hunt it down and kill it, and it yawned, cold breath icing over its clenched fists.

How it hated this place, this well-lit planet! It hadn't meant to come here; that had been an accident, one it couldn't have possibly foreseen. Eons ago, its ship broke through the atmosphere and burned with such ferocity that the Serpent lost control, tumbling, no longer able to steer. It crashed down at night, in the ocean, and quickly disintegrated, and as the Serpent swam to the surface, it realized there was no way home. Not yet. It would have to find a way to survive here until there was.

The water surrounding it was salty and full of life. Tiny organisms clung to the Serpent's scales; it sensed other beings swimming nearby, some large, some small. None were particularly threatening, but the Serpent knew it could not remain here long. It felt exhausted, in need of a firm, dark place to lie down and rest.

So it began to swim with the incoming tide, knowing dry land was nearby. How it knew, it wasn't sure. It knew so many things, its brain was filled with the knowledge of good and evil, but its intelligence was abstract, not concrete.

Although it was exhausted and had never swum before, the Serpent found itself a powerful swimmer. Its fingers and feet were webbed, its strokes strong, and when it came ashore, it coiled up on a ledge and fell asleep, awaking several hours later to a hateful, blinding light that burned its eyes and shriveled its scales. Was this the same light that had burned up its ship? The Serpent quickly sought shelter in the rocks on the beach, panting, frightened, afraid that it might die.

Its scorched scales flaked away when it brushed against the rocks. *I must find better shelter,* it reasoned. *But is there any such place on this vile planet?* At this point, it truly hated its Commander, the One who'd exiled it, sending it out with orders never to return.

It wasn't my fault, the Serpent fumed, grinding its teeth against the pain. Central Command had been falling apart, growing soupy in the center, its outer edges crumbling. Then came a great war between factions. The Serpent had been a leader, a general in the rebel forces, and seeing leadership disintegrate, contradicting itself time and time again, it had taken matters into its own hands. Sides were drawn, split and quartered, and the battle raged on.

They fought over the experiment, the one that had been started on the blue-green planet eons earlier, a test that had gone awry, the outcome different than anyone had anticipated. *Variables,* the Aelim called them and They embraced them all, but these were real problems to the rebel forces.

The scientists, the botanists, and genetic engineers who'd been sent had abandoned their main objective. Perhaps they'd become lonely, isolated from the rest of their kind, gradually losing touch—or maybe they'd begun fighting amongst themselves. Either way, a sacrilege had been committed: they'd begun to mate with the animals of this planet, and the offspring of such unions were of a kind unto themselves.

Not quite Aelim, not quite animal, these sons and daughters were capable of great intelligence, and proved to be strong and resilient. In their stature and beauty, they somewhat resembled the Aelim—but there was a serious problem: they were very, very violent, refusing to abandon the nature of their primal ancestry.

They killed one another without regard or conscience, waging war over items as trivial as a piece of meat. Or land. Or over the conquest of females. They even began to fight over the correct way to contact the Aelim. Clearly, they were greedy, proud, and lacked tolerance—and they were cultivating such fondness for their violence that they even killed the Ones the Aelim had sent—their own fathers and forefathers. Something had to be done, for in time, they too, would learn to reach the stars.

The leaders of the Aelim held a meeting where it was decided that one family of these hybrids should be allowed to survive. Only one; all others would have to be destroyed. Delegates were sent to determine which of the hybrids showed the best promise of survival, of intelligence, of heart.

But even so, after the deluge that killed most of the life on the planet, the offspring of the hybrids grew even more violent than the ones before them. The Aelim leaders were now in opposition concerning what should be done, and they broke off into two factions. On one side the Aelim, who wished to allow the hybrids to continue on their due course, trusting that they'd eventually embrace peace—and on the other side the Rebels, who wanted them destroyed before they could spread out and infect countless planets in the vastness of space.

The Aelim outnumbered the rebel forces, although many former leaders had joined up with the Rebels who questioned the judgment of the Aelim and had unanimously agreed it was time for a *coup d'etat.*

War waged in the outer reaches of the universe; the Rebels fought many battles in their rebellion against the Aelim, but in the end, they lost, and all were exiled, one at a time, after standing trial before the leaders. Stripped of their titles and charged with high treason, they'd been expelled in outdated, flimsy pod ships, spat out into the unending cosmos without ammunition and with limited life support. They were meant to die, their outer shells withering and falling away, their inner cores vulnerable and unprotected, lost forever. It would have been a far kinder fate if the Aelim had killed them outright.

The Serpent sighed with despair, wanting to rest but not daring to. What if that awful, blinding light found it again? It squatted in the shadows, waiting for it to come, growing wearier with each passing moment . . . then something strange happened. Miraculously, the light faded and died. Perhaps it was done searching? Would it come back? The Serpent didn't know.

But it knew it couldn't stay here in the rocks forever. It had to find a place where it could hide, should the light decide to return, so it crawled out of the rocks and made its way farther onto the land. There was another light in the sky, this one mellow and kind.

This was a strange planet. Brown and crumbly, beneath its feet, living things shot upward, brushing its ankles. The atmosphere was like the water it had landed in, cold and swirling, but considerably lighter. As it walked, the Serpent noticed the living things were larger, towering, wide and thick. It reached out and touched several of them tentatively, making sure they meant no harm, wondering if the Aelim had put them here as barriers or self-destructive weapons.

No, these were just simple, living organisms, much like the ones in the water, but different somehow: stationary, except for the air that moved through their outstretched limbs.

Hearing strange noises, it traveled closer to the source. It saw a new light now, a much smaller one than the lights in the sky. Fire! The Serpent grinned with recognition. Fire was one of the six chief elements, a component of life. In the distance, a band of hybrids were seated around this fire, conversing and eating. With its forked tongue darting at the air, the Serpent could smell the fragrance of the meat they'd roasted and as it crouched to watch them, it realized how very much it had in common with these hybrids.

No, they weren't covered with scales (the only ones they had left remained at the ends of their fingers and toes) and they lacked tails. Their limbs were shorter, and each had a strange, stringy substance adorning the tops of their heads, but they were communicating peaceably, unlike their animal ancestors. This had to mean they'd evolved, possibly maintaining the best traits of their forebears. Keenly interested, the Serpent drew closer to their fire.

Could they be taught new things? Would they be adept to technology? Perhaps, in time, they would help build a new ship for the Serpent . . . a better vessel upon which it could return to space?

No, it was obvious to see that those days were long into the future. The Serpent came to that conclusion by sheer observation. Each hybrid wore something ragged around their middles, it could see by the firelight that what they wore wasn't much different than the stringy substance atop their heads. The Serpent listened to them communicate, trying to fathom the meanings of their words.

They were afraid; it could determine so by their frantic

gestures and worried expressions. The way they tore into the meat, chewing quickly, eyes alert. The Serpent crept closer still, drawn to their fear and their fire.

They sense me, it reasoned, *and they are afraid. I can use this to my advantage.*

One of the smaller hybrids cried out in alarm, just then, pointing directly at the Serpent. It could no longer hide, so it stood to face them, content in the knowledge that no matter what they did, they probably couldn't cause it much harm.

Amazingly, all the hybrids fell to the ground, bowing before it, crying out in anguish. The Serpent raised its webbed hand, a gesture of peace, walked over, and sat down by the fire. It motioned for the beings to come and sit around it.

Thus it learned first-hand about life on Planet Earth. The hybrids called it "Serpent" and it rather liked the title, an expression of nobility from the Land of Sand far to the East. Some of these hybrids' most ancient ancestors had hailed from such places with exotic names such as Babylonia and Egypt. They'd navigated here by boat in days of yore, bringing with them the Cult of Set, the religion of the Serpent.

Hence, the Serpent began to teach.

2

The Aelim had already been here, the Serpent determined, educating these hybrids after the deluge, these "people" as they called themselves, teaching them how to live with one another and to respect—no, worship—the Aelim.

Because of its hatred for the Aelim, the Serpent decided

to educate them differently. It first had to convince them to distrust the Aelim, then it showed them methods of warfare to carry out against their neighbors. Teach them to fight, then teach them to fly. Let *them* wage war against the Aelim—surely that would show the Aelim the error of their ways!

The Serpent rewarded the hybrids' efforts with ambition and greed, making servants of the weaker, smaller ones, the women and children, while it taught the stronger ones the true meaning of power.

For a time, it became a god to the people, a deity to be worshipped, kept hidden in the shadows. They had given it a new name: Set the Wise, the great Dark Lord, and they presented great sacrifices of food, wine, and women. The people erected temples in its honor and, in return, it protected them. Teaching them, always teaching them. The people grew very powerful, their kingdom vast, challenged by none.

But the Serpent was not alone; there were other Rebels like it here on Earth. It could sense them, knowing they were all competing for ultimate control of the planet. They'd been comrades in the past, but now they were moving closer, old gods, each bent on the destruction of the other.

The Serpent bade its followers to fight against them and war cries filled the air. Blood soaked into the earth as the hybrids lost ground, enemies on all sides closing in for the kill. Then came the Aelim, flying down out of the sky, conquering, putting an end to the battles, driving the Serpent and its kind underground for a thousand years.

This angered the Serpent greatly. While it had masterminded the wars, the Aelim had only come in to sweep up the loot for themselves. Defeated and sore, the Serpent coiled in its underground den and began to sleep.

It dreamt hot, hate-filled dreams of a time long ago, when it had walked among the Aelim as an equal. An equal except for the fact that they never let it live up to its potential, always holding it back, never allowing it to create. *You are a warrior,* they said. A leader of warriors, guardian of the mother planet. *You can mimic, but you can never create. Leave that to us and do your duty.*

The Serpent did as it was told, until that fateful day when it decided to head the rebellion. Now this was its destiny? To hibernate, to slumber, a hero warrior buried in the earth, a great war general forsaken and forgotten?

No! Growling, the Serpent stirred, half awake.

Times were changing, it could sense such things from the surface. The hybrids were using the lessons it had taught so long ago and using them wisely. Something was going on overhead; the Serpent could hear the sounds of machinery. . . .

(*Ah, technology!*)

. . . and it could feel vibrations through the earth. Hybrids were building directly over this resting spot!

They weren't building a temple this time; the Serpent was certain of that. There were no soothing songs of worship, no offerings, no priests arriving to consecrate the ground. The Serpent listened closely, hearing the voices of men, their language much different than before, more elaborate than it had been in the days of yore when it had walked among them as teacher.

And it began to interpret what they were saying. The Serpent also found, quite by accident, that if it concentrated hard enough, it could also understand what the people were *thinking*. Their mental powers had increased so much that their brains were actually emitting signals.

The Serpent smiled. They remembered what they'd been taught!

But they hadn't changed that much since the old days. They still craved power, were still driven by their ambition and greed. They had much to learn and were years away from developing their wings—but these were thinking men in an industrial age.

Which of them would respond favorably to the Serpent, be the most willing to learn the secrets it could teach?

The Serpent examined them all and honed in on one man, a cruel, vile hybrid named Claude Trank Viperstadt. Now here was a prime example of purpose. Viperstadt, driven by dreams and desires, was a darker soul than any the Serpent had ever encountered before. And he took what he wanted, whenever he wanted. In another age, such a man would have been a leader. A greatly feared king, a cruel ruler. A tyrant.

The Serpent sighed with content, reading the man's thoughts, this hater of weakness, this destroyer of purity and love. Torture and rape were some of his many hobbies, and he relived his perverse fantasies, often playing them over and over in his mind before moving onto his next kill.

Exquisite! the Serpent thought, squirming in delight, remembering those sacrifices of long ago, the rich taste of hybrid blood and the tormented screams of its victims remembered. It decided it liked this man very much; in its former reign, it would have made him a high priest at the very least.

Will you be mine? the Serpent asked of Viperstadt—and Viperstadt answered yes.

I have always been yours, he admitted.

Then serve me, the Serpent whispered, *and all that you desire shall be yours.*

3

Claude Trank Viperstadt was up on a roof that day, laying bricks for a chimney, a degrading, backbreaking task made bearable only by the entertainment of his evil thoughts. A month ago, he'd kidnapped a red-haired woman and had taken her down to the cellar of his house. There he tortured her, shackling her to the wall, degrading her, reducing her to an empty shell of her former self.

She had been strong; she'd lasted four entire days, and Viperstadt rewarded her by dumping her body in the ocean. She'd been alive then, just barely, but she hadn't fought or struggled in her last moments. It was as if she *wanted* him to kill her. It was a perfect moment, the closest thing he'd ever known to be love.

He'd stood there on the dock, watching her sink, mesmerized by the torrent of bubbles in her wake, and his only regret was that he couldn't be down there under the waves with her, watching the fish tear at what was left of her flesh.

His thoughts turned to Madeline Roquefort. There she was, down there, at ground level, looking over her husband's shoulder at the blueprints laid out on a bench before them. Now there was a fine piece of work. Viperstadt fantasized about catching her, stripping away her dignity, wiping that haughty look off her face and replacing it with one of sheer terror. She'd beg him; they always did. At first, she'd plead with him to let her go, offering money and other consolation prizes in return for her life. Then she'd beg him to stop hurting her.

And if he was lucky, she'd finally plead with him to kill her, to end her suffering.

He watched her shield her eyes from the sun with her

hand as she glanced upwards. At him, as if she could read his thoughts and knew of his plans for her demise. Her mouth was turned downward in disdain. Madeline hated him and Viperstadt knew it.

With his luck, she'd insist that he move the chimney to the other side of the house now that he had it halfway built. Or she'd fancy using another type of brick. She was always and forever changing things; it drove him crazy. Viperstadt wanted to change things, too, where she was concerned.

First he'd rip her dark hair out of that uptight bun, where it would cascade over her shoulders. She'd be crying then, her smug look of superiority, of class, vanquished. Maybe he'd torture her with bricks. Then nails, before moving onto spikes. Yes, that's where he would start, as always, with the bricks.

She was pointing a dainty finger now, past him, and Viperstadt turned to look at the sky over his shoulder. It was still clear, bright and sunny, but something about the day wasn't normal. The air was taking on a brittle quality, seeming suddenly thin. He thought he could smell sulfur, but where was it coming from? Just then, every hair on his head and on his body stood straight up, tingling like pins and needles—or nail pricks—

—and that's when it hit him. A bolt from the blue, lifting him up in its incredible heat, cooking his eyeballs instantly, boiling his blood and blackening his skin, before slamming him to the ground, where he exhaled one last excruciating steamy breath. Then he fell again, slipping out of his body, and his soul became one with the Serpent.

4

So you are the first. The voice floated in the darkness, seductive and inviting, but strangely sexless. Claude Trank Viperstadt opened his eyes, expecting an agony that never came, and he blinked, trying to focus, but it was dark in here and so very warm. It smelled strange, too: a rich earthy rot, not entirely bad, but not particularly pleasant, either.

Someone was here with him. They'd just spoken but Viperstadt wasn't at all sure that he'd really heard it—or if it had come from his own mind.

"Where am I?" he asked, touching his body, surprised to find his skin intact and not burnt. The hair on his arms and head hadn't even been singed. How had that happened? There'd been a fire, a terrible fire, which he'd felt consume him. He would have expected to find blisters at the very least, missing limbs at the worst.

"Who's there?" he called out into the darkness.

My codename is Serpent, the voice hissed, sounding strangely metallic but deep and powerful. *And you are Viperstadt. Note the amusing similarity in our names. Viper. Serpent. You are part of me now.*

"I'm dead now, ain't I?" At the very thought of this, Viperstadt began to sweat, assuming he was likely lying at the mouth of some great abyss, about to be tossed into some Hellish, fiery pit.

Dead? Yes and no. Your mortal body went up in smoke a while ago, but not to worry. I've absorbed your soul. Fear not, you're safe, I assure you.

"Absorbed my soul?" Viperstadt repeated. "What the hell are you talking about? What are you? Some sort of demon?" He began to wonder if maybe he hadn't died at all, that perhaps this was all a hallucination and that he might be lying unconscious in a hospital bed. "Where am I?"

The voice chuckled. *Demons are imbeciles,* it said, still laughing, *so don't insult me. I'm no peon, I assure you. I am the Serpent. The leader of armies. An ancient deity, if you will.*

Viperstadt hugged his knees to his chest, trying to keep his teeth from chattering. Even though it was warm in here, he felt terribly cold and afraid, more frightened than he'd ever been before. He could feel the power of the Serpent, emitting fire and ice. "Where are we?" he whispered.

Listen. Tell me what you hear.

Viperstadt cocked an ear, straining to hear anything over the wild pounding of his heart, and he heard what sounded like distant voices, high up, coming from the darkness above. Gradually, he recognized Samuel Roquefort's low, stately tone and those of some of his co-workers. They were obviously upset. "Hit him right out of the blue," someone said. That sounded like that pansy, Lance Horton. *Master carpenter, my ass,* he thought to himself and the Serpent chuckled. "Lightning," another person said, "who'd a believed, on a day like today? Not a cloud in the sky."

Viperstadt groaned. "So I'm under the house now. And I was hit by lightning." Not a question but a statement.

Yes, and it is good that you came to me so quickly. You didn't suffer, didn't linger.

Scratching his head in confusion, Viperstadt tried to relax. Apparently, the Serpent wasn't going to hurt him. "What do you want me for?"

I need you to work for me.

Again, he groaned. "No more brick-laying, please."

Again, the Serpent chuckled. *No more bricks for you, I promise. I've known of your plans for Madeline Roquefort. You were going to be caught on that one, my fine man. Better that you come work for me.*

Viperstadt looked alarmed and his back stiffened. "How'd you know what I was planning to do?"

Why, I know everything about you. I could see into your mind then just as I'm doing now. Humans believe their thoughts are secrets, hidden away in the recesses of their mind. It might distress you to know that there are no such things as secrets. You might hide certain knowledge from other hybrids, but there are many beings who have the power to know. To unveil the secrets and ponder their meaning. To keep records of all thoughts, words, and deeds. Such data is reported to the Aelim for review.

Review? Viperstadt shrugged, a façade of bravado. Hybrids? Aelim? What was this Serpent-thing talking about? He didn't want to sound like a fool, so he stated, "Well, I never much gave a damn about what anyone else thought."

Au contraire. You would have loved to know what your victims were thinking.

Viperstadt licked his lips; they felt dry and chapped. That would have been nice indeed, being able to read the minds of those women, not just having to guess at their thoughts while he played his games with them. They voiced much of it in their pleas, but not nearly enough. He would have liked to know if, secretly, they enjoyed some of what he'd put them through. "Will you give me the power to read minds?" he asked.

I can.

"What must I do?"

Serve me.

"Serve you? How?"

As high priest. Yours is the first sacrifice. I need to absorb seven more souls. You can help me, but first you must prove yourself worthy.

"What are you waiting for? I'm ready."

All at once, the place where Viperstadt was, lit up in inky, crimson light. He could see now, just a little, and he found himself strapped down on what could be a mound or an altar made of hard-packed dirt. Looking up, he cried out, seeing what appeared to be a gigantic cobra, but at the same time, it was a man, too. Man and snake together. A human reptile. It towered over him, undulating, licking at the air with its forked tongue.

Do you fear me, human? Does my countenance not frighten you?

Wide eyed, Viperstadt nodded as much as he dared.

Good. Now are you ready to sacrifice in my honor?

"What happens if I don't?" Viperstadt cried out.

The Serpent roared, shaking this terrible place. *You want to see? You want to know what will happen to you if I hand you over to the Aelim?*

Viperstadt shook his head, unable to keep himself from trembling. "No, please no!"

The Aelim would have a fine time with you, my friend.

"You mentioned them before. Who are they?" The word sounded like A-ee-leem, and Viperstadt was aware that he was weeping, unable to stop. His tears felt hot, wet, and thick like melted wax, running into his ears.

They are ancient gods.

The Serpent turned and Viperstadt saw that it had a long, twisting tail with scales gray and colorless. Using its taloned finger, it drew a circle on the wall, then stepped aside, allowing Viperstadt to see.

Look upon this, hybrid. See how the Aelim discard those they have no use for.

Something terrible was forming in the center of the drawn circle, a vision of unadulterated fright, a visualization of what could only be the depths of Hell. Viperstadt saw throngs of people, huddled together in horror. One by one they were lifted into smoke-filled air by flying men . . .

(*Angels? No, they look like Serpents . . . like this Serpent, whatever the hell it is!*)

. . . and deposited into a fiery, molten furnace, steaming and bubbling, its color lurid orange. They tumbled, screaming, into the abyss below.

"I know what that is! That's H-Hell!" Viperstadt said, swallowing hard. "Take it away, please. I don't want to see any more of it."

The Aelim call it the melting pot, the Serpent told him, passing one webbed hand over the circle vision, which closed over like an eyelid. *It's where they recycle unsuitable souls.*

"Why?" Viperstadt screamed. "Why do they do it?"

Because that's what they do. They're big believers of recycling. And this fate is what awaits you, should I let them have you. But you're special and I can use you instead. Will you make me your god? Sacrifice willingly to me?

Viperstadt nodded, his face wet with tears and sweat.

Very good. The Serpent approached him and reached out with a single talon, touching his cheek, then running it down over his jaw, his throat, his chest. Viperstadt shivered, his bravado short-lived.

The talon stopped at his crotch and that's when the ripping began, a furious and blinding agony, causing him to bite off his tongue and swallow it whole. It hurt worse than the lightning, which had cooked his nerve endings in a fraction of a second. No, this was slow and excruciating. Blood bubbled out of his mouth, running from his lips as he screamed. No words. No tongue. This ocean of pain lifted him into an oblivion of anguish. Aware now of what was being done, unable to respond. Why? Why?

The Serpent chuckled from deep in its chest as the eyehole in the wall opened up once more, allowing it to toss in the severed, unnecessary parts of Viperstadt's body. Looking back down at his new disciple, the Serpent touched his mouth with a webbed, bloody hand. *You will have the power to speak whenever I command it, but your glands will no longer govern you. There, there. It's all done. Your new name is Viper. Snake. Sleep now, eunuch. Dream the dreams of the damned.*

5

The pain subsided to a dull throb as Viper knelt at the Serpent's taloned feet. In the past, he'd used his sex as a weapon, but the Serpent had taken that away and rewarded him with something better in return. A dark gift, perhaps the *darkest* of gifts.

Viper now had the power to read minds. He had certain limitations, yes, unlike the Serpent, who could inject certain thoughts and suggestions into a human brain, causing actions based on the altered perceptions it provided. The Serpent could cause people to believe they were actually seeing things that weren't there and Viper trusted that it could do anything. Anything!

I am the Prince of the Powers of the Air, the Serpent told him, but even with his limited understanding, Viper felt certain glee, an unholy joy. A feeling of belonging to something greater than himself, a sense of purpose. He cherished the gift he'd been granted.

The ability to hone in on someone's thoughts and know

exactly what they were thinking about . . . now that was the ultimate rape. Their philosophies, their schemes and desires—even their love—were weapons to be used against them.

And in Roquefort Manor, they often were.

The Serpent had told Viper he needed seven more souls and it was Viper's task to help collect them so the Serpent could absorb them. He'd first suggested Madeline Roquefort, that haughty bitch, but the Serpent didn't want her.

She's far too tepid, it said, coiling its body around Viper. *The seven I need are as follows: The Heartbroken, she shall be the first; The Hunter, he shall be next; then the Hanged, the Embalmed, the Necrophiliac, the Deranged, and the Impure. You will know these souls by the characteristics I've just named.*

Years passed and Viper grew restless. The Serpent had not said how long they'd have to wait for the right souls to arrive, only that they would come when the time was right.

In his impatience, Viper suggested the caretaker, Adam Walker, thinking he would have made a fine candidate; the man was a nervous little weasel, always conniving, always plotting and scheming. "He'd sell his own mother if he thought he could get away with it," Viper told the Serpent. "He's perfect."

But the Serpent shook its scaly head. *We could never trust him. He's far too weak. Let him believe he's serving me, if you wish, but never take your eyes off him.* A few years later, when Walker would hang himself, this would be at the Serpent's suggestion, for bringing that child into this world had been his final mistake. Did he really presume it to be a fit sacrifice?

Such abomination would have destroyed the Serpent, but Walker didn't know that and neither did Viper. At the shedding of the innocent blood of a Chosen Soul, the spirit of Gaia, the Earth, would have cried out at the injustice, shouting high to the Aelim—and they would know then that the Serpent had woken up from its hibernation. Rushing in, they would have put an end to its plan, making it sleep forever without waking. The eternal hibernation.

But the parents of the child, now that was another story. Both were runaway slaves, and the man, Stevie, had killed another in his struggle to get away. Although they weren't married (their owner hadn't allowed it), they'd lived together as man and wife. And for a time, they were within easy grasp of the Serpent, dwelling in a hidden room, in the attic of Roquefort Manor.

"Are they the souls you want?" the Viper asked the Serpent.

Yes, they are next.

Adam Walker, that bumbling fool, nearly foiled the Serpent's grand design—selling them to Beaumont, who'd planned to take them back to Georgia—but in the end, the Serpent got three souls that bleak October: Suki the Heartbroken, Stevie the Hanged, and Beaumont the Hunter all belonged to it now. Absorbed, just as Viper had been, decades earlier.

Beaumont was a willing servant and required little prompting, but the couple proved to be a problem. Stevie finally relented when the Viper promised not to harm Suki, then Suki gave in when the Serpent promised the return of her baby. If their preconceived notion of love bound them to this unholy union, imprisoning them within the Serpent, then that was to its advantage.

But they often fought within it, these three new souls. Struggling, causing turmoil in its belly. Beaumont enjoyed scaring Suki, making her relive that awful nightmare over and over again, chasing her through the house, even drowning her as Walker had done while she gave birth. Beaumont enjoyed playing such games with her, and Viper didn't mind, finding much of it amusing. His main objective was to keep Suki and Stevie apart as much as possible. The Serpent didn't trust their love for one another—or Suki's intuition. She was learning too much, too fast, and for this, the Serpent feared her. Sometimes, though, when it was asleep, she'd slip out, if only for the briefest moments, and because the Serpent required rest, Viper pretended not to notice.

For a long time after Walker's suicide, Roquefort Manor remained devoid of living people, while the Serpent waited in its lair, its bowels twisting with the chaos of what it had swallowed. It wanted more, needed others.

Leonard Roquefort, son of Samuel and Madeline Roquefort, became its next meal. Viper and the Serpent played upon his darkest fantasies, turning him onto opiates. Addiction followed, obsession leading to possession as Leonard began imagining the corpses he'd embalmed spoke back to him, and he liked what they had to say, especially the pretty ones whom he'd occasionally have sex with. They whispered of secret things, of dark and mysterious things that no mortal could have begun to comprehend. Through his conversations with the dead, he learned of his daughter's love affair with the Italian boy, Mario Delgado. The corpses made seductive promises, instructing him on how to solve that dilemma, getting rid of his problems for good. Roquefort never suspected, even after being swallowed, that those voices had come from the Serpent itself.

The Serpent and Viper had also worked on the teenager, Jacqueline, making her see things that weren't really there, like those faces in the wallpaper. They whispered to her, increasing her fear of her father, frightening her to the point that she obeyed when they told her to pick up the axe and kill her father, believing she had no other choice.

The Serpent claimed Leonard and Mario as its own but it couldn't take Jacqueline or her mother. Jacqueline had been spirited off to some distant hospital; her mother skipped town, never to return. And Roquefort Manor went back to being empty of the living.

Mario Delgado proved to be a problem, though, and the Serpent soon tired of hearing him whine for his lost love. Since his spirit was so hard to break, impossible to swallow all at once, the Viper imprisoned the boy's soul inside the cellar walls, in the very place where his corpse lie hidden.

"To keep you company," Viper had told the boy, leaving him in that tomb so the Serpent could digest him a little bit at a time.

His cries often echoed throughout the house at night.

6

September 25, 1930

It burned like hellfire rushing through his veins. Mario squirmed in his binds, screaming inside his head, begging and pleading for Jacqueline's father to stop the torture. He would have done anything, agreed to anything, to make it stop.

He grew even more desperate when he realized the mortician meant to kill him, embalm him alive. Mario watched Leonard's face, his eyes, dancing, sparkling with certain morbid elation. For an instant, he remembered a scene from one of the silent movies he'd seen last year.

A laboratory . . . and a monster assembled from parts of various corpses.

The grinning assistant, clasping hands, nodding, with the same look in his eyes as that of Mr. Roquefort. *It LIVES, Doctor! It LIVES!* the caption under the scene read in curlyque letters.

If this were a movie, said assistant would be declaring, *It's DYING! DYING, Doctor, DYING!*

Mario could hear his blood splashing and gurgling into some of the bottles lined up on the floor, but it was the stuff, some sort of chemicals that Mr. Roquefort had shot into his veins to replace his blood, now that was liquid fire, scorching his insides.

He wanted to scream that he'd promise never to see Jacqueline ever again, if that's what it would take to make Mr. Roquefort stop this madness.

Mario hadn't planned to put his hand down the front of Jacqueline's dress; it had just kind of happened. They'd been kissing, deep French kissing, down by the tool shed behind the rose gardens—and the button on his sleeve had caught in the laces of her dress's yolk. He'd tried to free himself, and in the process, the laces became untied.

"Go on," Jacqueline said in a low, husky voice. "Undo me."

Even in the most vivid of wet dreams, he'd never thought it would be like this . . . so natural, so unexpected, and so very taboo all at the same time.

With trembling fingers, he undid the front of her dress.

Her breasts had been small and pale, but perfect, and he'd kissed them, feeling their tips harden under his lips. Jacqueline's fingers wound in his hair and she was moaning softly, back arched.

There was no doubt that he'd have taken her right there, on the grass behind the tool shed, and there was little doubt that she'd have let him. It was a perfect moment, both of them caught up in a curious mixture of love and awkward inexperience and hormones run wild.

Just then, Jacqueline's fingers froze in his hair and she pulled his head away.

"Father!" she breathed in horror.

Quickly, Mario straightened up and stood in front of Jacqueline while she arranged herself.

Whether or not Mr. Roquefort had seen what they were doing, he didn't let on. "Jacqueline, your mother needs you in the kitchen," he said, pleasantly enough.

Mario watched her trot off dutifully, knowing he probably looked like he'd been caught with his hand in the cookie jar (and in a way, he had been). He could feel the burning flush in his face, creeping up from his neck.

Mr. Roquefort reached up and patted his shoulder. "Say, I've got something in my office I'd like you to see. Do you like photographs, son?"

Mario nodded. "Sure."

"Well, why don't you come down with me and have a look. I guarantee you've never seen nothing like these."

Mr. Roquefort's smile seemed genuine enough. Was it really possible he and Jacqueline hadn't been caught after all? Mario shrugged. "Okay, why not."

He thought it odd that Mr. Roquefort locked the door behind them, but maybe this was something he didn't want anyone else to see?

When he saw the photos, he understood why.

Jacqueline had mentioned something about her father taking pictures of her with his camera—but Mario didn't see any photographs of her in this collection. What he did see, though, were shots of women in various stages of undress. Their bosoms were fuller than Jacqueline's . . . and some of them were showing parts Mario had only imagined in his dreams.

"You like those pictures, son?"

Mario gave him a shy nod. Yeah, he liked them just fine, but this seemed very strange, the friendly way Mr. Roquefort was acting.

"You want to see Jacqueline like this?"

Blinking, Mario looked up, the color creeping anew into his cheeks. "Pardon?"

"You heard me. I saw what you were up to behind the tool shed."

Mario hung his head, clearly embarrassed.

"Now listen, son. I was young once. I don't blame you for doing what you did—but I don't want it to ever happen again. A promise just won't do in this case. No, I require something else from you."

Taking a step back, away from the desk, Mario fought the falter in his voice. "Sir, I don't think so—"

"I only want to take your picture, son."

Mario shook his head. "No way. Not if it's going to be anything like those." He glanced down again at the spread of photographs. The top one showed a dark-haired woman lying on her back, a side shot, casting a perfect silhouette shadow across the wall.

Mr. Roquefort gave him a funny look, as if he'd said something unthinkably crazy. "Of course, not! I wouldn't dream of it. I've bought some new film, you see, and I'd like to test it—but it's very important that the subject is human."

"Well, I guess it wouldn't hurt."

Jacqueline's father was grinning now. "Good. Now what

I need you to do is lie down here. This is a cooling slab; I know you don't understand, but this photo is for a medical magazine. That's right, just lie down there and get comfortable. I'm going to have to strap you in, but don't worry, you'll be all right."

Mario knew now that he never should have trusted Mr. Roquefort. The man was insane. Dying, he thought about Jacqueline. She was in great danger—he couldn't leave her alone with this nutcase of a father. He had to protect her, but how?

I'll help you protect her, the voice said. It was a slippery-sounding voice, silky-smooth and seductive.

But are you going to help me? Mario felt his heartbeat slowing down; it had been pounding in his ears just minutes ago. Now it was fading fast.

Stay here with me, Embalmed One. We'll protect Jacqueline together.

Who are you?

A friend.

As Mario slipped out of his body, he crossed the room and ventured into the darkest part of the cellar where the Serpent waited.

7

When the Faradays moved in, Geoffrey Faraday became lord of Roquefort Manor, ruling over his wife and daughter with an iron fist. A firm believer in corporal punishment, he never failed to spare the rod with his teenaged daughter. Things got even worse after Faraday began to drink heavily of his gin and absinthe, whose green fairy turned mean-spirited, inciting him to further acts of violence against his family. It didn't help that the bootlegger was demanding a higher price for his deliveries . . . or that Geoffrey required more and more of it in order to achieve the feeling of well being. As a result of his frustrations, he began beating his wife regularly, as well as his daughter.

Serpent told him it was aware that troublesome little Saxon already suspected the house was haunted, especially after her father burned her hands.

But she was strong, Geoffrey could see her fighting the Serpent's suggestions with every fiber in her being. If not for the War, fueled by another Serpent a continent away, Geoffrey knew Saxon might have escaped by marriage, ruining everything.

After death, Geoffrey Faraday's violent temper became so unpredictable that the Serpent seldom let him out. There was no logic to his rage; but one thing remained clear: He wanted his wife and little girl back. Not because he loved them but because he felt they'd done him wrong.

8

Geoffrey opened one eye (the other was damaged beyond use), to find himself sprawled across the cadaver table. Blood and brain matter were leaking from the bullet hole in the center of his forehead—but strangely, it didn't hurt. Maybe this lack of pain resulted from his years of self-medication; surely laudanum, cocaine, and liquor had accumulated in his system. He'd barely felt a thing when Saxon shot him, hearing only a loud pop in his head as his body was thrown backwards onto the table.

He'd sat up, gingerly touching his temples with his fingertips.

Saxon, you little bitch! What have you done to me?

It had all happened so quickly, too fast for him to try to stop her. He'd promised the Serpent he'd take care of things where his family was concerned—but he'd royally screwed it up. Calling his daughter down to his office for a talk, he'd honestly planned to sacrifice her right then and there, for hidden inside his coat, a formaldehyde-filled syringe was ready for injection straight into her heart.

But she'd outsmarted him, the nasty girl . . . packing a pistol in the pocket of her dress. Where had she gotten the gun? Likely, she'd stolen it from his desk.

Geoffrey sat there for a while, legs dangling over the edge of the table, wondering what to do. Should he go upstairs and beat the living hell out of Saxon—and her mother, too, just for good measure? He could kill them together and save himself the time of having to dispatch them separately. The Impure Soul and the Deranged delivered in one neat package, how convenient.

Geoffrey, I need you.

Huh? He looked around, recognizing the voice of the green fairy, the one he called Snake. "Is that you, my Lord?"

I am the Serpent. Snake is my loyal servant.

Geoffrey inhaled sharply. He'd never dreamed he'd ever be talking to the boss himself. The Dark Lord. "Sorry," he mumbled as his fingers found the hole in his forehead. It felt wet to the touch, the edges crunchy with sharp fragments of broken bone. "I tried to obey, but she got me instead. I'm real sorry about that."

I know you are. You want retribution? I can help you. All you have to do is come to me.

"Where are you?"

In the root cellar. Come, I'll show you things.

Geoffrey slid off the table and would have fallen if he had let go of the edge. His feet dragged on the tiled floor as he shuffled across the room. "She shot me. Shot me right through the head."

Does it hurt?

"No." Strangely enough, it really didn't. "But I can't see straight. Everything's all jumbled."

I can remedy that, the Serpent offered. *And then you can fix your family.*

Geoffrey opened the door and stumbled into the root cellar. It was comfortably warm and dark in here . . . and as he approached the place where the Serpent's voice had come from, he knew he'd never be the same again. The Serpent would replace the mind-altering substances he craved and fill him with something far more potent:

Eternal rage.

9

The Serpent used Geoffrey Faraday to its own advantage, so when Saxon returned, it was very pleased and yet surprised. She'd grown stronger, somehow . . . and now she'd made an alliance with two Pure Souls.

The Serpent was determined to fight to keep her here, and it readied itself for battle, morphing into its separate entities, regurgitating them one by one. It was nearly time to molt, to shed its skin and *transform,* to become something greater. Perhaps the greatest, most powerful being of all time; the Aelim would be no match for it, and they would fall as the Serpent had fallen: exiled, cast out forever.

Once that happened, every Serpent could emerge from their hiding places and walk among the hybrids, enslaving them, ruling over them until the end of time. They would learn to share the spoils and must always remember the fissures of leadership that had ripped the Aelim apart, but this planet would be theirs for the taking.

CHAPTER SIX

1

Roquefort Manor had changed over that hot, dry summer, growing ever darker and more gloomy, somberly sulking, looking more like a malignant mausoleum than a house. Saxon could almost feel it vibrate with Evil, and she balked, clutching one of the marble lion sentries while she waited for Moses to catch up.

This is crazy, she thought. *Who do I think I am, bringing a mentally handicapped boy and that poor old man here? What on earth can the three of us accomplish, except get ourselves killed trying to fight something we know so very little about? I made a mistake coming home; I know that now.*

As she stood there, trembling, something inside her triggered a resolute determination. *Four months ago,* she reasoned, *I came here to face my worst fears. I'd thought the problem was inside of me—but it's not. It's external. The Serpent wants me to think I'm insane. It's counting on me running away from it, but I won't. I can't. I've come so far already, there's no way I can stop. Still, I am afraid. What if I'm not strong enough—what if it's another trick?*

"Miss Saxon?" Clem's voice penetrated her thoughts, pulling them away from her inner struggle. "Miss Saxon, are you okay?"

Saxon let go of the lion and managed a slight nod. "Yes, Clem, I'm fine. Just a bit nervous, I guess."

Clem cast an uneasy glance at the house ahead. "Don't be scared of the ghosts. They need our help, that's all. The

Serpent's got them and we have to try to get them away from it."

She bit her lower lip to keep it from crying. "Why couldn't we have done it before? Try to rescue those trapped souls? Why did we have to wait until now?"

"The answer's plain to see," Moses spoke up, leaning on his cane for support. "The Serpent is about to regurgitate its victims; we wouldn't have stood a chance any other way."

Saxon turned to him in surprise—this was the same thing Rob had told her. "How do you know? How much do you know so much about the Serpent?"

Moses eyed the house with a jaundiced gaze and pointed to his chest. "The knowledge comes from here." His finger went to his forehead. "Not here. I know only enough about it to say we're not fighting anything that's of this world. Remember the old Bible story about Adam and Eve? How the Serpent tempted Eve, then God punished the Serpent, along with the man and woman? Well, it may be myth or it may be history—but I do believe something extraordinary, something supernatural occurred—and it involved humans, God, and a creature called the Serpent."

"So what are you saying?" Saxon asked.

Moses rubbed at the grey stubble on his chin. "Well, according to the Good Book, God told the Serpent it would spend the rest of its days crawling in the dust on its belly. Hence, it makes sense, doesn't it, that the Serpent at one time walked on legs? Maybe upright, on two legs, just like us. And if it had legs, it likely had arms. I'm in the way of thinking that the Serpent of old wasn't human—and yet, it wasn't God—but some sort of creature *in between*. One thing's for certain, it wasn't an ordinary snake. Especially after God cursed it."

Clem cleared his throat just then and said in a clear voice, "And I will put an enmity between you and the woman . . ." His words trailed off.

Both Saxon and Moses turned to stare at Clem, who was now staring at Roquefort Manor, transfixed. "That's right, Clem, that's what it says in Genesis. Are you OK?" Moses asked.

He nodded slowly, dragging his gaze away from the house. "I remembered that from Sunday School. I thought I forgot, but I didn't."

Saxon shivered and hugged herself to keep her teeth from chattering. The day was hot; every day had been warm since the drought started the big bake of 1947, but Roquefort Manor emitted a dank coolness that penetrated her very soul.

"It's the old adversary of all mankind," Moses said. "Call it the Devil or Satan, those are just names for the thing we know as Evil. The Serpent is that sort of creature. More cunning than any other animal on earth because it—and its kind—are *not* of this world."

"Its *kind?*" Saxon asked. "Dear God, what are you saying, Moses? That there's more than one?"

He nodded, his expression grave. "Some of the ancient texts claim thirty thousand angels fell from Heaven, when Lucifer was exiled for his pride," he told her. "Thirty thousand *Serpents*. Others might have landed elsewhere, but chances are if one found its way here, then there are more than one on this planet."

"So it *is* the Devil," Saxon remarked, rubbing at the goosebumps on her arms.

"Well, yes and no. I think it's *part* of what we call the Devil, if you consider that Satan may be a collective entity, not just a single being. That would explain a lot: why there's worldwide misery, murder, and unrest between nations. The Devil's not like God, not omnipresent, and certainly not omnipotent or omniscient. Satan cannot be everywhere at once, therefore, it makes sense that he is *many*."

"Like that demon," Clem chimed in. "The one Jesus cast out of the man in the graveyard."

"Legion. Yes, just like that."

Saxon scratched her head. "Omnipotent, omniscient, I don't understand. What does it all mean?"

"Omnipotent," Moses told her, "is unlimited power, what Christians, Jews, and Muslims attribute to God. Omniscient is complete knowledge, infinite awareness, another of God's powers, whereas omnipresence is the ability to be everywhere at once."

Saxon nodded, "I see. So the Serpent lacks these powers."

"I believe so. Remember the reason why Lucifer was expelled from Heaven—he wanted to usurp God, to take His place on the Heavenly throne. He wanted God's powers for himself."

"I know, but I don't understand the part about the Serpent shedding its skin," she said. "Why must it do that?"

"Evolution, dear girl. The very nature of this world is rooted in adaptation, the ability to change according to environmental influences. Survival depends upon it. I think that might be the way God set it up from the very beginning. It's no different for the Serpent, which is likewise about to transform."

Saxon couldn't hide her shock. "Transform? Into *what?*"

"I don't know and I don't want to find out. That's why we have to stop it. It will be at its most vulnerable just before it sheds, before its new skin hardens. Right after it regurgitates the souls in its belly. It will be, I suspect, like a new form of birth. Or rebirth."

"Do you suppose the other Serpents are doing the same thing? They'll all shed at once?"

Moses shook his head. "No. If that was the case, mankind wouldn't stand a chance at defeating them. I suspect other Serpents have shed in the past and were defeated; others will occur in the future, but this time, it's our turn to take our stand against it."

"Lucky us," Saxon said.

"Let's hope so." Moses pointed at the house. "Somehow, it looks different than the last time I saw it. Darker or something."

Both Clem and Saxon nodded; it *was* darker, full of malice.

"Well, let's go do this," Moses said, stepping forward with his cane.

2

Saxon led the way up onto the porch and into the parlor. Or rather what had once *been* the parlor. Changes had come, working their way from the inside out, and the interior of the house now looked like a mouth: a sunken, toothless cavern. It felt humid and alive, as if breathing its own dank breath, reeking with the sickly sweet stench of death and decay.

Gelatinous moisture dripped from the dark ceiling, running in streams down the remains of walls, and low rumbles come up the floor, shudders from deep within the earth.

"What the hell happened here?" Saxon whispered,

feeling faint, clinging to the arms of her friends. "It's all so different, like a cave . . . or a grave. How could this have happened so quickly?"

Moses looked around, his jaw slack. "Roquefort Manor," he said, "has become the Serpent's lair. It's making itself ready for its new master . . . thus the new monster slouches toward Bethlehem to be born."

"Not Bethlehem. *Eden,*" Saxon said, looking around in shock. "Its birthing room must be in the cellar. I'm not sure where exactly, but I know it's down there. That's where it's always been."

"Not for long," Moses said, "if we can't stop it. We'd best stick together. There's a reason why the three of us have been called here to do this deed for the greater good. I think the Serpent knows we're here—and why—and it will no doubt try to separate us. Pick us off one at a time, if it can. We mustn't let that happen."

"It's so hard to see anything in here," Clem noted, his eyes squinting.

"I've got a flashlight in the car," Saxon offered. "I can run out and get it."

"No. We'll *all* go," Moses suggested. "Like I say, we should stay together at all times."

They picked their way over the network of roots and rocks back toward the front door, but instead of swinging open on its hinges, it fell over like a drawbridge onto the porch floor, which was becoming spongy and soft, covered in a flurrying growth of moss and vines.

"We have to hurry," Moses said. "The house is changing, trying to keep us out."

Even the front yard was transforming now, mushrooms and toadstools springing up from the ground before them—an impossible, unthinkable feat, not just in time alone, but because of the ongoing drought. The yellowed grass, dull and brittle, began to grow, maintaining its lack of color. It already reached their knees. The sea roses to the left were changing, too, their dry, yellowed leaves falling away, revealing a multitude of thorns that lengthened into dagger-sized weapons as they twisted and raged. If the trio didn't move fast, the rosebushes would quickly form an impenetrable barricade, preventing them from getting back to the house.

Saxon and Clem were looking under the seat of her car when Moses called to them, "You'd better shake a leg! Look!"

Saxon looked up first and her jaw dropped as all color drained from her face. What she was seeing was unfeasible—her mind told her it shouldn't be there, couldn't possibly be there, but her eyes said the opposite. One of the marble lions had left its post at the end of the drive and was now approaching the car, its tail snapping and twisting, shoulders lowered, haunches lifted, working back and forth, ready to pounce. Her gloved fingers closed upon the flashlight. "Clem," she whispered, "Moses is right. I don't want to alarm you, but there's something out here and we're in serious danger if we don't hurry."

He nodded. "I know. The lion, I see it, too . . . but I don't think it can hurt us. It's a trick of the Serpent. It's trying to scare us away."

"Let's run back to the house," she said. "We'll grab Moses and carry him if we have to."

They didn't have to. Moses had turned and was quickly picking his way through the dead grass, now waist-high, with his cane, headed toward the house, which wasn't even a house anymore.

It had fully transformed. Where once stood the front

door, now yawned a great, dark hole. The porch roof had become a ledge, a swollen lip, overgrown with woody roots and leafless vines. The gabled roof with its sparkling, slate shingles had been replaced by a blanket of black loam, covered with spores from which sprouted large mushrooms and toadstools, grey, spotted, and malignant. There were no more windows, only holes tunneling into a structure that towered over them like a mountain. Together, the three of them made their way back into what had been the front parlor and Saxon switched her flashlight on.

In its beam, she watched Moses hobble over to a small portion of the wall that remained intact. The wallpaper there had grown mottled with mold and mildew, revealing ragged bits of damp plaster underneath. "Shine the light on this wall," he called out. "There's something here." He began to tear away the soggy wallpaper.

"There you have it," he said as Clem peered over his shoulder.

"666" was etched into the plaster; each number squirmed with a substance black and gelatinous.

"The Devil's number," Clem said, quickly making the sign of the cross.

"It's just trying to scare us off." Saxon came over and put an arm around him.

"No, it's more than that," Moses said. "That's the Serpent's mark. It's claimed this place as its own. We're trespassers here, that's what it's trying to tell us. We're in its territory now, and have no doubt, there are new game rules . . . the old laws of time and space, of physics and nature, don't apply here anymore."

"Where's the cellar?" Clem asked, peering around in the semi-darkness. The front parlor now sported a surrealistic façade; the furniture had become part of the walls—the front legs of a chair and half of its seat stuck out of the earth; vines intertwining around it. The top of the grand piano yawned open, spilling forth a pale growth of dusty millers, Indian pipes, and black mushrooms. Toadstools grew on the loveseat in a ghastly array of colors: orange, maroon, yellow, and black. Just then the phone rang, a strange, unearthly sound, causing everyone to jump at the same time.

"But the phone's shut off—" Saxon began, advancing toward it.

"Don't pick it up," Moses shouted. "It's a trick!" But it was too late; she lifted the receiver and held it to her ear. At first, she looked stunned, then her face crumpled and she began to weep. Clem hurried over and snatched the phone away from her, ripping it out of the wall by its cord.

"It was my father's voice," she managed to say. "He said something about eating my brains out. Or beating my brains out. It was awful . . . his threats . . ."

Moses rested a calming hand on her shoulder. "That wasn't your father. The Serpent's playing tricks on you. It will use your deepest fears against you—and, trust me, it knows all of them. You must have been scared of your father, so it's playing on that fear."

"But it was *his* voice!" Saxon said, wiping her face with a gloved hand.

"You have to remember," Moses told her, "the Serpent isn't all-powerful. It has weaknesses, and one of them is that it's incapable of creation. Oh, it's a master mimic, but it can't make anything on its own. It's a thief, taking what it can. For that reason, we must not believe *anything* we see or hear from here on out. Doing so may cause our downfall. It's only using tricks, mean little tricks, to try to get at us. Don't you believe any of it."

Saxon reached over to the nearest wall and pried away a handful of loose earth, twisting with worms, from the wall. She held her hand open and examined the dirt closely under the light. “Well, this looks real enough to me. Doesn’t it to you?”

Moses nodded. “It’s using a lot of energy to fool us into seeing things that aren’t here. Yes, the dirt looks real enough, but I don’t know about those worms. They just don’t seem right to me.”

Saxon examined them more closely and so did Clem. Neither had seen mustard-yellow earthworms before. Although they’d appeared to be alive, they weren’t. They crumbled in her hands like strings of gummy, half-dry paint.

“Point taken, Moses. The basement door is right over here,” she said, lifting her chin.

3

It seemed a long way down the stairs, the flashlight beam shining ahead of them, fading into a tunnel of darkness. Slowly, the three made their way downward, each close enough to touch the other.

The cellar steps had become spongy and soft. Rotten. Fortunately, the earth had mounded up beneath them, providing support.

All along the way, holes had opened up in the walls. Tunnels. By shining her flashlight into some of them, Saxon could tell they were deep. But why were they here and where did they lead? She didn’t want to find out. *Maybe the whole house has become a maze, some sort of demonic labyrinth,* she reasoned. *The Serpent's getting desperate . . . trying to buy itself more time . . . wanting us to get lost . . . but we won't if we all stick together.* She could feel Clem bump into her back from time to time, poor kid. She knew he was as frightened as she was, only he was trying to be a man about it.

And Moses? Frail as he was, he was her source of strength, her fountain of logic. She could feel her sanity waning thinner by the minute, and if not for him, she feared she might go stark, raving mad. This wasn't her house anymore, if it ever was. Only teasing, little parts of it remained. These stairs, for example. They were still here, but different now . . . and she wasn't at all sure where they led to anymore. It could be the basement . . . or it could be the very bowels of the earth itself.

At the foot of the stairs, her father's office door had changed drastically, into what appeared to be an arched, heavy-planked door coated in green and black mold. Slime dripped from the knob, which Saxon thought looked very much like a human bone, the end of a knee or elbow. She was staring at it, trying to summon the courage to reach out and turn it, to see what lie beyond, when Clem bumped into her again. Her nerves were frayed, on end, pulsating, and she turned her head, irritated, wanting to snap at him to watch his step, but what she glimpsed over her shoulder, out of the corner of her eye, caused her to spin around in disbelief.

Clem was gone—and so was Moses! But where? And how?

Her flashlight beam picked up a slow-swirling column of mist rising from the floor, and she stared at it, transfixed, unable to drag her gaze away. Logic told her this was another trick of the Serpent, and whatever it was, it wasn't going to be pleasant . . . and yet it was mesmerizing to watch. Land fog, swirling thick, curling upward. Turning . . .

. . . turning into . . .

. . . something . . .

. . . forming, thickening, *materializing!*

Feet, then legs, appeared as the fog drew upward. Now she could see a torso—that's when she began moving back, away from it. There was something sticking from its chest and, as it solidified, Saxon saw it was a handle, the dark grain of wood, sticky with crimson ribbons running down to drip off its end.

It was an axe! Now she knew what the mist was trying to become, and she turned away from it, struggling to twist the slimy, bony knob to open the door that led into her father's office. Her hand kept slipping; the damned thing wouldn't turn! Heart pounding, she glanced again over her shoulder.

Leonard Roquefort now stood in the same spot where Clem had been moments before—and she knew it was him (or some grotesque parody thereof). The blade of the axe with which his daughter, Jacqueline, had delivered that final fatal blow, remained buried deep in his right breast. His vest glistened with gore and she screamed at the horror of it; the sound of her shrieks echoed, trailing throughout the tunnels like a chorus of terror.

Roquefort, a tall, gaunt specter of pale, grey skin reeked viciously of the grave.

"Little vixen," he said with a gleeful growl, "you think you're going to beat us—but you're wrong. Let me take you down, sweetheart, down into the Serpent's belly." Before she could move, he reached out and grabbed her upper arms, pulling her to him in a perversion of a lovers' embrace. "You'll make such a tender morsel—and mmm, mmm, the things we will do together . . ." He licked his tattered lips in anticipation.

She tried not to breathe in his stench (God, he was vile—and so very tall!), her cheek wedged tightly against the axe handle. *This isn't happening,* her mind screamed in retaliation. *It isn't real—he isn't here—it's just a trick . . .*

"I'm going to take your picture," he told her, grinning down with long, yellow teeth.

. . . of shadows. The Serpent has . . .

She winced, trying to get away from him but the floor beneath her feet had become a greasy slope of earth. His fingers bore into her flesh, bruising her, as she struggled to free herself from his clutches.

. . . created him out of nightmares.

"Lemme go!" she screamed, struggling, and her words echoed, mocking her.

This can't be happening . . . but why does it feel so real? He's strong and he smells so . . .

"Never, you little hussy," he said, tugging at her blouse. "You're *my* kind of subject and you're going to give me everything I want—the Serpent promised me I could have you."

. . . bad! She shut her eyes at the sight of a thin, wet string dangling from the axe handle right in front of her nose. Another mustard-colored worm. *He's not here, not here, not here. . . .*

"NO!" He was trying to grope her and while fighting his cruel, cold hands, she screamed to Moses and Clem, begging them to come help her.

"You needn't bother, my dear. Your friends are dead, food for the worms," Leonard told her, his coarse laughter causing more worm-filled, stringy gruel to pour down over the axe handle.

Just then, something moved out of the earth from the

tunnel to her left; she saw it when she tried to move her face away from the axe handle. More of them? Dear God, no!

But this was no swirling mist. Behind Roquefort, a young man had appeared, crawling, then standing upright. Saxon thought he looked vaguely familiar—darker than Clem, and maybe a little shorter—but in her struggle she'd only caught a glimpse of him.

As if sensing his presence, Leonard whirled around, dragging Saxon with him, long fingers squeezing her throat. "You!" he shouted. "Return to the grave worms, you little bastard! Can't you see I'm busy?"

It was Mario! Saxon could see that now, although she couldn't comprehend any of this—how he'd gotten here—or how he'd approached Leonard, just like in the visions Rob had shown her, like a movie playing too fast, too choppy. With one hand, Mario pushed her aside and with the other, he yanked the axe free from Leonard's chest.

It all happened in a matter of seconds.

Saxon scrambled toward the door, crouching as Mario lifted the axe and swung it, cleanly lopping off Leonard's head. The body sank to its knees, hands clutching at the air over a neck spouting something that looked like ink. The head rolled across the floor and stopped, face up, the jaw working, snapping open and shut. Then it fell open and stopped moving.

Mario stepped over the body and lifted Saxon to her feet. His touch was frigid, icy fingers causing her to shiver. He gave her the axe and didn't say a word because he couldn't. She'd sewn his mouth shut when she'd prepared him for burial. "I'm so sorry," she said, but he just shook his head, stepping away from her.

It's all right now, she imagined him saying. *You rescued me and now I've returned the favor. The Serpent's waking up and I must go before it eats all of me.*

That's when she noticed the lower half of him was missing. Again, the quick, choppy strobe as she watched him float backward into the tunnel from whence he'd come. It was like watching a film in reverse—and then he was gone.

Saxon gripped the axe and turned toward the door. She could hear voices on the other side: Moses and Clem! Not bothering to stop to think about how they'd gotten ahead of her, she yelled out to them but they didn't appear to hear her.

Grunting, bathed in cold sweat, she swung her weapon at the door, and its blade met with the wood, puncturing through with a dull, squashy thud. It seemed to be made of something akin to pumpkin rind, although it looked like wood. Bad wood.

She kept hitting it until she'd made a hole large enough to step through. Picking up her flashlight, axe in the other hand, she made her way into her father's office.

The room that *had been* her father's office.

"Clem? Moses? Where are you guys?"

She ran the beam of her flashlight along the walls but didn't see her friends anywhere. Father's desk was still here, along with the chair, but both were heavily draped in cobwebs.

Spiders! The Serpent knew she hated them.

She sidestepped around the desk and hastened toward the workroom, hoping to meet up with Moses and Clem there. She hated the thought of being separated from them, and realized Leonard Roquefort had likely been a decoy, something to delay her. In all likelihood, the guys could be ahead of her now instead of behind her. She remembered what Moses had said about the laws of time and space and nature no longer applying.

The workroom door hadn't changed but it creaked open on its own power. As she entered, the light over the table snapped on, and the door slammed shut behind her.

On the cadaver table, Geoffrey Faraday sat up abruptly. His head hit the overhead light, causing it to swing drunkenly on its chain. Like Leonard Roquefort, Father had become an animated, rotting corpse exquisite in its power to revolt.

"You've been a very nasty girl!" he bellowed hoarsely, climbed off the table, which began to change . . . the thick glass top blackening dully, the stainless steel edges becoming gleaming chrome as it transformed into the kitchen cook stove—the chrome lining its edges was no longer smooth and sleek but studded with spikes and needles. The stovetop began to glow, its lids taking on a bright cherry red color, the lighter hue of white hot iron blazed in their centers, and above it all in gruesome scroll rambling across the warmer shelf, those terrible words: **Home Is Where the Hell Is!**

In horror, she backed away from it—and her father. Under her gloves, her palms began to ache anew.

"Time to take your punishment!" he shouted, advancing toward her, causing her to quake with fright.

Death had changed him, oh, how it changed him! Geoffrey was still very much a tyrant—but more powerful and scary than he'd ever been in life. His shadow seemed to expand, filling the entire room.

"Hold out your hands, nasty girl!" he ordered in a strangely metallic voice, reaching for her. "Hold them out and take your punishment!"

Saxon brandished her axe, painful memories flooding back to her.

I was only . . .

"You have no right!" she screamed. "You didn't then—and you don't now!"

. . . thirteen. . . .

"You'll take your punishment, or by God, I'm gonna eat your brains out . . . those lovely brains—I'll suck them out through your ears!"

I thought I was alone. . . .

She lifted her axe high in the air. "I was just a little kid," she said, her voice trembling with anger.

The radio was playing . . .

"You came into my room uninvited. You didn't knock, just barged right in."

. . . in my room and I . . .

. . . was touching myself, exploring for the first time . . .

. . . and it felt good: strange, but good . . .

. . . this new feeling. . . .

"Why did you treat me that way? Was I filthy, undeserving of privacy, of human dignity? I wasn't doing anything wrong. Children explore themselves; it's completely natural for them to be curious about their bodies, especially when they begin to change."

I was just a child; I didn't know it was a sin.

"But you couldn't stand it, could you, Father? Don't you think being caught was bad enough? You're a sadist, Father, a sick, depraved man. You come near me again, I'll slice you in half!" She swung the axe to show him she meant business, but he quickly darted aside and she missed her mark. She swore and swung again.

And missed a second time.

"Nasty," he hissed. "Nasty, nasty, nasty! You always thought you were so clever, hiding away, touching yourself when you thought no one was looking! Now look at you!

Not so smart now. Hold out your hands, nasty girl. This time they'll sizzle like bacon—I can almost smell them cooking!"

She could see where she'd shot him, the bullet hole in his head; the light shone straight through his skull.

In an instant, measurable only by fractions of seconds, he was upon her, knocking her off her feet, pinning her to the warm, dirt-covered tiles. She tried to lift the axe. Couldn't.

"Bacon . . . brains!" He grinned down at her, smelling sourly of absinthe and decay, thick lines of green, sticky drool dangled from the corners of his mouth.

"You're not real!" Saxon screamed up at him in defiance. "You can't be real!"

A glob of his drool struck her cheek, burning her skin as it trailed downward toward her ear. Something white was bubbling out of the hole in his head, hot and acidic, eating a path down the dead flesh of his face. She knew that if it dripped on her, its sting would be far worse than his drool.

"Nasty—" he began to say . . .

. . . and was interrupted by a loud, cracking noise; her father stopped as if frozen, eyes bulging, staring, the gunk coming out of his head in squirts. Droplets of it struck her forehead and she screamed in pain.

Then someone was pulling him off her.

Wiping at the acid on her forehead, Saxon looked up into the faces of Moses and Clem. "Oh, thank God," she said, her voice hoarse from screaming. "Where were you? How'd you find me? I was so scared!" She tilted her head to look past them. "Where's that damned stove?"

"What stove?" Moses asked, leaning on his cane, concern cutting deep furrows into his brow.

She rolled onto her side and stared at the place where the stove had been. It was gone, replaced by the cadaver table, and she couldn't begin to explain how it disappeared or why it had been here in the first place. How could she? What man in his right mind would punish his daughter for masturbating by holding her palms down upon a red-hot stovetop?

"Where have you guys been? I yelled for you when Leonard Roquefort showed up, and thank God, Mario Delgado rescued me. I thought you were right behind me."

"We were," Moses said. "Then something happened—can't quite explain it—but the whole place stretched, like pulling taffy. You were on one end; we were on the other, the distance between us growing longer, but there was nothing we could do about it."

"It tried to separate us," Clem said, offering her a hand up, and she accepted. Behind them, her father's corpse folded in on itself, as if made of coarse rubber, deflating and imploding.

"You see, it's not real," Moses told her. "It's only dark magic and the rest is left to our own imaginations. None of this is real, not in any physical sense, anyway."

Aghast, Saxon stared at him. "Then why does it hurt so much?" She pointed to the spots, the blisters forming on her forehead. "Father was full of acid. It burned me, so doesn't that prove it's real? And what of the axe? That's real enough. Look at it."

Moses lowered his eyes, shaking his head. "The blisters only prove that you *expected* to get hurt. As for the axe, I really can't explain it. Maybe it's real, maybe not. Regardless, it appears to work and that's what counts."

She groaned. "I know, I know. The power of belief, all that stuff, but I'm telling you, when it comes for you—it sure as hell feels real. The sooner we kill the Serpent, the sooner all this will end. Right?" She reached down and lifted the axe, but neither man moved. "Hey, what's wrong? Isn't this what we came here for?"

"Maybe we should just give up," Clem offered with a shrug, looking helplessly at Moses.

Saxon knit her brows, angry. Confused. "Moses? What's wrong?"

"It's been a lie all along," he admitted after a long pause. "I thought I knew—but I don't know anything. We can't fight the Serpent and expect to win. Who do we think we are, anyway?"

She could hardly believe what she was hearing. "What are you saying?"

Moses tossed a gnarled hand in surrender. "I say Clem's right. We should give up this foolishness. Turn around and leave it alone."

"I don't get either of you." She glared at her friends, feeling like throttling the pair of them. They'd been so cock-sure of themselves, of the mission that lay ahead. They were almost there—so why give up now? As far as she knew, the Serpent had only attacked her, using the bodies of Leonard Roquefort and her own father. Could it be that it was attacking them in a different way, playing now on their doubts? On their insecurities?

She peered closer at the old man and saw something wasn't right. She could see it in his eyes—his self-confidence was fading fast. "Moses, listen to me, please. The Serpent is getting to you. It's trying to talk you out of stopping it. Don't you see? It's *afraid* of us. It will do anything to make us turn away from what we have to do."

His eyes looked glazed; his words were weary. "No, it wants to kill us. Destroy our souls."

"Moses?"

No answer.

4

He could hear it, speaking in his mind, playing on his old fears. *You'll never make it out of here alive, old man. You've seen my power, but you know very little of my capabilities. Before we're through, I'll have you on bended knees before me.*

Shut up! He shouted at it inside his brain. *I won't let you have power over me.*

Moses, darling . . . it will hurt you! You've got to get out of here now, while you still have time!

Glory? Her voice sounded sweet; it had been so long since he'd last heard it, and his rheumy eyes filled with tears at the sound of it. *Glory, if it's really you, I'll leave. I'll do whatever you ask of me.*

I know you will, darling.

Daddy? Daddy, are you there? This was a new voice, a child's tone, and Moses recognized it instantly. In that painful past, he'd only heard one-syllable words, guttural and hard to understand, but he knew who was speaking now.

Yes, John, I'm here.

Daddy, you have to leave. If you turn around now, a safe way will be made for you. It will take you right out into the sunshine. That's where you want to be, isn't it? In the sunshine, so it can warm your bones. Everything will be okay if—

5

"—Moses!" Saxon's voice penetrated the fog in his mind, then his cheek stung so hard and sudden it brought tears to his eyes. "Snap out of it! It's trying to get to you—don't let it in."

Slowly, Moses nodded, the light returning to his eyes. "It—it must have been messing with my head. When we were separated, I thought we'd go crazy trying to find you. We could hear you screaming—we just couldn't tell where you were. After it finished with you, I think it tried playing tricks with me."

Saxon turned to Clem. "Are you OK?"

He gave her a quick nod and peered past her at the green light in the hole in the wall up ahead. She followed his gaze and saw a strange light that glowed intermittently, fading to bright, then fading again. "I'm just scared," he added.

"I think it's safe to say we're all scared." She set the axe down by her feet and reached out, taking Clem and Moses' hands in her own. "There's strength in numbers," she reminded them, trying her best to smile.

Clem smiled back at her but Moses frowned. Was he still unsure? She had the distinct feeling that he wanted to say, "Strength in numbers, yes, but remember, we're fighting *Legion,* an entity whose numbers are in the thousands." He didn't, though, and for that, she was grateful.

Past the mortician's cadaver table, the wall opened up into a great, glowing cavern.

"What is that light?" Saxon asked Moses, who'd stopped suddenly.

"That light . . . it's the light of the Serpent. It's ready to shed its skin; we may already be too late to stop it."

"We'll never know unless we try." Saxon handed her flashlight to Clem and touched Moses' shoulder. "Are you going to be OK?"

He gave her a strange look. "Are any of us going to be OK—ever? I can tell you, though, if we fail, the human race may as well kiss its ass goodbye."

"We won't fail." Saxon tilted her chin and stepped forward into the cavern . . .

. . . and was hit by something that swung down from the ceiling. It knocked her backward, off her feet, and she cried out in surprise.

They could hear a rhythmic creaking, a weird sound in strange, fluctuating light; Clem shone the flashlight in the direction the noise was coming from and everyone turned, gasping as they saw . . .

. . . the corpse of a black man swinging before them, hanging limply from a thick hemp rope attached to the cavern's ceiling. His eyes bulged from their sockets; his tongue, thick and purple, dangled over his chin. Losing momentum, the swinging slowly ceased. The rope had cut so deeply into his neck that the flesh swelled around it.

Saxon leapt to her feet, lifting her axe. "Oh my God, that's Suki's man, Stevie," she cried out. She swung and her axe sliced the air, severing the rope, and the body tumbled to the dirt floor. Immediately, she dropped the axe and struggled to loosen the noose around his throat. "He's still alive! I don't know how or why—but he is!" As she pulled the rope free, Stevie began to groan, clawing at his neck, trying to breathe.

Clem bent down to help; he propped him into a sitting position. "Geez, Mister. We didn't know you was alive. You looked dead, you sure did. Can you breathe now? Can you?"

Stevie nodded slightly, still gasping for air. "Suki," he managed to say. "Gotta save Suki."

Moses hobbled over with his cane. "Saxon, do you know this man?"

"Yes, I believe his name's Stevie, Stephen Freemont.

Don't ask me how I know that; it's a long, sad story."

"Suki?" Stevie's eyes, no longer bulging but very bloodshot, gazed up at Saxon, pleading. "Will you save her, please?"

"Where is she?"

He pointed into the cavern, toward the green glow. "Viper's got her. Torturing her again. When the Serpent gets done shedding its skin, it's gonna want to eat. He means to feed her to it." He tried to cover his mouth as he spasmed into a coughing fit. Leave me," he said, still choking. "Go save her."

Moses shook his head. "It's not safe here alone. How many more do we have left to fight?"

The man held up three fingers. "Viper and Beaumont, then the Serpent."

Saxon spoke up as she added it altogether in her head. "Well, we found four: Leonard Roquefort, Geoffrey Faraday, Mario Delgado, and you. So three more ghosts must be left before the Serpent. And one of them is your wife?"

Stevie nodded. "Sho' is, but you won't need to fight her. She's on the good side. Viper, though, he's the worst. Beaumont's no picnic either." Stevie continued to hack and cough. "I don't know about the other one."

"The other one?" Clem asked.

Saxon nodded. "The eighth, the Impure Soul, necessary to complete the Serpent's transformation."

Moses gave her a puzzled look. "Well the Serpent can't fully transform until it has the eighth soul—and apparently, it hasn't got it yet. At least we have that much on our side."

At this, Stevie began to cough again. He tried to stand up, but fell on his side before anyone could move fast enough to help him.

Saxon watched Clem give him a hand, easing him into a

comfortable position, half sitting, half lying down. "What are we going to do with Stevie?" she asked Moses. "He needs to rest, but we just can't leave him here—and we can't lug him in there with us."

Moses raised a frail hand. "I'll stay with him," he offered. "I'm not as steady on my feet as I used to be and the going looks like tricky footing from here on out. You and Clem go on, but for God sakes, stay together. Don't let anything separate you or frighten you apart."

"I dunno," she said. "We'd all agreed to stick together, no matter what. I think separating, even into groups, might be a bad idea. Remember, that's what the Serpent wants so it can pick us off one by one."

He gazed at her in amazement. Lord, this woman could be so stubborn! "Saxon, listen. We can't take Stevie with us. He needs to catch his breath, rest a spell. Doing so might just doom us all. Sometimes, we have to change the plans we agreed on beforehand. We didn't know we were going to find Stevie—how could we have known? When the variables change, accommodations must be made, lest the outcome be different than what's anticipated." Moses offered her a smile. "Now I'm sounding like a teacher. I'm sorry, but that's just the way I see it."

"Well, if that's the way you see it, and everybody else agrees, who am I to quarrel with your logic?"

"I'm afraid it's the only way, dear girl."

Saxon reached down and picked up the rope from the floor. "Well, Clem, we're going to have to tie ourselves together." She draped a loop around his middle and secured it with a knot. She did the same with the other end of the rope, tying it around her own waist. Checking the knots, she found them to be good and tight. It was scratchy rope, but thick and strong.

"Perfect," she said. "This way, we'll never be more than a few feet apart. There's no way we can get separated unless the rope is cut." Wincing, Moses got down on his knees to sit with Stevie, and Saxon shot him a concerned gaze. "You sure you're going to be all right here?"

Stevie nodded, coughing, still rubbing at his neck, and Moses answered, "Yes, we'll be fine. Between the two of us, we can look out for ourselves. There's something I need to give you, though." He lifted his cane and touched her hand with it. "Here, take it. You have her spirit in your eyes; I can see that now."

Shaking her head, Saxon took a step backward. "No, that's your cane—you need it more than I do."

"Red Feather," Moses insisted, "was a wise woman. She gave this cane to me decades before you were born and I believe she meant for you to have it. There's powerful magic in this stick."

"But how do I use it? Is it a magic wand? Do I look like a witch?"

Moses chuckled. "It's not a wand—it's a weapon. You'll know what to do with it when the time comes."

Bowing her head, Saxon accepted his cane, although she was unsure of the gesture. "I'll bring it back to you when I return."

"Just you make sure *you* come back. You and Clem both."

She glanced from him to Stevie. "We'll come back for both of you—and we won't give up until we have Suki with us."

Stevie shot her a grateful look, a coughing nod.

6

Moses and Stevie watched them go, walking slowly, becoming fainter in the shadows until not even the beam of their flashlight could be seen.

"What's it like?" Moses asked. "The Serpent, I mean. Have you seen it? What is it exactly?"

Stevie shrugged. "I seen it, but I dunno what it is. I don't like to look at it. No one does. Maybe the Serpent doesn't even know what it is. It's just always *been*. Way before In The Beginning."

Moses nodded. "Why are you here, Stevie? Did it trap you?"

"Yep. Me and my wife. Got us both."

"Did you work here at Roquefort Manor?"

Stevie shook his head. "Lordy, no. Just passing through. We was going to Canada. Gonna be free up there. Then Beaumont came." Stevie's eyes brimmed with tears and he made no move to wipe them away as they spilled over his lashes. "My Suki, she was giving birth—and Beaumont and Walker, they started chasing her, making her run. Like it was some kind of game to them.

"Weren't no game, though. Not for us. They chased her down to the pond and Walker dragged her out into it. Gonna drown her. She told him the baby was coming out, but he didn't care. He held her under while she gave birth, then after she's good and drownt, he lifted the baby out of the water like it's some kind of prize.

"So I shot Beaumont, trying to get to Walker to save my Suki and our baby. Shot him dead, straight through the heart, and I'm glad of it. I'd a'shot Walker, too, if I could have."

Moses rubbed his chin, thinking. Adding things up in his

head. Re-adding them. Yes, the numbers could be a match; the times were just about right. Still, he had to know for sure. "How long ago did this happen?"

"I dunno. Feels like we've been here for an eternity."

"What year did it happen?"

Again Stevie shrugged. "I dunno, never learnt to read, was never any good at ciphering numbers, either."

Moses pressed, "Was it before the Civil War? The War of Secession?"

Stevie gave him a blank look and coughed into his fist. "Never heard of that."

"Was the baby a boy or a girl?"

"A son." A fresh trickle ran down Stevie's nose.

"And he lived?"

"Far as I could tell. I only got one look at him before they drug me off."

"What happened to the baby?"

Now Stevie wiped at his tears with the thick back of his hand. "I dunno. I'm sorry. I just dunno."

Could it be true? These thoughts that filled his mind, his heart, with hope. There were definite similarities between him and Stevie. That vertical furrow between their eyebrows, the one that deepened whenever they were worried or angry; yes, both were the same. And each had a similar mole at the corner of their mouths. Their noses were shaped alike, for that matter, and so were their eyes.

If Moses hadn't known about his background, he might have been slower to accept the conclusion that was forming in his brain, but he felt a certain connection with this man—and he believed. He reached out and gently patted Stevie's shoulder. "I think I know what happened to your baby."

It would take a while, but he began recounting his life's story.

7

The cavern was huge, as wide and deep as a pond, an underground pond that had dried up thousands of years ago. Along its cool, dank walls, small, glowing worms clung to cover the surface, reaching as far up the high ceiling where huge stalactites hung like icicles, their sharp points facing downward. *They could be icicles,* Saxon thought, *as cold as it is in here.* She could see the puffs of Clem's breath in the air; he was sweating nervously.

That's where the glowing was coming from: the worms. They pulsated and wiggled, the glow inside them flashing on and off. At least it afforded them more light to guide their way. Clem went first with the flashlight, and Saxon followed with the axe.

The easiest way to get into the cavern seemed to follow a series of ledges that hugged the walls. They sloped downwards into nooks and crannies, full of shadows and vicarious angles, but if they were careful they could make it.

There were tricks in almost every shadow, in almost every crevice. It came close to scaring the life out of both of them the first few times they saw it, before they realized the Serpent had the power to make the rocks speak. Or appear to speak.

For Clem, it had been his father's face appearing in the rock ledge. The voice coming from behind him, forcing him to turn around, making Saxon catch him by the arm. She heard it, too.

"What do ya know, Joe? It's the retard!"

Clem blinked. "D-daddy?"

"You better not be going down there, boy." He glared with granite eyes at Saxon. "Not with that little hussy!"

"Daddy, that's Saxon Faraday from next door. She's a nice lady."

The stone eyes rolled back sarcastically. "Yeah, like mother, like daughter. You'd do well to get the hell home now, boy."

"I can't." Clem was beginning to sound quite crestfallen. Saxon could hear it in his voice and it alarmed her.

"Don't listen to it, Clem," she said. "It's not your father—and even if it was, I'd still tell you not to listen."

"You *can* and you will! Or it's bed for you with no supper—I'm not your grandmother and don't you forget it!"

Saxon tugged on his arm. "Clem, come on, let's go." In the semi-darkness, she studied his face. He was biting his lower lip and looked about ready to burst into tears. Then he nodded, letting her lead the way.

"You simpleton! Idiot boy! Don't you dare walk away from me—don't you dare go down there—you and your half—!"

"—Go to hell," Saxon shouted. "You're not even real!" She tugged on Clem's arm, then slipped her hand into his. "Pay no attention to that—that thing. It's a trick of the Serpent."

Hollow laughter followed in their wake.

"No Miss Saxon, the rocks are alive. Alive! Just look around."

That's when Saxon saw the faces. Hundreds of them jutting out of the ledges, with stony brows and jaws, mean, hardened eyes. Pock-scarred cheeks. Their expressions were fierce, full of fury.

"Why'd you do it, Miss Faraday?" one of them asked, in a voice filled with gravel. "Why'd you shoot your father? Do you still play with razor blades, Saxon?"

Saxon gritted her teeth, clenching her jaws shut. She wasn't about to give the Serpent the satisfaction of an answer.

"Those windows are atrocious!"

Saxon turned to see a stone caricature of her mother's face.

"Don't you turn away from me, young lady! Who do you think you are? Your father told me what you've been up to in your bedroom. Nasty, that's what you are!"

Saxon swallowed hard and squeezed Clem's hand. His palm and fingers felt sweaty but she didn't dare let go, needing him as much as he needed her.

Clem glanced back. "Hey, don't listen. It's not your mother."

"I know. It just sounds so much like her."

A crevice, deep and wide, lie ahead of them. They stopped on the edge, calculating the distance across the span.

"Think we can jump across?" she asked Clem, her eyes carefully following the beam of the flashlight.

Clem nodded, swallowing anxiously. "Yeah, I think we can. Hand me the axe."

"The axe? Why?" She passed it to him, then gasped as he threw it across the hole. It landed on the other side, spun around, then stopped.

"Because you'd never make it across in one piece," he told her, "if you jumped with it. What if you landed on it?"

Saxon put her arms around him and kissed his cheek. "That was good thinking, Clem."

He blushed and tossed his flashlight over. It landed near the axe. "Now if you untie me, I'll go first and help pull you over."

"I really don't want to do this," she said, reaching for the rope. "Are you sure it's safe?"

"No, but it's the only way."

Saxon undid the knot from around his waist. "Well, for God sakes, don't fall."

"I won't, I promise."

"He'll make it, but he'll let go of you," said another voice from the rocks. "He's an imbecile and that's what imbeciles do!"

"Don't listen to it," Saxon warned.

"I'm trying not to," Clem told her, wiping at his eyes.

"Now take it slow and be careful." She saw him nod; then he lunged forward.

"The retard's going to miss!" her rock mother yelled, and for a moment, it looked like she might be right. Clem slipped, losing his footing, but managed to cling to the side of the crevice. Laboriously, he pulled himself up.

"Close call," he said, panting as he peered over the edge.

"You ain't kidding."

"Your turn, Miss Saxon."

She looked down into the crevice. It had to be five, maybe six feet across, and deeper than she dared fathom. Falling meant certain death. She tucked the handle of Moses' cane into the loop around her waist, and took a few steps back to gaze at Clem, standing there on the other side, his back pressed into the ledge, one hand extended, ready to catch her.

She tossed him the end of the rope and he caught it. *I can do this,* she thought, running to the edge . . . and jumped, going airborne, reaching for Clem's hand.

And missed.

Her legs and belly scraped painfully down the side of the crevice, her feet digging in, struggling for a foothold. Stones beneath her toes crumbled away, falling; she could hear them shattering on jagged rocks far below. She could feel Clem pulling on the rope, pinching her middle.

Then her right foot found something solid, something to stand on. Would it hold? She didn't know, but she had no choice except to take the chance that it wouldn't give way.

Above her, Clem knelt, grunting with exertion. "Grab the rope," he urged. "I can pull you up."

She had no choice but to trust him with her life. With both hands, she grabbed the rope and held on for dear life. Using her knees as support, she climbed as Clem pulled, but she didn't dare breathe until she was up there beside him.

"You okay, Miss Saxon?" he asked.

"Yes, thanks to you. I don't think I could have made it without you."

That made him smile, and she hoped it washed away all the ugliness the Serpent had cast upon him. The insults, the name calling. After a moment's rest, they got up, retied the rope around Clem's waist, and pressed onward.

It took a long time to get to the other side of the cavern, where steps, wide and cracked, dripped with a strange, gelatinous substance. The steps spiraled downward onto another level that flattened out onto another ledge. Saxon, axe in one hand, clung to the rope attaching her to Clem and tried her best to follow in his footsteps.

As soon as they reached the ledge, they heard Beaumont, the heavy pounding of his boots shaking the ground, the noise of his terrible cursing bellowing from a tunnel at their right.

The flashlight Clem held darted crazily as he searched for an escape. But the ledge was too slippery, making any fast move dangerous. Saxon pointed at the tunnel, seeing a strange, white light swinging and arching, coming closer by the second.

"What is it? What—"

Just then, Beaumont came rushing out at them, toting a shotgun in one hand and a lantern in the other.

"You're all dead!" he cried out. "All dead, all dead!"

Clem stepped in front of Saxon; she knew he was trying to protect her, for George Beaumont was fearsome. The tails of his buckskin coat flapped behind him, his thick beard was crimson red, matching the stain on his chest—the stain around a gaping hole—but his eyes, those cruel eyes of his, were glowing as if lit by an internal inferno. Hell was inside this man, Saxon was sure of it.

She took a battle stance, parting both feet for leverage, and lifted her axe, ready to swing. "Clem, move out of the way. I've got this one."

Just then, Beaumont stopped, seeing that she was armed, and calmly set his lantern down on the ledge beside him. Sneering, he approached them, raising the barrel of his gun. "You think you can beat the Serpent," he told them in a booming voice, "but you're dead wrong. No one beats the Serpent."

Saxon saw his fingers feel for the trigger and she knew this was it; they'd only have one chance to beat him. With all her might, she threw her axe, watching the blade sail end over end, whistling as it sliced the air.

It found its mark, sinking deep into Beaumont's shoulder, causing him to drop the gun.

"You living bitch!" he screamed. "What have you done to me?" He fell to his knees, trying to pry the blade from his body. Blood coursed in streams down his hands and arms as he struggled with the embedded axe.

Saxon raced forward, sliding as she skirted past Beaumont, but she managed to pick up the shotgun.

"How many shots left in it?" Clem asked her.

She shook her head miserably, looking at the gun. "I don't even know how to check." Her father's handgun had been easy, just pull back the rod and check the revolving chamber; this old shotgun was totally different.

"Here, give it to me."

Saxon went to him and gave him the gun and, with a metallic click, he broke it open to peer inside the chamber. "One. That's it. Just one." He raised the gun by the butt, snapping it back together one-handed with another loud click.

"Shoot him, Clem," Saxon urged, pointing at Beaumont. "Let's finish him off."

"Nope. Gotta save it for the Serpent."

"Well, what about Beaumont? We can't just leave him like this? What if he pulls my axe out and comes after us?"

"It's a chance we gotta take. Don't think he's going anywhere soon," Clem said, cradling the gun in his arms. Saxon had never seen him look so much like a man before. There was something special inside of him, something calm, strong, and just, and she loved him for it.

She reached down to pick up Beaumont's lantern, but Clem stopped her. "No, don't touch it. That's not good fire."

Giving him a strange look, she reluctantly surrendered. "Well, maybe it's best we leave the light here with him—that way, when we come back, we'll know exactly where he is." She felt Clem knew a lot more than he was letting on, but she trusted him completely, especially after that long jump.

They left Beaumont groaning on the dirt floor, thrashing about in an effort to dig the axe blade from his shoulder, his dark blood soaking his coat, mingling with the crimson that was already there.

They went ever deeper, until it seemed they'd walked for miles. Gradually, the walls along the ledge began to widen until at last they stood at the foot of a precipice, a finger of a cliff sticking out over the middle of the dried up, ancient pond.

Two others were the end of this precipice, a man and woman, struggling one against the other. The man was big and burly, his head bald, his arms muscular, and Saxon recognized the woman he held in his grasp immediately.

Clem lifted the gun and Saxon called out, "Let Suki go!"

The big man turned toward them, snarling like a raging bear. "The hell I will! You don't know who you're dealing with!"

Together Saxon and Clem approached, weapon raised. "We know enough. You're Viper. The one my father called 'Snake.' After what I've been through, thanks to you, what makes you think I'd be afraid of you?"

Viper laughed, an evil belly laugh that reverberated off the walls. "Oh, you should be very afraid, little girl—you and your feeble sidekick!" He tightened his headlock on Suki. With her neck caught in the crook of his massive arm, the poor woman looked scared out of her wits, eyes bulging as she clawed and dug, trying to free herself from his grip.

"Let her go," Saxon demanded. She glanced over at Clem. "Shoot him!"

"But what if I hit the lady instead?"

She shook her head. "I've seen you skip stones out at the Witch Hole. You were a sure-shot, always able to hit the old tree out in the water. You were the best, Clem. I know you can do it!"

Holding her breath, she watched him peer down the barrel of the shotgun, finger pausing on the trigger.

"Maybe we should save this last shot for the Serpent?"

"No, Clem. We promised to save Suki. That's what we have to do right now."

She watched his slanted eyes narrow, positioning the bead so it lined up just right . . . and he squeezed the trigger.

The great blast from the shotgun blew him backwards, making him land on his fanny, but it also split the Viper's head apart. Black blood spouted from his broken neck and he fell across Suki, who scrambled to get out from under him. Frantic with fright, she ran to Saxon.

"Thank God you came!" she gasped, embracing her. "He was getting ready to throw me down there." Where she pointed, Saxon and Clem could see something writhing and twisting in the green light below. Something huge. "Down there, with *that.*"

"It's the Serpent, isn't it?"

Suki nodded. "Let's get out of here—it's awake now—and it's getting ready to shed its skin. We can't be here when it happens . . . Beaumont said it will need to eat. That's why Viper was going to toss me down there."

Saxon shook her head, standing her ground. "No, we have to defeat it once and for all. We mustn't let it complete its transformation."

"You don't understand—you can't defeat it. It's a god."

Clem cleared his throat. "No, not a god. It only *thinks* it's a god. It wants us to think so, too."

"How you gonna keep it from changing?" Suki demanded. "That thing'll eat you alive! It absorbs, that's what it does."

Peering over the edge of the precipice, Clem shook his head. "It won't. It's too busy right now. Besides, it hasn't got everything it needs in order to transform."

"That's right," Saxon affirmed. "It hasn't got the eighth

soul." *Mine, and I won't let it get me!* She couldn't tell Clem, knowing he'd try to prevent her from going down there to fight it. "We've got to end this right now."

Suki balked. "Uh, uh, ain't no way you're getting me near that thing!"

"Then you stay up here," Saxon told her. "And please pray for our victory—pray like you've never prayed before!"

Suki got down on her knees, hands clasped together, lifting her eyes upward, as Saxon and Clem picked their way down the side of the cliff. Reaching the bottom at last, they could now see the Serpent for what it was, and not just a distant, greyish lump writhing on the cave floor.

Saxon could see that Moses and Clem had been right all along; the Serpent wasn't of this world. It had human form, yes, partly, but its body was covered in scales, now turning from grey to translucent, crinkling and wrinkling all up and down its body. Apparently it did not see them, for the scales over its eyes had died, forming a milky mask.

Together, she and Clem approached it, the earth beneath their feet shaking with each breath the Serpent took.

It was a huge thing, a dark and terrible thing, this ancient monster, half man, half reptile. It wriggled and squirmed in its sac of dead skin and, as they drew closer to it, somehow it sensed their presence, for it rose to a crouching position, turning its thick head toward them, hissing.

"Impure Soul," it said in a strangely mellow voice. "At last you come to me. Nearer, woman, nearer." Its forked tongue darted at the air as it spoke; flakes of broken scales lined its awful mouth.

Clem grabbed Saxon's arm. "Don't get any closer to it—we don't know what it's gonna do!" He was shivering both from the drop in temperature and from fear.

She was well aware of her own fear; the Serpent was larger than she'd expected, well over seven feet long. It would have towered over them if it stood up, and it was grotesque in form: a rounded, triangular-shaped head, lidless serpentine eyes, a cruel slit for a mouth, and that terrible, black tongue flickering.

Clem dropped the flashlight and shifted the shotgun so that both hands gripped the barrel, still warm from its previous discharge. Gritting his teeth, he took another step toward the Serpent, ready to strike.

"Leave me be, little man!" the Serpent roared, its look of sudden, unfathomable rage rippling beneath the film of dead scales on its face. "I take issue with the woman alone. She has come to fulfill her destiny." It turned, apparently gazing at her again. "Come to me now. This is what you've been waiting for—our time is at hand!"

At this, Clem screamed, startling Saxon, who'd never before heard him raise his voice. He charged at the Serpent, intent on striking it, and pulling Saxon with him, for they were still attached by the length of rope, but just as Clem swung the shotgun, he was flung backward by an invisible force. The rope broke and Clem landed in a heap behind Saxon.

"Come hither, woman," the Serpent said, its tone mellow once more, ageless, sexless. "You shall see that I am not the beast you think I am. We can be great friends, you and I . . . be my mate, my consort, and I shall make you a queen. We will rule—"

But Saxon turned away from the Serpent and ran to Clem's side. He wasn't dying as she'd feared, for such a fall could have broken his neck, but he was trying hard not to cry out in pain, rocking back and forth, clutching his ankle. She could see his foot dangling at an odd angle; it had to be broken.

"I failed," he admitted, unable to hold back the tears any longer. "I wanted to save you and I couldn't."

Saxon bent down and kissed his cheek. "It's OK," she whispered. "Stay put and don't try to move." Clem nodded, then raised his hand, pointing past her, and she could see his whole arm was shaking.

"Watch out!"

She whirled around a second too late.

Clearly, she'd underestimated the Serpent's power, its ability to move, despite its condition. Its hideously long tail whipped around her legs, knocking her down, pulling her toward itself.

"Lemme go!" she yelled, struggling to free herself. Thrashing about, she barely noticed that she'd dropped her only weapon, the cane Moses had given her.

"That's my girl," the Serpent said. "Fight me. I haven't enjoyed physical combat in eons!"

She was almost close enough to touch the monster, and certainly within distance to smell its ripe, putrid stench. With its rubbery tongue, it lashed out at her forearm, drawing a slimy trail on her skin which blistered in its wake. She couldn't help but scream out in pain.

"Miss Saxon!" She heard Clem yell from behind but she couldn't turn away, not now. Her eyes were locked on the Serpent's dreadful face . . . those eyes now glowing red as its lower jaw unhinged, dead skin tearing, falling open to reveal long, yellowed fangs emerging, lengthening from the top of its mouth. An ichor of stringy venom dripped from their sharp points.

Its mouth became a cavern, large enough to swallow her whole. Looking into it, she could see the fire of its belly, burning and bubbling, the very depths of Hell itself.

"Hang on, I'm coming!" Clem sounded closer now.

Saxon shook her head, forcing her eyes away from the heat. "Run, Clem—get out of here! It's too strong for us!" She groaned, trying with all her might to pull the tail of the Serpent away from her thighs . . . but it was too strong, too constricting. From knees down, her legs had gone numb from lack of circulation.

Some of its dead scales ripped off in her hands, strips of cold, dead skin. It had all the strength of a rotten burial shroud, and underneath, the new skin glistened, pinkish-grey, a network of black capillaries pulsating. Could she possibly maim it before it swallowed her?

If I'm to be the eighth, the Impure Soul, she reasoned, *and if it is to absorb me before it can transform, perhaps if I alter the process, I can put an end to it? Its skin rips so easily, I should be able to at least hurt it, make it suffer. . . .*

She tore off her gloves and with her fingernails, she began shredding the skin of the Serpent as it pulled her closer to its mouth.

The heat on her face intensified, the force of it blowing back her hair . . . and she could hear screams rising up from the Serpent's belly . . . the awful sizzle and spit of its stomach acid.

This was the end, the very end; she was sure of it.

Its mouth began closing over her head, venom dripping, burning paths down the back of her shoulders.

Saxon closed her eyes. *Forgive me, Clem. Moses, too. I tried. I tried to fight it . . . I just wasn't strong enough.*

Just then, the Serpent stopped, drawing back its head, its long neck undulating. And it howled, the sound of its agony reverberating throughout the entire cavern. Some of the stalactites broke free from the ceiling, shooting downward to puncture the ground around her.

She felt the grip on her legs loosen and she rolled away from the monster . . .

. . . and into Clem, who was crouching, balancing mostly on one leg, holding Moses' cane before him.

Clem growled, drew back, and struck the Serpent again, and to Saxon, he looked very much like a fabled knight. Not in chain mail and armor, but in dungarees and a blue T-shirt, wearing his red ball cap backwards. No bright hero ever looked more dashing.

In that moment, she saw him for a man.

The Serpent screamed again, the most unimaginable, horrible bellow, twisting in its sack of dead skin. It writhed, trying to get away from Clem.

"You can't kill me! Your efforts are futile!" It twisted in vain. "Your own mother didn't want you—you know that, don't you? You were a mistake! Never meant to be!"

"Leave my mother out of this," Clem shouted, ramming the cane's tip into the Serpent's head, pinning it to the ground. "It's over," he said, his voice low and steady. "Face it, you've lost."

The Serpent stopped moving. It wasn't dead, but at least it was lying quietly between them now.

"You did it!" Saxon called out, rising, running to Clem and hugging him in triumph.

Slowly, the Serpent lifted what appeared to be an arm, tatters of dead, grey scales hanging from it. "Mercy, hybrids," it begged in a weak, croaking voice. "I am defeated; you've harmed me enough."

"We have to finish the job," she told Clem.

The creature's arm dropped back to the ground. "You can't kill me. No one can. The staff of Moses has neutralized me."

"Staff of Moses?" Saxon yelled, overcome by emotion.

"You make this sound like it's right out of the Bible!"

"It might be," Clem said. "I know my leg broke—I felt it snap . . . but then I picked up the cane and the pain went away. It don't hurt no more."

"The boy is right. That cane is made from the Staff of Moses, the same one in the Bible," the Serpent replied in a weak tone. "The Aelim put enmity between the woman and myself for all eternity. I didn't understand it before this; I thought I could win this time."

Saxon glared down at it without pity. "Why did you do what you did to me, to Jacqueline, and our families? What was the purpose in all of that? Tell me!"

The Serpent paused; she could see its new, unborn scales ripple slightly under the dead ones with every heaving breath. "I did what I did because it is my nature to destroy. I didn't plan to come here. I had no intention of staying so long—but as you can see, I'm grounded."

"So you thought you'd make everyone else as miserable as you are. Didn't you think that eventually someone would try to stop you?"

At this, the Serpent didn't answer for a long moment. Then it said, "I knew the Aelim were looking for me. I knew they'd send the brother and sister—that you would come someday. And together you have an undefeatable force. Congratulations on your success."

Brother and sister? "What do you mean?" Saxon demanded.

"You . . . him. Same mother."

She shook her head. "No, that's impossible." She glanced over at Clem, who appeared dazed and shaken by this statement. "Clem and I are neighbors, not siblings. I'm afraid you're quite mistaken."

The Serpent moved its head slightly. "No, it's true. Your

mother, his father. A secret affair and a deal made between husbands. No one was ever supposed to know—but I knew all along, even as it unfolded."

"It's a lie," Saxon told Clem.

Clem shook his head, blinking. "But what if it ain't?"

"Look at yourselves," the Serpent said. "Together in this space and time, so much alike but neither one can see it. The gift of clairvoyance runs through both of you."

"Stop it!" Saxon screamed. "Stop with the lies!"

"You want another great truth, woman?" the Serpent asked. "I tell you this, you think you've returned home, but you're so very wrong."

"This *is* my home."

The Serpent lifted one finger. "Nae, you're blocking things from your mind. I see much. Things you wish not to remember. There's something wrong with you. They said you could go home, but . . ."

"Enough, please," Saxon said, her outrage turning to confusion. "You're a liar—the father of lies—and I won't hear any more of this!"

As upset as she was, the questions caused her to pause . . . to think. What if the Serpent was right? Was she insane? She honestly couldn't remember going grocery shopping to restock her cupboards and icebox. She couldn't recall feeling thirsty enough to drink a glass of water, despite there being the worst drought in Maine's history. She barely recollected the drive home; it all seemed like a distant memory. But the past few hours had been like a nightmare, small wonder she couldn't remember anything. "You're confusing me; I don't want to hear anymore of your lies," she said, backing away.

Just then, Suki screamed from above. Saxon and Clem

heard the heavy thud of footsteps and knew it could only be one person.

Beaumont!

Saxon looked back at the Serpent. "It's over for you," she said, and closing her hands over Clem's as she glanced at him. "Let's finish this now."

"You can't kill me!" The Serpent had taken on the voice of Joe Tuttle, Jr. "Don't you even try!"

Clem frowned, his slanted eyes squinting. "I remember Grandpa telling about poor ol' Pat Sanders," he said.

"Pat Sanders?" Saxon had no idea where he was going with this.

"Yeah, way back in the logging days. Pat Sanders caught rabies and that's real bad. The other loggers, they tied him to a tree because he told them to. He wanted them to shoot him, can you believe that?"

Saxon nodded. She knew hydrophobia was one of the most deadly diseases; it almost always ended in death.

"My father's a jerk, but I think he's got that same kind of spirit." Clem glared down at the Serpent. "If this thing was really my dad, he'd be begging me to end this."

"I think you're right." While Saxon had no use whatsoever for Joe, Jr., she knew no one was one hundred percent bad. Clem carried half his father's genes; there had to be some good inside the man.

"Young lady, you don't know as much as you think you do."

That voice belonged to Moses, and the Serpent continued using it, "You're wrong about me. I am a god. Maybe even *the* one true God. You kill me, and you could be dooming all mankind."

She shook her head, glancing at Clem. "I've had enough of the games. Let's end this now."

Clem knew what she meant to do, and together they leaned, pushing the tip of the cane, driving it down through the brain of the Serpent. It took every ounce of their combined strength . . . and then finally . . . shrieking, it twisted in its bag of dead skin, impaled, then lay still, twitching slightly.

"You and your kind will pay dearly for this . . ." it said in its own voice, trailing off as Saxon pulled the cane free from its head. Its jaw dropped, steam spilling from its tattered lips, as green fluid gushed in to fill the hole in its skull.

She and Clem raced over to the side of the precipice and began to climb. Beaumont was coming; they couldn't see him yet, but now they could hear him muttering curses and groaning as he advanced. At least he didn't have his gun now; that was lying down near the Serpent, its ammunition spent.

Suki reached down and pulled them up to where she'd been praying. "We gotta get out of here NOW!" she shouted. Together, the three of them raced toward the ledges.

Beaumont was there, waiting for them, the blade of the axe still embedded in his shoulder. Cursing, he reached to grab Suki, but all he caught was her sleeve. It tore off in his hand, and swearing, he followed them, the lantern by his side, swinging.

8

Moses and Stevie heard the others coming and both managed to stand up, holding onto one another, father and son.

"We have to get out of here," Saxon called out to them.

"Hurry! Beaumont's after us!" She ran over and touched the handle of the cane to Stevie's throat and instantly his coughing stopped. He gave her a surprised but thankful look as he pulled his wife into his arms.

She tried to touch the cane to Moses, to heal his legs in a similar manner, but he waved it away. "It won't work," he told her. "There were many times I thought about using it on myself—but self-healing is a selfish reason to drain its magic." He gave Saxon a hopeful look. "But tell me you killed the Serpent?"

Saxon shook her head. "Kill it, no, I don't think so. But we beat it, disabled it. I don't think we'd ever be able to kill it entirely—we only stopped it from shedding its skin. It won't be able to transform now."

Moses swallowed, his eyes rimming with pride. "Well, that's going to have to be enough, isn't it?" He looked over at Suki embracing Stevie. "Mother?"

Suki turned to gaze at him. "What did you just call me?"

"He's our boy," Stevie told her. "The one we thought we'd lost. That's him, all right. All growed up now."

Saxon watched Suki's brows knit, the questioning stare of her eyes. "But how can this be? He's an old man!"

"I know. We've been trapped here a long time," Stevie said. "But he lived. Walker didn't kill him." He motioned to Moses with his hand. "Come, give your Ma a hug."

Hesitating, nearly overcome with emotion, Moses hobbled over. Suki smiled, her brows smoothing out. Could she see the family resemblance? Saxon thought so.

Then she took him in her arms, folding them around him, holding him close.

This was what he needed, what he'd longed for, for so many years. Burying his face in the crook of her neck, he wept like a baby.

And behind them, Beaumont roared, charging ahead in great, loping strides.

"We gotta go NOW!" Saxon yelled, breaking the touching moment.

Hanging onto one another, they all forged onward, managing to outdistance Beaumont, but not by much. The last leg of the journey through the tunnels led them upward to the parlor of Roquefort Manor.

It was changing back to normal, the vines slithering back into the walls, the mushrooms and toadstools curling in on themselves, crumpling, the mold and mildew vanishing, the dirt and grime fading. The wallpaper, old as it was, began to return to normal, and as they passed through the parlor, Saxon could see that the faces were no longer there.

The power of the Serpent was over, spent.

Hearing the creaking and groaning of the house, they hurried outside, a relatively safe distance away from the porch. And in the light of the late afternoon sun, they found that the world had changed back to normal.

"Oh, thank God," Saxon cried out, falling to the grass, now soft but still dead and dry from the drought. She kissed the ground, so happy to be alive, to have not only survived the ordeal—but she'd done what she'd come here to do. Now she could get on with her life.

Behind them, the house continued to groan, beams snapping, boards and windows breaking. As they all turned to look, it caved in on itself and a cloud of dust ballooned over it.

"It's finally over," Saxon said with a sigh of relief, rising to her knees, clutching Moses' cane.

Moses shook his head. "Not yet. Look."

Someone was coming out of the rubble and as they stood up in the swirling dust, Saxon saw it was Beaumont, the axe still in his shoulder, the lantern still in his hand. He scowled as soon as he saw them and began his advance anew.

Only something was wrong—he wasn't as slow as before. Hatred was nourishing him, making him stronger. Grunting with effort, he pulled the blade from his shoulder as he quickened his march. The bloody axe swung beside him, keeping tempo with the swinging of his lantern.

"He's unstoppable!" Saxon said, scrambling to her feet.

Suki's face froze in terror. "No, he's the Hunter. He won't stop until he gets what he came for: me and Stevie."

This spurred Stevie to action; he grabbed Suki and Moses. "We gotta go somewhere. I ain't letting him get us." He glanced at Moses. "Can you run?"

Moses shook his head. "I've used up every ounce of energy I have. You and Suki go on ahead. Save yourselves. It's you he's after, anyway."

Suki reached out, clutching his shirt. "We can't do that! We've waited too long for this. C'mon now, Stevie will carry you, won't you?"

He gave her a nod as he gently heaved Moses over his shoulder.

Saxon and Clem were pulling at them. "We gotta hurry—he's getting closer!"

As a group, they ran down the slope of the driveway, and Saxon couldn't help but notice her car wasn't there where she'd parked it. Where had it gone? Had someone stolen it?

She didn't want to take the time to worry about it. Behind her, she could hear Beaumont swinging the axe, cursing, swearing that he was going to kill them all.

But someone else was standing between the lions at the entrance, and when he turned, Saxon saw that it was Mario Delgado. "Where's Jacqueline?" he called out, no longer looking like a corpse, or a ghost, either. He was just a boy dressed in his best clothes, holding a bouquet of dried flowers in his hand, ready to court his sweetheart.

Saxon hurried over to him, the others close behind. "There's no time to explain—"

Mario lifted his chin. "Beaumont's coming. Don't worry about me, I'm sure I'll find her." He pointed down the road. "Go that way toward Fresh Meadow; I'll try to delay the Hunter."

She looked back over her shoulder as she ran with the others. Mario stayed true to his word; he was taunting Beaumont, trying to get him to fight, and deftly sidestepping each time Beaumont swung the axe. It reminded Saxon of a bullfight, but she knew Mario couldn't win; he was only trying to buy them some time.

Moments later, she heard Beaumont coming again.

"We have to move faster," she called out to the others. They were nearing Dolliver's Dump, where retired, old cars took their place beside broken wringer washers to wait out their final demise. Just beyond the dump, Saxon realized Mario was right, the cranberry bog in Fresh Meadow might afford them the best route of escape. It was bone dry, but the ground was still soft and spongy. As strong as Beaumont was, she knew he wasn't quick. And he was heavy. Maybe he'd get stuck in the bog, break an ankle or a leg? That would slow him down.

"This way," Saxon yelled, leaving the dusty road and slowing down so she could catch her breath. "The going gets real hard from here on out," she told the others, "but it should slow Beaumont down. Just watch where you step."

Carefully, they picked their way through the side of the bog nearest to the dump. Saxon hadn't been wrong; the footing was unstable at best, full of dips and spongy hills, hidden by dead, dry shrubs.

Beaumont had just entered the bog when he fell to his knees, cursing anew. His lantern tumbled over on its side and immediately spilled, catching the grass on fire.

The effect was instant.

Flames shot upward, feeding voraciously on the dry bushes, and they engulfed Beaumont, who screamed and danced, trying to get away from them.

Then all fell silent, and the Hunter was gone as quickly as if Hell itself had reached up to claim him. Perhaps, in a way, it had done just that.

The flames, though, continued onward, forcing Saxon and her friends across to the other side of the bog to safety.

They wanted to rest, needed a breather, but something extraordinary had taken place during their journey in Fresh Meadow; Moses had changed. He was no longer an old man, slung over the back of his much younger father, but had become an infant, cradled in his mother's arms.

"Moses?" Saxon went to Suki and gazed down at the baby. Those eyes! She would have recognized them anywhere; undeniably, they belonged to Moses Brady, and had the look of someone old, someone who'd seen it all before. He peeked back at her, blinking in the glare of the afternoon sun . . . and smiled a sweet baby smile.

Was this a reward for his sacrifice, for never healing his afflictions with the cane, but saving it for a greater battle? Could be.

Now she understood why Miss Geddy had wanted her to read *The Book of Riddles: Mysteries of the World and Universe Revealed* so many years ago. That section about the physics of time and space that had certainly been beyond her grasp then; she was just beginning to understand now. *Time really is irrelevant,* she thought. *It's a human invention, a means of measurement, and nothing more. We put so much stock in it . . .*

instead of living life the way we were meant to, one moment at a time, savoring each for what they are: gifts and lessons from the infinite—

Clem was tugging at her sleeve, begging her to explain to him what had happened to his friend and teacher.

"I'm not sure," she told him, "but I think maybe this is the way it was supposed to happen. Maybe the way things might have been if there had never been a Serpent in Eden. Does that make sense?"

He said it did, but she wasn't really sure he understood, and there was no time to explain. They had much more to worry about now, for the southwest wind began to pick up, fanning the growing flames in the bog, working them up into a wildfire. This was one of the worst things that could have happened; because of the long summer drought, the bog was bone dry.

After managing to reach the safety of the road, the friends split up into two groups, each going their own way.

Stevie and Suki decided to head toward Norway Drive and head North as they'd planned to do almost a hundred years earlier . . . only this time they were taking their baby with them. Saxon and Clem wished them the best of luck, and, wanting to be sure that Beaumont hadn't harmed him, Saxon and Clem decided to go back and check on Mario.

The date was Friday, October 17, 1947, the time, 4 p.m.

9

A 150-gallon fire truck rolled to a stop by the Cranberry Bog in Fresh Meadow. The flames were extinguished before they could stretch across to Salisbury Cove, but even so, the bog continued to smolder. Sixteen hundred feet of hose had been unrolled from the truck and spread along the ground, in hopes that the heat in the dry earth would soon be vanquished under the sprays of water. Back at the station in town, the sign indicating the fire danger level was changed from "VERY HIGH" to the fifth, the highest degree: "EXTREME."

Was it really over? Was Bar Harbor now safe from that terrible, underground demon? Roquefort Manor, Death House, was gone; the earth itself had reclaimed it, drawing it in upon itself. Firemen arrived to put out the fire in the bog, so it would seem that the worst was over, that once again, all was right with the world.

Saxon and Clem were unable to find any trace of Mario Delgado. Had Beaumont killed him, destroyed his spirit? Saxon prayed it not so, but until she found him, she knew she'd always continue to wonder. If not for his help, Leonard Roquefort would have killed her, she was sure of it.

After hours of searching for the boy, Clem convinced Saxon to return home with him to his house and she relented, although she didn't care much for his rude father. Fortunately, Joe, Jr. ignored her completely, which was fine by her. She couldn't imagine her mother having an affair with the man, but after the way her father treated her mother, who could really blame her for jumping the fence? *Perhaps Clem really is my brother,* she thought, and that wouldn't be bad at all.

Four days passed and this time went slowly for Saxon. Her house was gone, her car, everything, all her belongings. All she now owned were the clothes on her back, and this gave her plenty to think about.

What if the Serpent was right? What if something really is wrong with me? She watched Clem and Joe eat. Clem really knew how to pack away the food, but she wasn't hungry at all. *Nerves,* she told herself. *Nothing but nerves. Makes sense, after all I've been through.*

Winds of change were coming, though; she could feel them in the air.

It wasn't just the fact that the wind had changed quadrants from southwest to northeast and was picking up in velocity; it was something worse. She had the saddest feeling that something special, an era, was about to die, despite their victory over the Serpent.

She listened closely, standing at the window on the other side of the room, as Joe told Clem how a small fire, a hotspot, had been spotted in the cranberry bog, just beyond the reach of the hoses that had been left there. "Apparently," he said, "the heat and dryness made a virtual tinderbox there. You don't know anything about that fire do you, Clem? Someone mentioned seeing you out to the bog a few days ago."

Clem shook his head. How could he begin to tell his father about Beaumont or any of the other paranormal events he'd experienced just days ago? Joe would never believe him, anyway. He looked up at his father instead and asked, "What's a hotspot?" The mercury had climbed to a mild sixty-three that day, nothing particularly *hot* about that.

Joe grunted as he refilled his pipe. "Hotspots happen when a fire goes underground. Fire's like water, boy. It follows the path of least resistance. You take as dry as the ground is, and all those roots, fire can travel underground as fast as it can above."

Silently, Clem nodded. Saxon knew he was doing his best to comprehend all his father was saying.

"It's the wind that's got me worried. A Nor'easter's

brewing, sure as shit. Feel it in my bones." Joe sat suddenly forward, lighting his pipe. He gave it a couple of puffs to get it going, then asked, "You know what'll happen if the wind blows a gale, don't you?"

"Batten down the hatches," Clem whispered. That meant closing the shutters on the house and putting away lawn chairs and garden tools.

"No, you fool, it means—" Joe threw his hands in the air, spreading his arms wide, gripping the tip of his pipe between his teeth—"KA-BOOM! Fire's already out of control in the bog. Bar Harbor will be toast, if we get that gale, mark my words."

Toast? Clem blinked. Saxon wanted to explain that it was a figure of speech, but the last thing she wanted to do was get caught up in an argument with Joe, Jr. What if he kicked her out of the house? She had no other place to go.

But Joe wasn't looking at him just then. He was gazing out the window, a plume of blue smoke swirling over his head. "They called for assistance, you know," he added, still not looking over at Clem. "Fire crews from Ellsworth, Bucksport. Got 'em coming in from as far away as Camden and Brewer."

"Who?" Clem asked.

"The firefighters. It's gonna be a disaster, the fire and the wind coming. You seen those Army trucks rolling by?"

Clem shrugged.

"Well, them's the boys from the Dow Field Army Base in Bangor. You know things are serious when they call in the troops."

"Fire in the bog," Clem said, scratching his head. "It's real bad, ain't it?"

This time, his father whirled around to face him. "Have you been listening to anything I've said? Yeah, it's real bad.

It ain't only in the bog anymore. Last I heard, it was headed for Norway Drive. You know those pastures out on Prosperity Hill? They're all black now."

"Fair Acres?" Clem asked.

His father nodded. "Didn't get the house or the barn, though. They hosed 'em down good. Fire rushed right on past."

"What about Mr. Moses' house?" Clem asked.

Joe opened up both hands. "Poof, gone."

"The old folks? They got out, didn't they?"

His father gave him a brief nod. "Ayup, they evacuated everyone in the wrinkle hotel. Fire's crossed the road, though. Up McFarland's Mountain and headed for Eagle Lake."

Clem gave a low whistle. He knew those places by heart.

"Yep, they say it's jumping from tree to tree up there. Forty, fifty feet high. Leaves are so dry, may as well be made of crepe paper."

Just then, the power went out.

Saxon jumped as Joe shot up out of his chair, pipe in his fist. "Dammit! Well, just don't that beat all?" He stomped across the room to the cellar, opened the door, and went down the stairs. Clem could hear him down there, stirring around. He knew better than to ask what he was doing.

Moments later, Joe returned up the stairs. "Well, it ain't a blown fuse. Power must be off. Probably because of the fire."

"It's that close? Will it get our house?" Clem asked, looking alarmed.

His father answered him with a disgusted glare of silence.

10

Saxon heard every word of the exchange between father and son, and although it didn't surprise her that Joe didn't show any affection toward Clem, it didn't fail to anger her.

Still, Joe Tuttle, Jr. was her best source of information. She could have left the Tuttle residence to find out first-hand what was happening around town, but she just didn't feel like going anywhere. Her battle with the Serpent left her quite drained of energy. Besides, there'd been a lot of traffic on the road, lately, Jeeps mostly, and she didn't want to get in their way.

The next evening, on October 22nd, as the southeast sky glowed unmistakably red, Saxon listened to Joe and Clem's conversation after supper. Joe had been away from home all day, from dusk to dawn, to help fight the blaze.

"Fire tore up Sargent's Mountain today," he was saying, dipping a lit match into the bowl of his pipe. "Forest rangers all the way from the Smokey Mountains came in to help, and from Florida, too." He took a few puffs, and added, "A ton of school kids—they're letting 'em skip school. Can you believe that?"

"Can I help, too?" Clem offered, his eyes eager.

Joe shook his head, frowning. "Nope, the fire's bad enough without everyone having to worry about some re-tard running around. Besides, I feel better knowing that you're home, just in case something happens."

"Like what?"

Joe rolled his eyes. "Jesus, Mary, and Joseph! There's a wildfire out there. *Anything* could happen! I wouldn't be surprised if we have to evacuate."

Clem frowned. "Evacu-what?" He'd heard his father use

that word before, but he couldn't remember what it meant.

"Leave!" Joe shook his head. "Sometimes, boy, I swear you're dumber than a bag of hammers, but other times, I think it's just an act. I never quite know what to make of you." He pointed the stem of his pipe at Clem. "Now you listen up: if someone official-looking, like one of those Army guys, shows up here and tells you it's time to evacuate, that means it's time to go. Pronto. No fooling around."

Clem nodded, quickly absorbing the gravity of the situation. *Go,* he thought. *Wherever the Army guys say to go. And pronto.*

"And don't forget to take the bag on top of the cupboard, either."

Clem knew which bag he meant. He'd helped Joe pack it the night before. There wasn't much in there, some old photos and war metals, no great value to him, but he knew it meant a lot to his father. He wouldn't forget something important like that.

That night the wind shifted again.

This time, it turned the direction of the fire, making it bear down toward Bar Harbor village, but it swung around again, driving the giant blaze toward Hulls Cove.

For Clem, it was a terrifying night. The sky was all lit up outside his bedroom window, and he sat there on his bed looking out at it. Saxon sat beside him, talking to him, trying to soothe away his fears.

"You suppose we're really brother and sister?" he asked in a whisper so Joe wouldn't overhear.

She shrugged. "I don't know. Could be, but then I wouldn't trust anything the Serpent had to say. He's the father of lies, the old deceiver."

Clem fell silent for a long moment, then looked over at

her. "Well, if I could choose a sister, I'd choose you."

Saxon smiled and squeezed his toes. "And you'd be my first pick for a brother. Now go to sleep, Clem. Try to get some rest."

"What about you?"

"I'll be fine," she told him. "I'll keep watch over you tonight. Now close your eyes."

He obeyed and was asleep in a matter of minutes.

Her gaze moved from his round freckled face, gone slack in slumber, to the window. The reddish glow was brighter than before and it had her worried. *What if there's an evacuation and someone forgets to let us know? What if we're completely surrounded by flames, unable to escape?* This was compounded by the other nagging question, the one that wouldn't go away no matter how hard she tried to force it from her mind: *What was the Serpent trying to tell me? Something's wrong with me, I just know it is. I only wish I could figure it out.*

11

The next day, in the middle of the afternoon, the wind flunked out. It was a momentary reprieve, nature's tease, for when it swept back up, it spawned a flash fire, borne by northeast winds blowing in excess of sixty-five miles per hour, nearing hurricane strength. It was the last thing any of the islanders wanted, the worst weather conditions that could possibly happen.

Joe had been right to worry.

In less than three hours the wildfire moved six miles, leaving behind a swath of destruction three miles wide. The fire whistle began to blow continuously. Seven, seven, seven. That was the evacuation signal, and it sounded eerie, disturbing, with the promising threat of danger.

"It's time to go," Saxon told Clem. "We're not waiting for the Army guys to show up. Grab an extra change of clothes and your father's sack off the cupboard."

"But where will we go?" he asked, jamming some of his clothes into the sack.

"I don't know. Someone will tell us where to go, and we'll have to do what they say. But it's real important that we leave now."

"What about my dad?"

She shot him an impatient look. "He'll be fine. He's working with the firemen, and there's no way we can reach him. He'll know where we've gone when he comes back." She didn't mention that there might not be a house left to come back home to. Clem was worried enough already; maybe that's why he was dawdling.

The evacuation whistle continued to blow.

"Hurry up, Clem."

He nodded. "I'm hurrying, but I can't decide what to do. Do I lock the doors or not? My dad will be real mad if he comes home and we're gone and the house isn't locked."

Saxon waved her hand. "Leave them open. That way, if the firefighters need to get in, they won't have to break down the door. Joe will be madder if he has to replace the door, trust me."

That seemed to make sense to Clem and he followed her out of the house, clutching the small sack to his chest. The Crooked Road was jammed with cars, trucks, farm wagons, and Army Jeeps. A nice soldier in a Jeep offered them a ride.

"Where you taking us?" Clem asked. He'd climbed into

the back to allow Saxon a front seat.

"To the Athletic Field, Son. That's where all evacuees are going." The soldier was an older man with silver-lined temples. He looked dusty and tired, but kind.

"They play softball there," Clem said. "One, two, three strikes you're out."

The man nodded, smiling. "I'm sure they play ball there. Nice big field, too." He didn't say anything to Saxon, barely even looked at her for that matter, and she figured he was just shy around women.

Saxon looked at the people alongside the road. Some were alive, but many of them weren't. The dead were dressed in their grave clothes, mingling among the living, and some of the ladies were carrying bouquets of flowers. Long dead cemetery flowers. They shuffled along in the direction of the traffic—and she knew it must be bad when even the dead evacuate.

Just then, Saxon heard a noise, the pitiful wailing of a child, and it seemed to be coming from the house they'd just passed by. Clem heard it, too. "Can you stop here, Mister?" he asked the driver.

"Why?"

"I have to check on something."

Someone's child . . .

"Well, I guess so. You'll have to catch a ride to the Athletic Field with someone else, though."

. . . is trapped in that house!

Saxon wasted no time getting out of the Jeep. Clem jumped out of the back and took her by the arm. Together they pushed through the throngs of people on the road. Some of the dead were reaching out to them, knowing they could see them, and Saxon gave them wide-eyed glances.

"They're ghosts, Clem . . . there's so many of them."

"I know."

The house the sounds were coming from was just on the outskirts of town. It was a little rundown but not yet shoddy. A washing machine sat on the front porch and a black wreath hung on the door, along with a gold star. That meant the family who lived there had lost a loved one during the War.

Clem knocked but no one answered, so when he opened the door and went inside, Saxon followed.

The house looked as though it had been deserted. *Evacuated,* Clem reminded himself. Nothing on the walls, nothing on the countertops. No furniture. Empty.

Empty except for the sound of a crying child.

They called out—anybody home?—no one answered but the child continued to cry, so they followed the sounds upstairs.

The rooms were as empty as the ones downstairs . . . except for the smallest bedroom. It had been a nursery, complete with a small bed, a crib in the corner, a colorful dresser . . . and sobs coming from within the closet.

Saxon hurried over and opened the door.

A child of four or five years looked up at her, a dirty little face streaked with tears. Saxon reached down and picked her up. "Well, hello there. What are you doing in the closet?"

"Hiding," the child said, sniffing as she snuggled against her. "I woke up and Mama was gone. I got scared. All those whistles."

"It's OK," Saxon said, smiling over at Clem. "We'll help you find your mama."

The little girl clung to Saxon, smiling with hope despite her tearful eyes. Clem, however, bit his lip and turned away. "We will find her, won't we, Clem?"

When he turned back around, she saw something in his eyes, something she'd rather not see: dread. "What's wrong?"

"I'll talk to you about it later," he said. "But first, we've got to get out of here."

They caught a ride on another Army Jeep; again, Saxon sat in the front, but this time she held a little girl on her lap. Clem sat in the back. The soldier driving them kept looking at Clem in the rearview mirror, and Saxon would have thought he should have at least said something to the little girl, but like the other driver, he only talked to Clem.

Clem, who looked absolutely miserable. *Is he worried about the fire?* Saxon wondered. *Or is it something else? Something he's not telling me. Maybe he can't tell me because he's afraid of upsetting the child?* She hoped that was all it was. The Jeep took them through the middle of town and Saxon couldn't remember ever seeing it more busy, more filled with people, than today. Anxious faces, looks of dread, haste everywhere . . . and the choking smell of smoke in the air.

The Athletic Field was full. Saxon later learned there were well over 2,500 people waiting here, sitting on the grass or upon heavy trunks packed with their family heirlooms, photographs, cherished items that could never be replaced. This is where the soldier let them off, in this field of people.

Saxon no longer cared that she wasn't wearing her gloves; she'd taken them off to fight the Serpent and hadn't bothered to put them back on. It didn't bother her anymore, what people thought of her hands. *Something inside me has changed,* she decided, and maybe that was for the best.

It was such a strange and frightening sight; all those kitchen appliances, furniture, trunks, boxes, cars, trucks, and wagons scattered over the field where just a week ago games had been played. Now the cheering section waited while the home team was out fighting to keep the fire from ravaging their homes and businesses. Women and children, and men too old or sick to battle the fire, sat down—anywhere they could find a seat—and those not sitting were nervously milling about. Everyone, sitting or standing, was talking about the fire.

All at once, the little girl wiggled out of Saxon's arms and with a yelp of joy, ran toward a woman dressed in black, who turned and dropped the bouquet she'd been carrying, opening her arms wide to receive the child.

"Is that her Mama?" Saxon asked Clem.

He nodded. "Yeah." Without another word, he walked off, not looking back to see if Saxon followed. But she did—she had to. He was her friend and she was supposed to look out for him.

"What's wrong with you?" she asked, catching up with him. "Why are you acting this way?"

He stopped and turned to her, and she could see that his eyes were wet, his face blotchy. "I saw the way you were acting with that girl. I know you love kids. You probably thought it would be nice to keep her, huh?"

Clem was puzzling her; why had he said that? Was he jealous?

She answered him softly. "I thought that, yes, for one fleeting moment. But I'm glad she found her mother."

He folded his arms, frowning. "Her mother is dead. A ghost. Same for the little girl."

Saxon nodded, expecting more of an explanation. "And?"

"That doesn't bother you?"

"No, why should it?"

Clem screwed up his mouth and shook his head, blinking back more tears. "Never mind. Let's go find someplace to sit for a while, OK?"

They found a grassy spot, near two women and another young girl, and from the looks of them, Saxon surmised that either the ladies were related or neighbors and the girl belonged to one of them. Probably the darker-haired one, that was whom she best resembled. She was cute as a button, too, and when Saxon smiled at her, she smiled back with a little wave of her hand.

Maybe Clem had a point; it did make her feel a bit sad. She would have made an excellent mother, loving and attentive. If only Rob had lived. . . .

The smell of smoke was thick in the air now. Strong gusts of wind tossed leaves about and carried them high into the sky. If not for the fire, the day would have been gorgeous, still warm and sunny, perfect for a walk in the park or for kite flying, still clinging to summer with a temperate sixty-four degrees. A perfect Indian Summer day.

Oh, but because of the fire, it was far from perfect.

From the Athletic Field where the evacuees awaited further orders, tall columns of flames could be seen shooting straight up into the sky from Strawberry Hill. At every up burst, the evacuees screamed, mothers covering their children's faces as sparks flew overhead, smoke billowing, ballooning outward, upward, ever higher. People watched flames shoot skyward in the vicinity of the Glen Mary Road.

"It's the end of the world!" a young woman shrieked, tearing at her hair. "We're all going to burn just like it says in Revelations."

Quickly, a handful of people moved in to calm her down.

"Are we going to die here?" Saxon asked, suddenly alarmed, caught up in the overwhelming emotional tension of those around her. "We're on an island, for crying out loud! There's nowhere left to go except into the sea."

Clem reached over and patted her shoulder. "No, we'll be just fine. The Army guys know what to do to keep us safe. And don't worry about what that woman said. She's just scared."

"I know. I'm scared, too."

The roar of the blaze, even at this distance was incredible, almost deafening. Although they couldn't see it from the field, the fire was mowing down many of the mansions, the summer cottages, skirting the shores of Frenchman Bay. By morning, sixty-seven vacation homes of the rich and famous would be destroyed, and while the fire flanked the business district, it would reduce one hundred and seventy permanent residences along with five historic hotels in the area surrounding downtown Bar Harbor to little more than ashes and blackened bricks.

"I wish I'd gone to the Trenton airport instead," a nearby man in a wheelchair said. He was about to say something else when his words stopped short. He was looking up and his mouth dropped open, awestruck.

Saxon and Clem followed his gaze upward.

The sky had taken on a strange, golden hue and the wind was now coming in great, blasting gusts of hot air, like that from great bellows being pumped—like breaths from a huge set of dragon lungs. People froze in their tracks, their faces skyward, and no one said a word. Silence washed over the field. Everyone knew they were watching something akin to the wrath of God, and one of the two women Saxon was sitting near remarked in a hushed voice, "It must be the fire—it's making its own wind!"

That had to be what was happening now.

Just then, evacuation instructions were announced over loudspeakers placed atop Army trucks, combating the constant droning of the fire whistle. "Everyone is to proceed to the town wharf immediately. Buses are waiting there for you. Repeat . . ."

Saxon stood up as everyone rushed about trying to gather up their belongings. "What about my things? How will I get all this stuff on a bus?" someone asked. Another inquired about her car. "There are Naval vessels on the way to pick up the cargo," the Army men assured them.

Saxon took Clem's arm and walked, following the two ladies and the girl they'd sat near earlier. Although she didn't know them, they seemed like nice folks. One of the ladies carried a radio, a Philco just like hers, tucked under one arm, and a shopping bag in the other hand. Her daughter held her hand with the radio and, as they got closer to the wharf, the lady and her daughter veered off toward the telephone exchange.

"I need to check on my older daughter," she said to her friend.

"Well, you tell her I said hi and to be careful," the other lady called out.

"Will do."

"See you down at the wharf."

The daughter gave a quick wave to indicate that they'd heard and they hurried into the building.

Saxon and Clem continued walking to the wharf. It was such a strange thing; she couldn't ever recall a time when she'd seen more people packed into a single place; it was even more crowded here than the Athletic Field had been.

The buses were quickly filling up with passengers. Every time Saxon and Clem tried to board a bus, the driver would shake his head, "Sorry, filled to capacity," and the door would close.

After several tries, Saxon shook her head. "It's just no use," she said, trying not to sound miserable but unable to help it. "We're going to die here, I just know it!"

Clem put his arm around her shoulder, patting her upper arm. "Don't worry. The buses will be back soon."

She gazed at him, unable to control her tears. "What if the roads get all burned up? What if the buses have to turn around and come back? What will we do then?" She shook her head, squeezing the tears from her eyes. "I'm sorry. All this is so very stressful."

"Here," he said. "Lean on me."

"Clem, what would I do without you? Huh?" She rested the side of her head against his shoulder, grateful for the comfort.

He patted down her hair. "See? It's gonna be OK."

"You know," she said. "I've been doing a lot of thinking these past few days, and I've been meaning to talk to you about this. I remember a time when Mother had to go away for a while. I was real young, but I remember being told she was sick. Father worried a lot; he didn't want to talk about her much. That was about sixteen years ago."

Clem's eyes lit up and he pulled back to look at her face. "Sixteen? I'm sixteen."

Saxon nodded. "Yes, I know. Everything's starting to make sense now. Could very well be that Mother went away because she was pregnant . . . she had you, then came back home . . . and tried to pretend nothing happened. That would explain why your father never liked me, wouldn't it? After all, I was the one she kept, the only child she owned up to."

Clem's arm tightened on her shoulder. "My dad never liked me much, either."

"I know. It always killed me, the way he treated you."

"So you're really my sister?"

"I think I am."

A soldier interrupted their conversation. "Listen up: we're telling everyone left here to go to the Reading Room now," he said. "Hopefully, it will only be a short wait before more buses arrive." He waited politely for Clem to indicate he understood, then he moved onto alert the next group of people.

"Have you ever been to the Reading Room, Clem?"

He shook his head. "Gosh, no. I'm not very good at reading, I'm afraid."

She chuckled softly. "It's not a place to read, although I suppose anyone could, if they wanted to. It's kind of a cross between a restaurant and a country club. It's very nice, has a beautiful view of the ocean. I think you'll like it." She held out her arm. "Would you be so kind as to escort me there?"

At this, Clem gave a little bow and placed her hand in the crook of his arm. As they walked inside, she couldn't help but notice him looking all around at everything.

"Wow, it sure is big in here . . ."

She gave him a smile. "Grand, isn't it?"

"Fancy-schmantzy," he said and she giggled.

All at once, her expression dropped.

The woman she'd seen when she'd last visited the Bar Harbor Inn, was still seated at the same table where she'd been sitting before. Again, Saxon feared melting under her glare.

"Who's that?" Clem asked. "And why's she looking at you that way? Did you upset her? Is she mad at you?"

"I don't know her."

He looked over at her, studying her for a moment, his

gaze never wavering. "Maybe it's because she doesn't understand," he said.

"Understand what?"

"Her lover's been dead a hundred years now. Same for her, too, only she don't know it yet. She's been waiting for a very long time."

"You mean she's a ghost?" Saxon felt the color leave her cheeks.

Clem nodded.

"Can you help her?"

He shrugged. "I dunno. Maybe, if she lets me."

"Will you try?"

He let Saxon lead her over to the table by the window. "Hello, Catherine," he said in a pleasant voice. Saxon noticed the candle's flame in the middle of the table made her features look quite eerie.

She stared rudely at Saxon, ignoring Clem. "Oh, go away and leave me alone!" Her tone was glacial.

"I think my brother can help you. Won't you talk to him?"

She turned her well-coiffed head to stare at Clem. "Well, have you seen the Captain?"

Clem shook his head silently.

"Then you're of no help to me."

"Wait," he said, reaching across the table. "Please, will you touch my hand? If you do, I might know something about your Captain. Maybe I can tell you something?"

She smirked. "If I do, will you and your pesky friend leave me alone?"

Clem nodded and Catherine sighed and laid her thin hand upon his open palm. His fingers closed around hers and he stared into her eyes.

"This is going to be hard to hear," he said, slowly. "I'm

really sorry to tell you this: there was an accident at sea. Your Captain was on his way home but he didn't make it. He drowned. If you don't trust me, you can find his grave at Summit Hill."

She snatched her hand away and turned to gaze out the window. "You lie! That's no grave; it's a memorial stone."

"That's true. He's not there." Clem pulled his hand back and stood up. "You should give up waiting for him. Whenever you decide to, he's *waiting* for you. He wants you to join him."

Catherine gritted her teeth, refusing to look at Clem. "Foolish boy! You think you know so much!" She whirled in her seat to glare at Saxon. "Why don't you tell *her* the truth, if you're so full of it? Hmm?"

"Tell me the truth about what?" Saxon asked.

"Nothing," Clem said. "She's just a bitter woman. Come on, let's leave her alone."

Saxon backed away, pulling Clem along with her. "Well, some people are beyond help," she told him.

"Don't ever become one of them," he said.

"I won't. Besides, I've got you to help me."

They managed to find a couple of unoccupied chairs at the far end of the room, and someone handed Clem a lit candle to hold. Now that they were fairly sure they were actually brother and sister, neither knew quite what to say to the other. After a couple attempts at conversations, they each gave up and were content just to listen to what other people were saying.

Rumors ran amuck that evening, fueled by fear. There was a terrible buzz about the possibility that the huge oil tanks at the Clark Coal Company on West Street, not 700 feet away, would catch fire and explode. "Blow Bar Harbor clean off the map if that happens," one woman in a big, flouncy hat declared.

"Did you hear about houses being dynamited to keep the fire from spreading?" someone else asked.

"Oh, yes, it's quite true."

"Well, I don't know about the rest of you," the woman in the hat said. "But if the oil tanks catch fire, we might have to jump into the ocean to keep from burning to death."

"Oh, I couldn't do that. I'm wearing my Sunday best."

"People have been burning to death inside buildings," someone else chimed in. "I'd sooner take my chances in the ocean, thank you."

"But it's a storm out there—didn't you see the size of those waves?"

"Did you hear about the TNT stored over at How's Park? Caught fire and exploded like the fourth of July times about a million."

"Did someone blow up the DeGregoire Hotel?"

"Staff was still in there. They wouldn't let 'em out."

"You don't say—my God, that's terrible!"

Unable to bear hearing any more of it, Saxon buried her face in her hands and leaned against her half brother. Over the din of voices, the wind shook the windows, vibrating the entire room. Through those windows, the sky beyond was lit up in red, orange, and pink, vivid colors broken only by plumes of grey and black smoke.

The sky over the big Malvern Hotel on Kebo Street boiled as it burned. From the Breakneck, the huge blaze topped Great Hill, racing up one side of Cadillac Mountain and down the other, engulfing Sieur de Mont Springs and a sizable part of the Jackson Memorial Laboratory as darkness fell.

Megaphones managed to cut through the noise and

shock. "Evacuees, please proceed now to the town wharf."

"Oh good, the buses must be coming back," Saxon said, lifting her head.

"Not buses," Clem said. "Boats. I saw their lights, red and green, from the window. I've been watching them come in near the pier."

The Reading Room emptied its occupants into the driving wind.

Saxon held Clem's hand as they walked down Main Street. They passed the telephone office where the woman with the young girl had gone into to check in on her older daughter. Saxon hoped she'd be all right. She hoped *everyone* would be all right. Looking up, she could see faces in the office windows looking down at the crowds.

Down at the town wharf, boats were tumbling and tossing in the waves and the gale-force winds. Many of them had problems anchoring so close to the wharf, near the ladder where they needed to be.

These weren't military vessels, but ordinary fishing boats. Fishermen from Lamoine, Hancock Point, Sorrento, Sullivan, Gouldsboro, Prospect Harbor, Winter Harbor, and other nearby towns had braved the winds and the waves on a rescue mission for the people of Bar Harbor.

The tide was low; the ladder, long and treacherous, slippery down past the tidemark.

Saxon watched people line up and climb down into boats very cautiously. Some of the ladies backed away, crying because they just couldn't handle the steepness of the ladder in their fine dresses and heels. Saxon felt their panic and wondered if she'd be brave enough to try it.

And she shivered. Gone were the mild temperatures of day; night had fallen and it was cold.

Behind them, in the distance, the Building of Arts, a

grand example of Greek architecture with its towering columns, had been smashed flat, like the charred ruins of a Hellenic temple. Every house on many of the streets—the Eagle Lake Road, the Highbook Road, Forest Street, Oak Street, Pine Street, Kebo Street, Cleftstone Road, Prospect Avenue, Rockwood Avenue, Mountain Avenue and Brookside Avenue—became ravaged by fire. Homes along Eden Street and Harbor Lane lay in ruins. With nothing more than chimneys left standing in blackened cellar holes, smoke, ash, embers and flames, it was a hellish scene of total and utter desolation, the aftermath of Dante's inferno, a no-man's land. Sparks flew overhead and live coals glowed for miles in every direction except over the ocean.

At the end of the worst of it, the fire blew itself out over the Atlantic in a massive fireball, exploding upward, embers and cinders tumbling to the sea in a sky of ever-moving sparks.

Four hundred were rescued by boats that day.

Saxon Faraday felt lucky to be among them.

Just before climbing down the ladder to a boat, she passed Moses' cane to Clem. It had never left her side, after defeating the Serpent. "Here, I think you should have this," she said. "I really do. Someday, maybe years from now, you'll give this to someone. Pass it on to the next generation to protect them from the Serpent."

"But what about you?" Clem asked.

"I won't be needing it again," she assured him. "But someday in the future, someone might. You'll know who, when the time is right."

Clem took the cane but his eyes were full of tears.

Climbing down that ladder was one of the hardest things she ever had to will herself to do. Confronting the Serpent, yes, that had been very difficult—but she'd had friends with her. This, she had to do by herself.

Her smooth palms and fingers threatened to lose their grip and slip, and every rung felt like sheer agony as she hunted for the next with the toe of her shoe. The ladder was moving, too, which didn't help, shaking and vibrating, banging against the pier with every wave. After what seemed an eternity, someone grabbed her from behind and swung her onto the deck of a boat.

A lobster boat.

There were already about a dozen people aboard. Saxon looked up at the pier for Clem. "Are you coming?" she called out.

"No. Not on this boat," he told her. "I'll catch the next one." Even from this distance, she could see a strange look in his eye, a determined courage despite his tears. He'd be fine, just fine.

She nodded emphatically, not sure he could hear her very well over the wind and the roar of the fire. "OK then, I'll see you over on the other shore."

Clem nodded back with a wave. She blew him a kiss and he caught it in his hand.

I'll never see Bar Harbor again, except in ruins, she thought as the boat pushed away from the pier. *And now, without Clem, I am completely alone.* As the boat pitched in the waves, she managed to cling to the edge of the washboard to keep from tumbling across the deck. It was a terrible scene: the boiling ocean with its foamy waves, the screaming wind under a night sky that had taken on a lurid, golden-orange hue.

Are any of us going to survive this? she wondered, shivering in the cold. Unable to witness any more of the destruction, she turned toward the others on the boat, their faces illuminated in soft, golden hues by the fire on the land. How could they be so calm, just standing there, watching their homes go down in flames, their town desecrated, blackened beyond recognition? All at once, she wanted to shake each one of them by the shoulders; they were in shock, she was sure of it.

The boat was very crowded, so much so that she feared it was overfilled, that the waves would swamp them, and that they'd all die in the cold, ink-black froth that night, the last sight they'd see being the flames from the shore.

As her eyes scanned the faces, she was filled with growing despair. *We're all going to die—and they know it! Such a waste. We've gone through so much—and for what? Why did we have to fight the Serpent? To what end?*

Her gaze fell on a black couple in the corner of the boat. The lady had a baby in her arms. Was it them? Suki, Stevie, and Moses? Yes, she was quite sure of it. Somehow, they'd found their way to the pier, to this very same boat. In this moment, she realized that the infant she'd heard crying in the attic hadn't been a ghost at all but an essence, energy left over, expended, Moses' energy, which became part of the house that awful night he'd been born.

Saxon stepped forward, giving the family a wave and a shout: "Hey, I'm here! Over here!" Overcome with elation, she started to make her way over to them, but someone tugged on her sleeve and she turned to look.

She could hardly believe her eyes! It was Rob Carmichael—not a disembodied specter—but *him,* here in the flesh! Smiling, he held her at arm's length, just looking at her . . . and he was still in uniform, as handsome as she'd last seen him. She nearly fell to her knees as the boat shifted, but he caught her and pulled her to his chest, his hand smoothing her wild, tangled hair.

She sought her voice and found it. "Oh, Rob, can it really be you?" she asked, clinging to him, vowing never to let him go. "I thought you died at Pearl Harbor!"

"It's really me, darling," he said, tilting her face upward toward his.

"But how? If you were alive, why didn't you come back to me?" Tears spilled down her cheeks, mingling with the salt spray that clung to her skin. "I thought you'd died—they said you were missing in action—then your ghost, it came to me in my bedroom . . . only I couldn't see you then. I heard your voice and I thought, I thought—"

"—Hush now, love. I told you I'd come back for you and so I have," he said, setting her lightly down on her feet as the boat lurched from side to side in the foamy waves.

Out of the corner of her eye, she noticed Mario Delgado standing nearby with Jacqueline on his arm. He mouthed the words: *thank you,* then turned and kissed Jacqueline.

"You've done good," Rob said, kissing her forehead. "I knew you could do it."

Saxon looked up at him, her face shadowed in confusion. "But Suki, Stevie, Mario, and Jacqueline—they're dead. Does this mean we're—"

Rob nodded, his smile steady. "We're dead, too."

Saxon's dropped. "But how—how'd it happen to me? I don't remember dying!"

"You sure you want to know?"

Was she? Saxon wasn't at all certain that she wanted to hear how it happened, but it was something she felt she needed to know. No wonder Clem had been acting so strangely; he knew, he just couldn't tell her because he didn't want to hurt her.

"Yes," she said at last, "I'm sure. Did I die in a car accident on the way home from the hospital? Is that the reason why my car wasn't in the drive after we took care of the Serpent? What happened to me? I need to know!"

Now his smile faded. "All right, I'll show you, if you insist, but it's not going to be easy to take. Are you sure you want to see it?"

"Yes . . . as long as you hold me so I can feel your arms around me, I'll be OK."

"Then close your eyes, love. I've got you and there's no way I'll ever let go."

Saxon shut her eyes, hugging him tightly. She could feel the warmth of his body, the strength of his embrace, and she felt safe.

"It will be like the visions I sent to you in your bedroom when I warned you about the Serpent and the ghosts, the history of Roquefort Manor," he told her. "All you need to do is concentrate."

She did just that, and slowly the noise of the gale faded, along with the heavy slapping of the waves and their vibrations, the rocking of the boat in the storm, the buzz of conversations around her . . . it all diminished . . . along with the comforting feel of Rob's arms around her.

The blackness of her closed eyes brightened to grey, then white.

Stark white walls and a white tiled floor. Saxon looked around, trying to figure out where she was and what she was seeing . . . then it came to her.

She was back in the hospital—the hospital for the insane!

But something was in her hand, and looking down, she saw it was her purse. She was no longer wearing cotton, hospital-issue pajamas . . . no, she was dressed in her navy skirt and silvery grey blouse. She had her trusty black gloves on, along with her sensible black pumps, and her Hollywood sunglasses, along with the hose she'd saved . . .

★ ★ ★ ★ ★

. . . and it all came rushing back at her, the memory of it.

"They were sending me home!" she breathed. "I was so happy, so thankful to finally get out of there!"

One of the janitors mopping the floor at the end of the hall glanced up as she passed, then took a second look and smiled. "Miss Faraday! I'd heard they were releasing you today—hey, watch it, the floor's wet—"

His warning came seconds too late. Yes, the floor was wet, the tiles slick with soap and water . . . and Saxon began to slide, unable to stop herself, the soles of her pumps so hard and smooth slipping, carrying her along toward the stairs.

They were wide and there were so very many of them.

She reached, grappling for the banister—and missed. Then the steps came flying up at her, two by two, the pain of hitting them instant and severe. As she tumbled down them, she could hear the wet crunch of bones in her neck, snapping, vertebrae shattering, disks in her back jarring.

Sounds like loose gravel, she thought, screaming, tasting blood in her mouth; then, feeling something that *felt* like loose gravel on her tongue, she bounced to the landing where the stairs stopped.

Looking up, unable to move, she only saw the end of the banister post towering over her and out of the corner of her eye, spotted the janitor at the top of the stairs, his face as colorless as the grey of his uniform. His mouth dropped open and then he dropped his mop; its handle hit the floor with a clattering thud, a harsh noise. She shut her eyes against the waves of pain rushing through her body.

His voice floated down to her. "Miss Faraday? My God, are you all right?" And she heard (and felt) his footsteps approaching. She opened her eyes as he stood over her, yelling for the doctors. Now her face was at eye level with his work boots. They were heavy, round-toed, and she saw that he'd double-knotted his laces.

I'm hurt, she tried to say, but the words wouldn't come out. Blinking, she tried to sit up.

Couldn't.

Others were racing to the stairs; she could hear them, feel the vibrations they made as they rushed toward her. At the very top of the stairs, she could see a gathering of patients standing there in their pajamas and hospital-issue slippers . . . looking down at her in apparent shock. Some of the ladies were crying.

She didn't want, didn't need, their pity.

Yes, she was in great pain, terrible throbbing pulsating through her body . . . but the last thing she needed was people gawking at her. She couldn't feel her legs and hoped that her skirt hadn't ridden up too high.

Gradually, the agony began to dull, and she was able to stand up.

"You see?" she told them, smoothing down her skirt. "I'm all right."

But the janitor beside her just kept looking down, completely ignoring her. His hands were shaking, Saxon noticed this and let her eyes follow his gaze.

Someone was lying there! A woman, whose neck was bent, twisted at an unnatural angle. A wet, white shinbone protruded from one of her legs, its sharp end poking up through her nylon hose—and the spreading red . . . blood running across the floor.

Poor lady, Saxon thought. *I must have fallen on her when I landed. I didn't mean to—didn't want to hurt anyone. . . .*

She bent down and picked up her purse as a team of

doctors in white overcoats raced over.

I'm so sorry about this, she said, stepping aside. *It was an accident. I didn't mean to hurt anyone.*

They ignored her, kneeling to check the injured woman's pulse, then grimly shaking their heads.

Oh no! She's dead—and I killed her, Saxon reasoned. *They'll say it's my fault—and they'll lock me back in here—and God only knows for how long!*

I can't let them get me!

She hurried toward the door, past the front desk where two nurses looked up. The younger of them stood up, covering her mouth with one hand, pointing a finger with the other.

"Did you just see that?"

"No, what are you talking about?"

Saxon raced past them, pushing open the door. She stepped out into freedom, and the sunshine on her face felt good, its warmth spreading through her. It had been such a rainy spring, but now, on the day of her release, the sun was shining to celebrate with her.

"Saxon, darling?" She could hear Rob's voice penetrating her thoughts, her vision.

"Saxon, you're not getting it, are you? The woman who died on those stairs . . . that was you."

No! She shook her head in dismay, refusing to believe it. *Why are you telling me this? I didn't die back there—I landed on someone.*

"Saxon, it's true. That's how it happened, only you wouldn't accept it then, just like you're not accepting it now. You have to believe me in order to move on."

"Then make me believe it's true," she said through gritted teeth.

★ ★ ★ ★ ★

The vision of sunshine faded once again to white and she was back in the hospital. Only it wasn't the same one. This was a medical hospital. The morgue inside a medical hospital, deep in the basement, like her father's workroom had been . . .

. . . only the cadaver table was stainless steel and there was a sheet-covered body upon it. A doctor came in and drew back the sheet. He was a young man, his manner businesslike, his face expressionless. He gazed for a moment at the corpse and jotted something down on his clipboard.

Because he was between Saxon and the table, she couldn't see the body. Nor did she want to.

Rob, why am I here? Why are you showing me this?

"Go look under the sheet, then you'll know."

I've seen corpses before. Why should this one be any different?

"Saxon, please. Just go look at it. Do it for yourself. You need to make a clean break. Do it for us."

Us?

She took a hesitant step toward the table, then another, until she stood beside the doctor. A pale, waxy-looking face stared up at her, one that was a mirror image of her own . . . only this one was dead. Slack. Broken.

One eye bulged outward, so bloodshot that not a speck of white remained. The nose had been crushed, its bridge flattened, and the mouth hung open, revealing bloody, broken teeth.

But Saxon recognized her own hair, the only thing that stayed intact, although it was a bit mussed up. She'd never quite been able to tame those long, dark curls.

Father used to tell me that my hair was a gift from his great grandmother. She was a famous Italian opera singer. He'd say that back in the days before we moved to Roquefort

Manor, before he became possessed.

Glancing over at the doctor's clipboard, Saxon read the name on the death certificate. Now she knew Rob had been right . . . this was what he'd been trying to show her, what he needed her to believe.

I understand now, she thought. *And I can accept the fact that I died. I had to return home as a ghost. It was the only way to defeat the Serpent.*

She opened her eyes, brimming with tears and looked up at Rob as he brushed them away with his thumbs. "Clem knew all along, didn't he?"

He nodded. "Clement and Moses both knew. And they knew you didn't know. Neither one had the heart to tell you."

She looked around, eyes darting from face to face. "This is a ghost ship, isn't it? Every one of us, we're all ghosts here . . ."

"—Ghosts?" shouted the captain of the boat, his strong hands gripping the wheel. "Heck, no! I feel alive as ever! But I've had just about enough of this storm!"

Saxon recognized his voice at once. "Georgie Marshall?! You're here, too?"

He turned from the helm, grinning. "Yeah, girl, it's really me! Soon as I got to the Great Hereafter, they gave me a lobster boat of my own—how about that?" His grin softened into a smile. "It's really good to see you, Saxon. Glad you could make it." Keeping both hands on the wheel, Georgie called out, "Hang on, folks. We're going skyward."

The bow of the boat tilted upward slightly, then it was lifted into the air, floating ever higher over the sparks, the smoke and ashes. Through thick, misty clouds and into a blanket of stars shining bright, twinkling.

It was so very beautiful up there.

12

While that awful fire cleansed the land above, the Serpent squirmed deep into the bowels of the earth. It was in agony, its skull shattered, alone and without allies.

The hybrids would pay for such pain, the Serpent decided, coiling its body around itself. *The Aelim won the battle, but they didn't win the war.*

Things were far from over, but the Serpent was weak. Sighing, it fell into a deep and fitful rest . . . where, twisting and turning in its tatters of dead skin, it slept a sleep full of hot, hateful nightmares, a dream of a future time when it could awaken and rise to power once more.

It would not be so easily defeated next time.

AFTERWORD

On November 14, the Bar Harbor fire was finally and officially declared out . . . yet four feet underground, even after the first snow of the year had fallen, it still burned under Sieur de Monts Meadow. It would take a long, long time, perhaps even until the dead of winter, for it to die out completely.

It would also take a long time for the island to recover. Some parts never would. Many of the great estates of the opulent rich would never be restored or rebuilt, due to rising taxes (income tax had just been invented) and a dwindling post-war economy. Most of the magnificent pines and spruces were gone; white birches would eventually grow in their place. Many of the burned residential homes, however, would be rebuilt on their former foundations and much of the lumber used for reconstruction came from charred trees salvaged from the fire, lumber that had been wintered in Eagle Lake and Witch Hole Pond. This wood smelled smoky, as it always would, for it had captured the overpowering odor of the fire, locking it deep within its fibers.

Almost 20,000 acres of land burned in that fire, claiming nearly one-third of Mount Desert Island. Exploring deep enough, one may still come across the remainders of blackened stumps in the forests.

In all, over 1,500 people battled the blaze. Approximately 175 residential homes, several inns and grand hotels, 67 summer homes, and 45 garages and greenhouses were consumed before they could stop it.

By May 1948, 18 homes had been rebuilt and 60

more were under construction.

Over the years, most of the scars from that disastrous fire healed over with new growth as Nature gradually restored the former beauty of the Island, Acadia National Park included. This is God's country. You'll know *it* when *it* finds you—and yes, it will leave an impression on your soul.

As for the Bar Harbor fire, no one ever determined how it started. There were rumors and tales, even ghost stories, but that's up to the reader to decide how much of any one story to believe.

The fact remains, though, that this fire made international headlines and it wasn't alone in its fury. The summer of '47 brought forth a drought throughout the entire state of Maine, igniting many terrible wildfires that October in towns from Wells to Waterboro to Machias and up into Aroostook County. There had been a terrible hurricane in 1936, and there's little doubt that the debris from that storm, the downed trees and limbs, helped fuel the wildfires eleven years later.

Statewide, 205,678 acres, 851 permanent homes, and 397 seasonal cottages were destroyed in a period that lasted only about ten days.

The famous Smokey Bear campaign has been telling us since 1944: **Remember, only YOU can prevent forest fires**.

That's right. *Only* you.

—T. M. Gray, July 2003
Downeast, Maine

ABOUT THE AUTHOR

T. M. Gray was born in Bar Harbor and lives in Downeast, Maine with her husband and children (one of whom is a polite but neurotic foxhound named Chance who hides in the bathtub during storms). Gray has a keen interest in reading, movies, genealogy, video games and history. Her short stories have been published in numerous magazines and anthologies, and recently published novels include *Mr. Crisper* and *The Ravenous.* Because of her warm personality, Gray is sometimes mistaken as an author of children's books, but we assure you she's not. T. M. Gray is a member of the Horror Writers Association and is hard at work on her next novel (and yes, it's scary!). Visit her on the web at: www.tmgray.tk.